CW01506473

ZEUS

A
CONTEMPORARY
MYTHOS NOVEL

ZEUS

CARLY SPADE

ZEUS

A CONTEMPORARY MYTHOS NOVEL

Copyright © 2022 by Carly Spade

WWW.CARLYSPADE.COM

Published in the United States by World Tree Publishing, LLC

WORLD TREE
PUBLISHING, LLC

This is a work of fiction. References to real people, events, establishments, organizations, or locales are intended only to provide authenticity, and are used fictitiously. All other characters, and all incidents and dialogue, are drawn from the author's imagination and are not to be construed as real.

Cover and Interior Formatting by We Got You Covered Book Design
WWW.WEGOTYOUCOVEREDBOOKDESIGN.COM

CONTENT WARNING

Excessive swearing, sexual situations, and a sexy god-king
determined to steal your heart…and maybe more.

*Dedicated to my husband, who inspires me
on a daily basis far more than he realizes.*

Proud is the spirit of Zeus-fostered kings—their honor comes
from Zeus, and Zeus, god of council, loves them.

HOMER

Heavy is the head that wears the crown.

WILLIAM SHAKESPEARE

ONE

ZEUS

SHE DIDN'T THINK I heard her slip out of bed in the middle of the night. Didn't think I saw her nab a twenty from my wallet before ducking out with a light click of the door. At least she had the decency to look at my ass peeking from the sheets before leaving. It *was* a nice ass.

She also probably didn't think I remembered her name. Elena.

I didn't bother locking the door behind her. In fact, it'd be entertaining for someone to barge in and try to kill me. The King of the fucking Gods. It'd been far too long since I'd seen the terrified look on a mortal's face when they realized who I was. Any attempt to announce it in the modern age…they'd look at me like I was insane. Fucking mockery.

And I know what you're thinking. This scenario isn't surprising. Dickhead Zeus sleeps with yet another woman, cheating on his wife. Shocking. There *is* more to that story, but I digress.

This time…I'm not the asshole. This time, I fucked her fair and square. Hera left me. Gave up her Queendom, sneered at me, and left.

And I let her.

Despite the humiliation. Despite the absolute fury. It hadn't been the first time she rebelled against me, only this time I didn't care. Because in a bizarrely fucked up way…I admired it. It grew old and tiresome pretending things were as they'd been all those ages ago. She changed. The world changed. And most importantly, hold onto your asses, *I* changed.

I shook my head at the notion, rattling away whatever fog clouded my brain.

Besides, I couldn't remember the last time I was single—a bachelor. She may have unleashed a monster. A short-lived one anyway.

I crawled out of bed, slipping on the boxers I'd haphazardly tossed to the floor earlier, making my way to a back room. Lightly touching the knob, I cracked the door open, greeted by a large wet black nose.

"Come on, boy," I said to my white Labrador, Levin.

Yes, I did name him after an archaic word for lightning. Shouldn't be surprising. What *may* surprise you, however, is that he's a rescue. I "stole" him from an abusive home and gave him a better one. Think of me what you wish, but beating up innocent beings simply because you *can*? Not on my fucking watch.

He forced his shoulders into the door, sprinting down the hall, slipping and sliding with each passing step. I smiled to myself, patiently following him. No woman I'd ever brought here deserved to meet Levin. He was the only being in the universe who'd ever seen past all the bullshit, didn't give a fuck about my past, and loved me unconditionally. When I rounded the corner, he was already making circles on the bed, finding a suitable spot to curl up and sleep for the night.

Before crawling in myself, I paused at the edge, taking his large head in both of my hands, scratching behind his ears. His wide pink tongue flopped to the side of his mouth, panting.

"Good boy." After turning off the light, I climbed into bed and felt Levin's furry warm body shoving against my back after only thirty seconds.

Morning seeped through the cracks of the black curtains in my sleek downtown New York apartment, making me grumble. As much sleep as I got, and it never seemed to be enough. Ironic considering I'm a god, right? It's what happens when you partially hold the entire cosmos on your shoulders— always on your mind. The important thing was to *never* show it on my face in front of my people. And I hadn't for millennia.

Ruffling my hair, I shoved my face into the pillow, ignoring the scent of Elena's shampoo, or fragrance, or whatever the fuck it was she'd left behind. The metal eagle statue in mid-attack protruded from the wall, staring down at me from above my headboard. Levin was sprawled on his back, curled to the side with his legs spread, sleeping away. Slipping out of bed, I paused to stretch my arms to Olympus, gazing at my reflection in the mirror—cut, toned, tanned, and immaculate. A physique that never changed, and I had to do absolutely nothing to maintain—perks of being a Greek god.

My face. The closest semblance I could replicate to the true me. Unless, of course, I enjoyed the sight of each mortal I passed on the streets catching flame. A younger, more ruthless me might have grinned at the thought. But no, I've learned to admire the poor bastards. My mortal guise was a version of me that existed before fighting for and *earning* the right of chief deity. But my eyes…those would never change.

Where was I? Ah yes. My small window of bachelorhood. Thanks to the overpowerful bitch of a grandmother of mine, Gaea…there's a stipulation to my Kingdom. At all times— there must be a Queen. If the expiration date lapses, I not only lose my title but part of my power to go with it. We couldn't have that, now, could we? And to be honest, I'd never given the clause much thought. There'd only ever been Hera. I didn't think she'd give up her crown. At any rate, I'd take the next few nights to "live it up," so to speak, and then pick the nearest mortal woman who was pleasing to the eyes to be my Queen. Done deal.

Any and all of them would pine over the idea of it. And why wouldn't they? To become not only a goddess but an immortal Queen? Not to mention I could walk down the street and have any one of them if I so desired. Fuck—if I had a thing for man-ass, I could have that too. The world was my oyster, and I'd shucked my share. But I'd be lying if I said the ease of the conquest on the rarest of occasions never felt…hollow.

Sneering, I turned for my walk-in closet, the light automatically illuminating as I entered. Hundreds of pristinely hung suits lined the walls, dozens of glossed dress shoes resting on matching shelves. Displays held a different Rolex for each day of the week and several shined and glinting pairs of silver and gold cufflinks.

I could conjure clothes with a snap of my fingers, but for as long as I'd roamed the Earth one starts to appreciate the smaller things—things mortals take for granted. A uniquely tailored suit created to fit you like a glove. The feel of it as you slip it on like liquid sex. Even the scent of the fabric calmed me far quicker than any steaming hot shower. And I never wore the same suit twice. Ever.

I donned a light grey ensemble with a white shirt and dark blue tie. And, yes, I did up the tie as well every time. Peering into the full-length mirror, I did the necessary overlapping and pull- through to secure the perfect knot in the silk tie, smoothing it down. I turned my face to the side, running a hand over the light beard on my chin. My godly King form was far less…clean. Ironic that between my brothers and I, Hades' true self was the only beardless one.

Upon securing the gold Rolex on my left wrist, I attached the gold "Z" cufflink to one sleeve, a lightning bolt on the other, and paused to stare at the New York City skyline through the wall of windows near my king-sized bed. Mortals of all varieties busied the streets, appearing as ants in a structured maze. Chins tilted down, eyes glued to their phone screens, missing half the world around them. It was no wonder they didn't believe in us anymore. They were far too busy worshipping technology and the media. Eons ago, I may have asked Poseidon to wipe the slate clean by making Earth's oceans swallow it whole, but I no longer interfered that deep. There was an entire universe to oversee, and if you think the Greek gods are the only deities from "mythology" in existence—you'd be sorely mistaken.

I turned to Levin, who was still snoring, fast asleep on

the bed. With a smirk, I snapped my fingers, making raw meat chunks appear in his dog bowl in the kitchen. Levin's body writhed, and his head shot up, nose sniffing the air. He jumped off the bed and scurried over to me, sitting but shaking, waiting for permission to eat. Crouching, I scratched under his chin and gave a quick kiss to the top of his head.

"Be good. Go on." I motioned with my head at the kitchen, and with an excited yip, he trotted off to eat.

New York. I've lived in many, many places. Aside from Olympus, aside from Greece, New York felt like a kingdom to be ruled—even if they had no idea who walked amongst them. Slipping my hands into my pockets, I made for the elevator and began my daily stroll to the firm's building. I could've had a chauffeur, *me* knows I could afford it. Could've even simply ported there. But there was something about feeding on the energy of mortals—their expressions. Their reactions as pure raw power waltzed right past them. A pity they didn't believe in the old gods anymore. We could all have *so* much more fun.

It was time to don the mask. A façade forged through the ages that mortals molded and adapted to fit their own needs. Their own agenda. Same old song and dance. It'd become as much a part of me as the warmth of a perfectly aged scotch settling in my stomach. Could I have taken the time to convince a world there was more to me than the endless parade of women? More than the meddling god-king who cared for nothing or no one else but himself? Sure. But I had an entire fucking kingdom to oversee. Hundreds of gods beneath me and seemingly more even within the last few months. We'll get to that tiny detail later. There were far more pressing matters to deal with over a reputation I've grown to accept. If it gave them comfort to hate me, I'd be their sounding board because I'm a leader. The alpha. A godsdamned admiral.

The Jupiter Bistro. A coffee shop directly below my penthouse apartment. The fucking irony, right? I breezed past the line leading out the door, and they all let me—because they wouldn't dare otherwise.

The barista, Claire, grinned as she set a steamy paper cup on the counter, slipping a cover on. "Dark roast, black, Z. All ready for you."

Taking the cup from her hand, making sure to drag my finger over her knuckle, I winked. "Thank you, as always, my dear."

She bit her lip after letting out a shaky breath. Immediate putty in my hands. Not uncommon in the slightest. But anymore? Almost too easy.

After tapping my card on the reader, I turned with the cup in hand, spying a buxom red-head giving me a sultry smile. Her emerald gaze dropped to the impression of my cock through my pants. Making a piece of paper with my address appear between two of my fingers, I slipped it into her palm as I passed, sending a light current of electric shock against her skin. She gasped, and I exited with a broad smile.

Storm clouds rolled in, and with a quirk of my brow, they froze. I couldn't walk into the firm looking like a soaked rat. As soon as my feet hit the foyer carpet of the thirty-story building owned by Crane, Crane, and Wallace Law, rain poured down in buckets with another raise of my brow. A satisfying crackle of lightning streaked the sky.

Why is the King of the Gods practicing law, you ask? A part

of me might say the power and irony in controlling mortals in such a way intrigues me. Another part of me might say it's a genius way of keeping badly-behaved mortals in my sights. And an even smaller part of me might say—because I'm fucking bored. Not to mention how much it annoys my brother, Hades. Sure. I keep his ass happy so he does his job, but at the end of the day…I'm going to have a little fun in the process.

Let us not forget that besides my kingly status, I also oversee law and justice. Defending a known criminal may not exactly be viewed as justifiable. Still, my status as chief deity of the Greeks not only meant sovereignty over the gods but a responsibility to humankind as well. Such is the role of *any* chief deity—Greek or otherwise. And I'd learned through time, the best way to help mortals is to witness them at their absolute worst.

Removing the lid from the coffee cup, I tossed it into the trash, blowing on the hot liquid as I made my way through the bullpen.

"I swear this piece of shit gives me a blue screen every other month. Can't the firm spring for new computers?" An intern, Larry, with far more humility to learn and a set of balls to grow, spat from a nearby cubicle.

With an idle sway of my hand, I sent an electric pulse into the device, rejuvenating its life for precisely another two months. At some point, he'd finally break down and humbly ask one of the partners' assistants to request a new computer. Until then, I entertained myself watching him prolong his own misery.

My assistant, Ruth, came trotting from around the corner, sporting her usual attire of a modest skirt that went to her mid-shins, flats, and a cardigan sweater. Her cropped brown hair bounced as she ran, a pen resting on her ear, notepad clutched to her chest. She adjusted her squared glasses as she stopped in front of me. When she smiled, it extenuated the mole above her lip. At a petite five-foot even, she had to crane her neck back to look me in the face.

"Mr. Vrontí, there's a new case file for you to review," she said, her hazel eyes beaming.

I caught her gaze over the rim of my cup as I sipped. "Ruth, you can call me Zane or Z. We've been over this, sweetheart."

"Yes. Of course, Mr. Vron—I mean—" A nervous, shrilled bout of laughter poured from her throat.

Smirking, I pointed toward my office. After a tiny jump, she turned on her heel and power-walked.

I'd never slept with my assistant. Not because I didn't want to—Tartarus, no. I always did love the small ones you could toss around in the bedroom. No. It was due to us seeing each other several days a week for hours. I couldn't risk her becoming…attached. And it's not as if she never tried with her varying moments of brushing her tits against my arm or undoing several buttons on her blouse to give me a view as she bent over to place paperwork on my desk.

I sat in my leather-back rolling chair, resting the coffee on a mahogany coaster. I'd kept my workspace simple and clutter-free. Aside from my gold nameplate, a desktop calendar, computer, pen holder, and stapler, nothing that would hint at my electric personality nor anything from my personal life was displayed.

Whose photo would I put on my desk anyway? Apollo? Sure,

if I wanted every other client to start probing about my son being the rockstar "Ace." Athena? A woman in ancient Greek armor could look strange. She was one of the few who didn't bother to show herself to mortals. No. I preferred keeping that part of my life completely separate from the mortal lawyer. It made things far easier to deal with—to pretend for several hours a day I didn't carry an invisible boulder on my back like fucking Atlas himself.

Without disappointing, Ruth "discreetly" adjusted the collar of her shirt before trotting over to me with a folder. She leaned forward, squeezing her tits together, and dropped the papers in front of me with a flourish. Obliging her, I stole a glance at her cleavage before scooping the folder into my hand.

She smiled, chewing on the end of her pen before standing straight. "Murder case."

"Oh?" I flipped through the papers, eyeballing mugshots, receipts, internet history printouts.

"Killed her husband."

Ah, the ancient tale of a wife murdering her husband for one of a dozen reasons. And this one didn't look much different.

"Shoved him in a tub of acid."

Without looking up, I continued to shuffle through more digital evidence paperwork in the folder. "To dispose of the body?"

Ruth cleared her throat and squeaked before saying, "Alive."

I paused, shooting my gaze to hers. "Fuck."

"Right?" Ruth lifted her hand and dropped it, slapping her thigh.

Well, now things just got far more interesting.

I picked up the paper with the accused woman's mugshot. A portly woman with curly hair and a glare that could curl the paint from a fence. "Have they announced the lead prosecutor yet?"

"Yes. Keira Bazin." Looking away, Ruth scratched the back of her head with the pen.

A woman. This would be a first.

I tossed the paper to the stack. "Why have I heard that name before?"

Ruth snorted. "You should have. She's *never* lost a case. I've heard some other lawyers call her 'The Bulldog.'"

After a quick Google search, I pulled up several full-body photos taken by the media. Starting at her tanned, toned legs peeking from her skirt, I panned up to her perfectly rounded ass, and landed on a gorgeous face with bright blue eyes, plump red lips and a head of *very* light blonde hair.

A conquest if I ever saw one.

After raising my coffee in a cheers gesture to Ruth, I said, "This'll be far too easy."

TWO

KEIRA

"THIS ISN'T GOING TO be easy. Did you say who I think you said is on the defense?" I asked my paralegal and best friend, Olivia, through the phone as I paced back and forth in my apartment.

"Eric Carter, yes. But you shouldn't be so bloody nervous, Keira. You've never lost a case. Why would who's on the defense change that?" Olivia murmured something, sounding like she held the phone away from her face.

I narrowed my eyes. "Are you with someone right now?"

It *was* three in the morning, but given Olivia and I were both night owls, her calling in the middle of the night to relay the news wasn't surprising.

"No…" Her answer sounded more like a question.

I knew she was lying, not only because of the lilt in her voice but because I had what some would refer to as—empathic powers. Anyone I was near, I knew all the emotions they were feeling, the emotions they projected versus bottling up, and when only hearing them versus seeing—the truth fluttered through my ear like static raindrops. It was the main reason I stayed at the office late and arrived super early. The fewer people I encountered on my walk to work, the better. Ironically, I'd ended up in one of the continent's most populated, bustling cities.

"Ollie, you know you can't lie to me." I zig-zagged through the boxes strewn about my living room floor. Boxes I hadn't unpacked since I moved in after my divorce. I was rarely in my apartment except to sleep anyhow. Work was my significant other—which was undoubtedly the main reason Tyler left me.

"How is that exactly, hm? Do you have ESP?" Olivia's "you" sounded more like "ya" given her Australian accent. She'd been in the country for over seven years, but her accent remained thick as molasses.

With a deep sigh, I moved to my window that faced the luxury apartments across the street. The apartment building that Zane Vronti, a slimy criminal defense lawyer, lived in. The universe's idea of a cruel joke. "Go hang with your man of the hour. We'll talk about this in the office tomorrow."

"Aye, aye, ma'am," Olivia said with an American drawl. She giggled and told someone to "stop it" before hanging up.

I rested my chin on top of my phone, watching a woman with long black hair walk from the apartment building's lobby barefoot, letting her heels dangle by the strap from her finger. The woman hailed a cab at three in the morning, and there wasn't a doubt in my mind she was one of Zane's regular fuck toys. On many late nights, I'd see him with a variety of women on his arm, waltzing them up to his penthouse apartment. And every morning, they'd leave, never staying long enough for breakfast.

Typical New York playboy—always dressed in a pristine suit, hair slicked back with gel and a swagger that suggested he owned the world. I'd only ever seen him from afar and the occasional blips on the news that I mostly ignored. I loathed defense lawyers. I'd be lying if I said what I *had* seen wasn't attractive, but honestly…how could any self-respecting person be perfectly sound with a revolving door of partners?

I couldn't even remember the last time I'd had sex. It wasn't because I didn't enjoy it, nor because I wasn't capable of seducing someone. Not only was my brain far too wrapped in casework up to my ears to care, but sensing every passing emotion from your partner during the act could be overwhelming and borderline exhausting.

Scooping the Melissa Daniels case folder into my hand, I slipped off my heels, scrunching my toes into the carpet as I paced and read. As a criminal prosecutor, especially in New York, it took every bit of cunning and finesse a lawyer had in their arsenal to win cases like this. Wife kills husband. Jury, making preconceived judgments that the husband had to do something to drive her to such a state, sympathizes with woman. And maybe the husband *did* do something. But it also took a special kind of evil to shove a human being, living or not, in acid and shove the barrel in a storage locker.

Not looking down, I stepped over the box I knew rested between where the carpet ended, and the tile began, leading to my kitchenette. I set the stack of papers on the counter as I grabbed a bottle of water. My eyes felt heavy, and sleep tugged at my brain. Half-past three in the morning. An hour of sleep and then straight to the office.

The obnoxious alarm sound chimed from my phone at four-thirty in the morning, and I rolled out of bed, showered, styled my hair, slapped on some make-up, and slid into my work uniform—pencil skirt, heels, an eggplant-colored button-down shirt, and jacket. With my briefcase strap tossed over one shoulder, pea coat draped on my back, I made for the street, walking the four blocks to the courthouse. The subway or bus was almost always out of the question. No matter what time of day or night, public transportation seemed to be perpetually packed with people. Walking allowed me to pick alternative routes if the current one suddenly grew too busy for comfort.

As I stopped at a crosswalk, the emotions started flowing like a ruptured dam. The man on my left talking a mile a minute on his cell phone was anxious, panicky, and confused, making momentary jitters flutter over my skin. I shrugged the feelings away and an overwhelming sadness seeped into me from a woman behind me. Her eyes were dark and sunken, hair greasy and disheveled, pieces sticking straight out from her low ponytail. A deep depression nestled into my bones, weighing on my brain like cement.

I turned around to face her. "Ma'am, are you alright?"

"Excuse me?" The woman's chin lifted along with her eyebrows, and a tiny spring of hope bubbled in her chest.

"I asked if you were alright?"

"I—" The woman pulled her shirt sleeves over her hands. "No one's ever asked me that before."

Oh, dear.

Quickly glancing at my analog watch, I canted my head at her. "Would you like a cup of coffee? Maybe a chat? I have some time before I need to be at work."

It would mean walking the remaining two blocks during peak hours, but the heavy cloud hanging over this woman frightened me.

"You'd do that? For a complete stranger?" The woman's eyes glazed over as if she were about to cry.

The gratitude and sheer surprise beaming from her made my chest tighten.

"Absolutely, come on. There's an outside café right on the other side of the street."

Part of my abilities allowed me to inherently know what a person needed—how they wanted to feel but may not have been able to get there on their own. Some closed themselves off with a mental shield, and although I could still sense their emotions, it was challenging to help them. I don't know how or why I'd received this gift, but I'd make the most of it in any way I could.

Choosing a corner table outside nestled under the dimly lit sky, I motioned for the waiter as we took seats across from each other. The woman ordered a plain black coffee, the same as I.

She wasn't used to someone caring and simply needed someone to listen. I couldn't read minds, so I never fully knew why they felt the way they did, but I gave them every opportunity to explain—if they wished.

"Do you always randomly buy coffee for strangers at crosswalks?" The woman folded her hands atop the table after smoothing the disarray of her hair with a palm.

I extended my hand. "My name is Keira."

"Beth." A warm smile slid over her lips as we shook.

"There. Now we're not strangers."

The waiter returned with our coffee, and Beth curled her hands around it, relishing the warmth.

"Life hasn't exactly dealt me the best hand lately." Beth lifted the cup to her nose, letting the steam collect on her cheeks.

I sipped my coffee, keeping quiet, not pressuring her to elaborate.

"I lost my job last month, and I'm weeks away from losing my apartment. I'd moved here for a now ex-boyfriend. Left everything and everyone I knew in Nebraska."

This story sounded familiar. I'd given up my life in Canada to move to New York for my now ex-husband. The only saving grace has been taking the bar to practice law in New York and building an image that would last me a lifetime. It didn't mean I didn't miss a steaming pile of delicious poutine now and again.

She sipped her coffee, wincing when the heat passed her lips. "It took me months to find a job, and we argued about it almost every waking day. And finally, I got a waitressing job at this little diner. The tips weren't great, but I made enough to help with the bills."

With each moment, her demeanor calmed and brightened. I could never be sure if I could pass emotions from myself to another. It was always a fine line to tell someone about my abilities, let alone ask if I could use them as a guinea pig. Still, it never stopped me from trying. With Beth, I dug into every vibrant memory I could bring to the surface—showering her with positivity and warmth.

"One day, I came home from an overtime shift. Two o'clock in the friggin' morning and there was George, packing a suitcase." Beth's eyes glazed over.

I reached a hand across the table, lightly touching her forearm but still saying nothing.

A small smile crept at the corner of her lips, and she patted my hand before leaning back. "He said he needed more out of life, and neither this state nor I was going to be part of it."

A knot formed in my stomach, and I wanted nothing more than to sucker punch this "George" in the gut. As a wrinkle formed between Beth's eyes, I pushed the thought away, concentrating on the moon still looming in the sky above us instead.

"He left me with a rent I couldn't afford on my own, in a place where I knew no one, and with a broken heart." She scraped her thumbnail over the side of the ceramic mug. "I tried to explain it to my work, to get more hours, and they informed me the diner was losing business and shutting down. I also tried to talk to my landlord to work out some kind of payment plan until I could find another job and all he could do was make snarky comments about other ways I could 'pay' him."

A hope fluttered from her, settling over my skin like warm fleece.

"Will you let me help you, Beth?" I peered at her over the rim of my mug.

Beth shifted in her seat before her spine straightened. "I—

you'd do that?"

"We all need a lifeline now and again. I have the means to help, so I will if you let me."

Most would never come right out and ask for it, but the decision to allow help still needed to be theirs.

"I honestly don't know what I did to deserve such kindness, but I will gladly take whatever help you're willing to give." Her eyes glistened from built-up tears.

Resting my mug on the table, I slipped a business card from my pocket and slid it to her. "I work for the state. A prosecutor. There are several jobs open, and I'd be happy to give you a reference if you're interested."

I'd sensed enough of her good character to vouch for her. The poor woman just needed a break.

"I—" Beth started, but the words caught in her throat. She launched from her chair and hugged me, sobbing. "I can't thank you enough."

I wasn't what you'd call a "hugger." But for those I'd helped through the years, embracing seemed to be the only form of gratitude they could muster. It still was enough to make my body stiffen at their touch and triggered a mental game of suppressing the discomfort leaking from my pores.

"Everyone deserves a chance to be happy, Beth. Especially when life puts us through trials, attempting to derail us." After throwing several bills on the table, covering both her coffee and mine, I stood. "When you apply, be sure to add my name. I guarantee with my recommendation, they'll hire you so long as you show the bright side of you in the interview."

"Yes. Absolutely. I'll do you proud, Miss Keira."

I slipped my briefcase on my shoulder and offered her a warm smile, and after pocketing several sugar packets from the dispenser on the table to consume later, I left.

The walk to the office was borderline nauseating. There was so much anxiety seeping from everyone I passed, I felt antsy and dizzy by the time I'd made it to the foyer. I needed to make it to my office to decompress. Everyone and their mothers greeted me when I entered, and I offered small waves and meager smiles in return.

I breezed into my office, whisking the door behind me. Instead of the gratifying clicking sound it should've made upon closing, it muted against a fleshy palm.

"There you are. I was about ready to send out a search party, and then I thought—" Olivia gasped with a hand over her mouth. "Maybe she got laid last night and needed to sleep in from hours of nastiness."

After tossing my briefcase on the desk, I flopped into my chair with a roll of my eyes. Olivia considered my sex life, or lack thereof, a side mission to *her* everyday life. Why she cared so much about the fate of my vagina was beyond me.

"Only one of us got lucky last night, and that one of us wasn't me." I shuffled the papers on my desk, attempting to force my brain to focus and work past the stir of emotions I'd soaked in like a sponge during my walk.

Not bothering to shut the door, Olivia strode in with a manila folder pressed to her chest and her face glued to an e-reader. Olivia had accentuated curves in all the perfect places with a confidence about her that could make any woman envious. My admiration for her never failed, and I'd hired her on the spot the day she applied for the position. I'd have called it a done deal within five minutes but prolonged the interview to checkmark all the necessary boxes. Not to mention, having her around with the glowing positivity she gave off, always refreshed me.

"What are you so intently reading?" I pointed at the tablet.

Without even cutting her eyes to me, she replied, "A book."

"A book? I thought you were reading a paperback. *The Hating Game* or something?"

"Yeah. That's my subway literature because it's got the cute illustrated cover. My e-reader now that is where all the filthy, dirty smut lives." She popped her glance to me long enough to give a sidelong grin.

"Alright, I'll bite. What are you reading?" Tapping my pen against the desk, I rested my chin in my hand.

She bit down on her plump bottom lip, smiling. "It's a cyberpunk romance called *Rescued by Her Enemy*. Action, intrigue, and the best part? Sex. Lots and lots of sex."

"You? Reading such explicit content? Shocking."

She flipped the cover shut on the tablet and rested it on my desk. "I know, right? Speaking of lucky, it's one thing not to want to deal with the peskiness of getting a man involved, but it's another to ignore *her* completely." She pointed below her belly button. Slipping the folder under her arm, she gave one toss of her light blonde bangs and removed her phone from her dress pocket.

Raising a brow at her, I paused mid-flip through a stack of papers.

"Look. This one has a Fifty Shades theme, vibrates, and has

this little rabbit deal-y that stimulates your—" She'd held her phone screen out to me, showing a picture of said sex toy, but paused when I nudged my chin behind her at a group of men leaning in their chairs, straining to listen.

"I appreciate your concern, Ollie." I lowered the phone from view. "I really do, but the last thing we need is one of them filing a complaint about us talking—devices—in the workplace."

Ollie pursed her full lips together, those bright green eyes narrowing before tipping her chin over her shoulder. "They should be taking notes. Maybe you blokes will learn a thing or two."

"I'm going to assume that the folder shoved in your armpit is the acid case?" I pointed with a grin.

She jumped to attention and removed the folder, fanning her palms over the crease down the middle. "Rest assured. I *did* put on deodorant this morning."

"How fortunate for the entire building." I smirked and snatched it from her.

Olivia's jaw dropped as she slid into the seat across from me. "Someone's fiery this morning."

"If you say it's because I'm horny, I'm kicking you out of my office." I offered a small smile but kept my gaze on the case files.

"ESP. I told you. I bloody told you." She snapped her fingers before taking out her cell phone again. "Don't forget you have your client's wedding soon."

I groaned. "I did forget about that. Who invites their lawyer to a wedding? Honestly."

"Keira, you kept him from falsely going to prison. I'd say he's, I don't know, grateful?" Olivia stuck her bottom lip out.

"Where is it again?"

"Argentina."

"Jesus. They couldn't keep it more local?"

Her face fell, deadpan. "Only you, of all people, would complain about having to go to Argentina for a wedding."

"I'm in the middle of a case."

"That won't go to trial for at least lord knows how long. We both know this."

I grabbed a pen from the holder at the corner of my desk and tapped it. "Did you already book the flights?"

"You'll leave the morning of and fly back the day after. In and out."

I twirled the pen between my fingers. "See if you can reschedule for the red-eye flight the same day. That way, I'm only wasting twenty-four hours."

She stared at me wide-eyed, her jaw dropping. "Are you human? I swear sometimes you're an actual robot."

Chewing on the tip of the pen, I ignored her question and raised my brows. "Ollie."

"Red-eye. You got it." She nudged me with her elbow. "Who knows? Maybe some hot Argentinian guy will tango with you."

"Tango?"

"Yeah. Didn't you say you took ballroom dancing classes at university?

Sighing, I shook my head. "One course. One. It was an elective, and it was required. Trust me. I would've taken something English-y or science-y if they'd have let me."

"Alright there, Buzz Killington." Olivia folded her arms in a huff.

"I still can't believe the defense hired Eric Carter." I bit my thumbnail, stopping on the paperwork that outlined preliminary evidence.

"You're telling me. If I can manage not to drool a lazy river and happily float down it in his presence *and* actually get some work done, it'll be a miracle."

The lust wafting from her like vapors made the small space of my office suddenly cave in.

"I'm sorry, what?" I snapped my gaze to hers.

She leaned forward, slapping her palms on my desk, making her six Alex and Ani bracelets jingle together. "Don't play coy with me, Keira. Any woman in her right mind knows that man is attractive. Gross defense lawyer? Sure. But still wouldn't stop me from riding him like an ostrich."

I scrunched my nose and let the papers fall to the stack. "Oh, come on. I haven't even had breakfast yet."

Olivia's phone chimed from the desk outside of my office, and she leaped for the door. She talked, but I was far too busy rummaging through the case file paperwork to concentrate on what she said.

Her head poked out from the doorframe. "Um, apparently, the defense wants to have a pre-pre-trial conference to discuss their client and any evidence currently held."

"We can have a pre-trial conference with the judge same as any other trial as soon as I've had the time to look through the damn case."

"They want to meet within the hour." Olivia scratched the side of her deeply slanted nose with a nervous smile.

Sighing, I slammed the folder shut. "It never fails. It's always the prosecution that has to bend over and take it in the ass."

"Until The Blonde Bulldogs wipe the floor with them in the trial itself," Olivia added with a brightened grin.

"And this is why you're my wing woman, Ollie." We fist-bumped as we made our way through the cubicles.

On the cab ride over, I'd pored through as many of the files as I could. It wouldn't be the first time I'd had to come prepared on a whim. My heart thundered against my ribcage as we neared the conference room. These conferences were never easy and most often a struggle to maintain professionalism. I'd never cracked under pressure or lost my cool with a defense lawyer, but I'd be lying if I said there hadn't been numerous points of temptation. They were the enemy in that courtroom, and it all started here—the pre-trial conference.

The room was empty when we entered, and I took a brief moment of reprieve to calm my nerves, regain composure, and browse through the evidence folder one last time.

"You're bloody adorable," Olivia said, taking the seat next to me.

Concentrating on the list of audio recordings, I dragged my finger down it. "Why do you say that?"

"You've gone over the evidence a dozen times. You know it. You're fine." She closed the folder with my hand still on the paper.

"How long have you been my assistant?" I didn't move my finger, saving my spot on the list.

Olivia puckered her plump, glossy lips. "Years? I've lost track. Time flies when you're havin' fun, right?"

"Two years, six months, and eleven days."

Olivia sat up straight and counted on her fingers, mouthing numbers to herself with a perplexed brow.

"My point is, we've known each other a long time. This is my system. It works, and—"

A deep, masculine voice from the hallway seeped through the window. It sounded familiar, but I couldn't place where I'd heard it.

The door opened, and a man entered the meeting room—a man who was *not* the assigned defense lawyer. This man was infamous. One of the best. The nerves I'd fought to calm ramped into overdrive at the thought of going up against him.

I locked gazes with a pair of deep-sea blue eyes, luring me in to hurl me to the depths and crush me.

Zane Vronti.

What was worse?

The man. Was. Gorgeous.

Shit.

THREE

ZEUS

THE JAIL SET ME up in a private room and I sat at the table, mindlessly scrolling through dozens of images of my opposing counselor, waiting for my client's arrival. It was no wonder the media had a field day with her. She was practically a supermodel practicing law. But one thing I noted, despite over a hundred images, in not one of them did she smile. And she was always alone. Was she depressed at all times? Angry? Putting on a serious demeanor for the sake of the cameras?

And why the fuck did I care?

The door burst open, and I immediately turned the phone screen black, resting it on the table in front of me. Adjusting in my seat, I smoothed down my tie and waited.

Melissa Daniels. Late forties. Dark hair with exposed grey roots in wiry disarrays of frizzy curls. Double chin. And that same scowl from her mugshot.

I nudged my chin at the officer, signaling he could leave. As

Melissa maneuvered into the chair across from me, the cuffs on her wrists jangled. Removing the folder from my briefcase, I slapped it down between us, locking eyes with her.

"They say you're the best," she said, her voice gruff and lifeless.

"They say a lot. But on that, they'd be correct. It's a wonder you didn't hire me in the first place." I flipped open the folder, shuffling the papers like the professional I was.

Melissa snorted, sucking snot back into her throat through one nostril like she was getting ready to spit a godsdamned loogie. "You've cost nearly every penny I have."

"It's a worthy investment, trust me." I paused to watch her for a moment as she unabashedly stuck half a finger up her nose, digging. After sucking on my teeth, I flipped the folder shut, garnering her attention. "We're going to need to work on your— manners while we're sitting in court. I'll also make arrangements for your—" I flicked my wrist at her head. "—hair."

She frowned and dragged a hand over the bird nest atop her skull. "What's wrong with my hair?"

"Everything. You want sympathy from the jury? They need to see you at least give one out of two shits." I held my phone up, acting as if its presence in my hand had a correlation to our conversation.

In reality, I worked up an e-mail asking for a meeting with the lovely prosecution. Considering I'd already lost time given the last-minute change of attorneys, the prosecution would have no means to deny the request—not that they *ever* had the means. Not to mention, the sooner I had Keira within my sights, the sooner I could have her—underneath me, on top of me, in front of me...

I grimaced at the amount of evidence already piling up against her as I flicked through the folder. "Did you tell your hairstylist you could kill your husband and get away with it?"

She tapped her pudgy fingers against the table. "People say a lot of things."

"That they do." Grabbing a pen, I jotted notes. "It's not recorded, so we have that going for us. The dozen answering machine recordings however, are a little harder to skirt around."

She rolled her eyes as if her time spent here was an inconvenience.

"Was your husband abusive? Physically? Emotionally? Was he a bad father?" I tapped the pen on the paper, making dozens of dots.

I'd briefly skimmed family and friend testimonials, all stating that he was, in fact, a good father. But I needed to understand her angle. If she even had one. The serpent-like glint in her gaze—the hollowness I could sense through her mind suggested she may have simply "snapped."

"Being a dad to our kids was about the only damn thing he was good for. He'd watch them while I worked and made all the money." She rolled her shoulders with a sneer. "I'd be lucky if half the time I came home to a cooked meal. Not even sure what the bastard did all day."

Rubbing my chin, I kept my gaze fixed on her, noting the aloofness when she spoke about him. No guilt. No remorse. I'd venture to guess she couldn't remember most of what she and her accomplice carried out that day—acting and reacting on pure rage.

"Is that the reason you left the voicemails? Angry at him for not upholding his stay-at-home-dad duties?"

The words sounded fucking ridiculous out loud, and it was the part of the job I hated most. As a defense lawyer, it wasn't my job to judge or cast blame. All were innocent until proven otherwise, right? Fuck me. At least I knew what waited for her at the end of the river Styx when she arrived in the Underworld.

"It says here, months before the incident, you landed a rather large contract with one of the largest pharmaceutical companies in the country. That true?" I leaned back, pinning my gaze to hers, studying her.

She glared at me. "Yeah. So?"

Tossing the pen on the table, I held back an exasperated sigh begging to escape from my chest.

The selfish harpy wanted all of her newly hard-earned cash for herself—especially with a looming divorce started by her dearly departed husband. She couldn't give me a legitimate means to defend her even if she wanted to, which meant it would rely heavily on the dismissal of evidence. A notification blipped on my phone, and I stole a glance at the reply e-mail from the prosecution agreeing to meet.

"Let's cut straight to the chase, Daniels." Staring at her, I lowered my phone. "Did you do it?"

She blinked. Silent.

"Mrs. Daniels. Did you murder your husband?" I purposely emphasized the 'Mrs.' part of her name, knowing full well I'd hit a nerve. The divorce was never finalized before his death. Therefore, she still legally bore the name of a man she hated enough to kill.

Am I already accusing her? Yes. Ninety-five percent of the criminals I represented were guilty of their crimes. In all honesty, it made winning a case easier than if they were innocent.

Melissa's face distorted into a grimace, her hands balling into fists on the table, making the metal cinched against her skin squeak.

"Nothing leaves this room, but it makes it easier for me to formulate an argument on your behalf if I know the truth." My electric powers sizzled over my skin, desiring nothing more than to force the confession out of her.

Her dark eyes panned to mine, an unspoken evil floating within them. "Yes. You're damn right I killed him, the fucking asshole."

And there we have it.

I nodded once, sliding the folder off the table and back into my briefcase with one swift motion. "There should be no need for you to testify, but now under no circumstance are we letting you get on that stand." Standing, I pulled my jacket sleeves down, realigning them with my cufflinks.

"Are we done? That's it?" Melissa looked around the small room.

"That's it. Now I get to work. If I need any clarification on the evidence presented, I'll arrange for another meeting." I pressed a button, alerting the officer to retrieve Melissa.

Melissa Daniels was evil incarnate. One had to be to do what she did over the simple fact of "not liking someone." But again, it wasn't my job to judge them. And I certainly didn't condone murder. It didn't matter what my personal scruples were. She was a human being, and with that came certain rights. Rights that needed protecting. Guilty or not, someone has to be willing to say, "I'll defend you." And it might as well be me. A certain strength was needed to take the burden from others onto your shoulders. I'd been doing it for eons.

I stood in the men's restroom of the courthouse, only several rooms, and across the hallway from the assigned meeting room. I'd arrived early but purposely waited three minutes over the agreed time—an excuse to make an entrance. Peering at myself in the mirror, I traced my hand over my beard and adjusted my sleeves. A snap of my fingers put every hair back into place atop my head, the cufflinks and watch sparkled with radiance, and not one hair within my beard was left untrimmed. As easy as I had it with the mortals I set my sights on, certain women took extra care—extra steps to ensnare. Given Keira's reputation, I fully expected a pacing lioness. With a glance at the clock hanging on the wall, I'd become fashionably late and smiled to myself before exiting.

Slipping my hands in my pants pockets, I made my way down the hall, halting by the meeting room's window. A man walked past, and I greeted him, not knowing who the fuck he was but needing an excuse to say something. She'd hear the boom in my voice through the wall—the power lacing every word. And within a few seconds, the daunting realization would crawl through her. That deep voice—*my* voice, didn't belong to the previously hired defense lawyer.

Adjusting the knot of my tie with one hand, I opened the

door with the other, focusing my gaze on my glossed shoes as I entered. "Apologies for being late. I had some…catching up to do on the case."

It was subtle, but the smallest of feminine gasps escaped her throat.

Finally lifting my eyes to hers—was like being punched in the gut. The media hadn't done this woman one ounce of justice. She was fucking gorgeous. The buxom and curvy blonde woman next to her widened her green eyes at me and squeezed Keira's knee below the table.

"Keira. That's Zane Vronti," she loud-whispered, staring at me.

Keira slapped her hand, her nostrils flaring, heat flushing her light skin. "I can see that, Olivia," she spat through gritted teeth, trying desperately not to glare at me.

Oh, the fire exuding from her like a backdraft.

Keira stood, smoothing her hands over the faux designer suit jacket hugging her tits. "I'm sorry, you failed to mention a counsel change in your e-mail request."

"I figured this meeting would serve both purposes. Is there an issue, counselor?" I leaned a hip on the table.

Keira rolled her shoulders back, making herself taller before jutting her hand out. "Not at all. Keira—"

"—Bazin," I finished for her. "Trust me. I've researched you." Slipping my hand into hers, I sent enough electricity over her skin to elicit a reaction but not enough to hurt her.

Her face stayed neutral save for the slightest twitch of her upper lip.

Huh. Peculiar and incredibly…irritating.

Keira recoiled her hand and wiped it on the front of her pin-stripe skirt as if my palm was covered in shit. A grin tugged at my lips as I took a step back.

A femme fatale disguised in imitation Versace.

"My paralegal, Olivia." She referenced the eager shorter woman to her left.

Olivia threw out her hand, a radiant smile plastering her face. "An absolute honor——" Her eyes cut to Keira and back to me. "—er, a pleasure to meet you."

Squinting at her, I shook her hand, sending the same current through her as I had Keira. Olivia's reaction was more to my expectation. She gasped, her neck flushing. A nervous bout of laughter floated from her belly, and she dragged her fingers through her wheat-colored waves of hair.

"Love the accent." I pointed at her and winked, inciting another trail of bubbly giggling.

"Cheers," she responded before plopping in her chair and fanning herself.

Keira sat down and folded her hands on the table, not sitting back.

All the more curious about her.

Moving to the opposing side of the table, I sat on the edge, gaining the high ground over Miss Bazin.

The suit jacket shifted as her shoulders tensed beneath the fabric. "You don't want to have a seat, Mr. Vronti?"

"I'm fine right here." I patted the glass table. "And please. It's Zane." Flashing as charming of a grin as I could manage without spraining something, I gauged her reaction.

She undid the top button of her purple blouse and rebuttoned it. "I assume you have evidence you propose to dismiss, Mr. Vronti?"

This. Woman.

"That confident, hm? No plea deal?" I plucked a pen from the holder in the center of the table and twirled it between my fingers.

Olivia's gaze fell to my hand, and her palms flattened on the table.

"Not a chance." Keira flipped the folder open. "Evidence you wish to challenge?"

For the love of me, give me something.

Pushing from the table with a smug grin, I rocked back on my heels before pacing the length of the room. Olivia's eyes trailed me like a bouncing shiny red ball. Keira glanced only long enough to stifle an eye roll before removing a pen from her jacket and slapping it to the awaiting paper.

"The answering machine recordings," I challenged.

Keira started to write but paused, furrowing her brow. "All of them?"

"All of them." I tapped my fingertips to the table as I passed.

Keira rested the pen on the table. "There are several recordings of her threatening to kill her husband. Why would it be agreed to withhold those?"

"Fine. Keep those, but dismiss any where she goes into a name-calling barrage."

Keira's chest lifted as she sighed but kept it inaudible. "They're still threatening."

"Oh, come now, Keira." I jiggled the keys in my pocket as I turned on my heel. "You're telling me you've never dropped a curse word or two while arguing or—" Her gaze met mine. "—in the *throes* of passion?"

"Dear God," Olivia whispered.

Not quite.

Keira undid two buttons on her shirt, taking several more seconds this time around before doing them up again.

I may not have broken through yet, but perhaps…*cracked* her invisible shield.

ƑOUR

𝕃𝕃𝕃𝕃𝕃𝕃𝕃𝕃𝕃𝕃𝕃𝕃𝕃𝕃

KEIRA

HIS EMOTIONS WERE A tidal wave repeatedly hurling me against other incoming waves. It took everything in me not to show the turmoil surging through me on my face. Since I was a child, I'd had my empath ability and experienced all levels of emotion from hundreds of people. His were the most intense I'd ever felt—burdened, arrogant, powerful. *Very* powerful, but most of all? Insatiable lust. In the passing minutes, it'd become so overwhelming I couldn't sift through his emotions versus my own.

The bastard refused to sit down—no doubt a power play against me. I undid the top button of my blouse, touching my fingertip against my skin before doing it up again—a habit I'd formed to calm myself. It pissed me off to no end that the man was undoubtedly attractive as well. I'd done my best to avoid lingering on news stations talking about him. It was bad enough spying him across the street from the safety of my apartment window. But now those sapphire eyes I'd glimpsed only on a TV screen lingered in front of me—probing me, seducing me.

Slapping my palms on the table, I shot to my feet. "Mr. Vronti, I'm not entirely certain where you get off talking to me in such a manner. It's entirely unprofessional, but furthermore, you want *half* of the recordings dismissed?" I tightened my jaw, not letting my eyes tear away despite the lust pouring out of him in droves. The devious glint in his gaze had my insides twisting. "Fine. We have plenty of other ammunition."

In truth, I did not want him to request *anything* dismissed. His requesting dismissal of evidence would have to be brought up before a judge, further postponing the trial.

Irritation and confusion bubbled over him but were soon overshadowed by determination, which dissolved them in the thick air hanging between us.

A jackal's grin pulled at the corner of his lips. He crossed the room with deliberate steps, his serpentine gaze fixed on me. "You know how this works, Keira." He stood in front of me, scents of sandalwood and cologne permeating the air. "You're required to reveal *all* the dirty laundry at your disposal." He bit on his lower lip, eyes squinting.

Standing this close to him had my brain whirling while simultaneously making the hairs on my arms stand on end. Rather than peel my eyes away, suggesting he had some form of power over me, I distanced us by taking a step back.

Olivia tugged the hem of my jacket.

Thankful for the reprieve, I bent at the waist, lowering my ear to her mouth.

"I think my undies melted," she whispered…very loudly.

I loved Olivia. Really, I did. But her filter was Swiss cheese on the best of days.

My eyes snapped to Zane's satisfied smile.

"I have that effect on *most* women, Olivia." His gaze roamed my body before lazily lifting back to my face. "Don't hate yourself for it."

Squaring off my shoulders, refusing to let him see the effect he *could* have on me, I slid the folder across the table. "And you know how this works, counselor. You can review with prosecution present."

His eyes dropped to the folder, a challenging smirk creasing his mouth. As he slid a large tanned hand over the manila, his pinky brushed the tip of my finger. The same mild static shock I'd felt when he shook my hand earlier shot through my skin. My right nostril bounced, and I ignored the tingling sensation his touch left behind as he scooped the folder into his grasp and started to flip through the papers.

He waltzed around the room with a pinched brow, squinting here and there as he sifted through the evidence files. Hiding my hand beneath the table, I tapped it on my knee, suppressing an annoyed sigh. Zane started to hum a song, his tone deep—baritone. It sounded familiar, but I didn't want to focus on his voice enough to decipher it.

Olivia leaned over. "Is he singing Acca Dacca?" She poked my ribs, her large green eyes even larger as she stared at the criminal defense lawyer circling us.

We really needed to discuss proper whispering decibels.

"Why, yes, I am. *Thunderstruck* by AC/DC for some reason

always helps me concentrate." He paused and shot his gaze to mine, impaling me with it. "You know?"

"Whatever speeds this up. I'll even play it on my phone if it means spending less time in a six-by-six room with you." I slipped my phone from my jacket pocket and rested it on the table with a smug grin.

"Not a fan of my serenading?" He leaned on the table across from me.

Pulling up a streaming service, I queued up the song. "Why settle for second best?" I pressed the play button, keeping a challenging stare fixed on him.

The opening guitar riff to *Thunderstruck* blared from my phone's speaker. Olivia scrunched her face and threw up rock horns on both hands.

A wicked glint flashed in his eyes, a hint of a smile hiding over his lips. His emotions shifted—intrigued, more irritated. But the lust? Amplified.

I just. Didn't. Get it.

Leaning back in my chair, I folded my arms and held my hand out to him. "Please continue."

The tip of his tongue skirted his bottom lip before he finally lowered his gaze back to the papers and began his proximity march again. At my side, Olivia switched from the air guitar to drums, her blonde bangs falling over her eyes.

Slowly turning my head, I cocked an eyebrow at her.

Out of breath, she froze mid drumstick twirl and tousled her hair. "Too much?"

"Maybe a tad." I gestured my hand up high and lowered it, asking her to bring it down a notch.

"Right." She cleared her throat and tugged on the hem of her jacket. "Serious mode."

Despite her best efforts, she sat still for the most part, but her foot kept tapping. She'd fist pump under the table during specific lyrics and attempt to subtly lip sync.

I bit back a smile. Olivia could be such a goofball, but I wouldn't have had it any other way. Her presence alone helped me cope every day.

There was a knock at the door, and I quickly shut the music off. Zane glared at the door with one hand rubbing his chin.

"Mr. Vronti? Sorry to bother you, but your three o'clock appointment is here," Ruth said, pausing with her hand on the door handle and adjusting her glasses.

"I still have work to do here." Zane's tone was abrupt. Turning his back to her, he returned to the paperwork.

"But sir, it's your br—"

Zane snapped her a look over his shoulder, and flipped the folder shut with a loud *thwap*.

"Right. I'll let them know you'll be late," Ruth squeaked before closing the door behind her.

Impatience. Ever-growing irritation.

"There isn't any reason to drag this out, Zane. Everything is there for you in black and white. Either request a hearing on the evidence with a judge or let me get back to work." Scooting to the edge of my seat, I folded my hands on the table.

Zane opened the folder and dropped his gaze to the papers. "Such impatience for a woman's life hanging in the balance."

"Don't try to act as if you care about the client. You care about winning." I narrowed my eyes at him, and crossed my legs under the table to ignore the throbbing happening between them.

Lust. Anger. Desire.

"Regardless of your preconceived notions, for once, it isn't about me, Keira." He tossed the folder on the table and shoved his hands in his pockets.

"Are you trying to imply you inexplicably grew a conscience?" I panned my gaze to the awaiting folder.

"Fine. I'm formally requesting a hearing on the evidence before a judge."

Heat surged up the back of my neck, molars cracking as I gritted my teeth. Olivia sighed beside me, jotting down notes on a legal pad.

He jiggled keys in his pocket, his jaw tightening. "Are we done here?" Glancing at his watch, he started for the door. "I have more important things to do."

My jaw wanted to drop, but I forced it to stay put and, instead, squeezed the life out of the pen in my hand. "But you—" I cut myself short once his brow raised to the heavens.

This guy was one colossal mind fuck. And he *knew* it.

Standing, I shoved the folder under my arm and stormed at the exit with my chin held high.

"Looks like I'll be seeing you soon for the evidence trial—" His gaze lowered, lingering over my chest. "Counselor."

Impatience. Smugness. Attraction.

He made no move to shake my hand, so I gave a simple nod. "May the best man win."

A chuckle—low and smooth—flowed from his chest. The sound vibrated to my toes, making my lips part as if they had a mind of their own.

His eyes dropped to my mouth before turning away, not muttering another word.

The further he got away from me, the more relaxed my mind, my nerves, my *everything* became. Rubbing my forehead, I leaned against the doorframe, exhausted as if I'd just run a marathon—twice.

"You okay?" Olivia nudged me.

"Yeah. Tired is all. I think I'm going to head home." I caught sight of Zane disappearing into another meeting room down the hall and sighed with relief.

"Woah. Home? And at half-past three in the arvo?" Olivia slapped a hand on my forehead.

Used to Ollie's antics by now, I let her palm my face. "Ollie. What are you doing?"

"Checking for a fever. Pretty sure this hasn't happened since the Fueller case."

She wasn't wrong. On any given day, I'd barricade myself in my office and pour myself into my work until the wee hours of the night. Sometimes even well into the early morning. After the overwhelming emotions exuding from Zane like a damn geyser, however, the only thing my mind would excel at currently would be absolutely nothing.

"I'm tired." Removing her hand, I pushed past her, heading down the hall. "I want my bed, a fluffy blanket, and Barns Courtney music. Tomorrow, I'll be good as new."

"Holy shit. Does this mean I have an early day?" Clapping, Olivia bounced on her heels.

"Knock yourself out. You've earned it." I whisked through

the foyer to the sidewalk outside, grimacing at the flood of emotions hammering my brain from every corner.

"Catch you later, Keir-Keir." Olivia held her fist up.

With a weak smile, I bumped mine against hers. "Blonde Bulldogs, out," she shouted, fanning her hand out before turning away and almost barreling into a businessman briskly walking.

He sneered at her, and Olivia threw her arms at her sides.

"What? It's a thing we do, alright?" Olivia said to the man's back, who made an active effort to ignore her.

My smile faded into a wince as bouts of anxiety, anger, fear, and worry flooded me from New York's inhabitants.

Was no one happy anymore?

Yanking earbuds from my briefcase, I slipped them in to cue up music. With any luck, it'd drown out most if not all of the emotions running rampant in the streets. *Tonight (I'm Lovin' You)* by Enrique Iglesias blasted into my ears. Concentrating on the beat, the feel of the concrete beneath my heels, and the bitter cold crispness in the air, dulled the floating feelings around me.

Stopping for a red light at the next crosswalk, I patted my hand against my hip, continuing the rhythmic distraction. I swiveled my hips ever so slightly, unable to control them. Lust washed over me in waves—a faint whimper collecting at the back of my throat. I opted for the explicit version of the song where "fuck" replaced the word "love." Because let's be honest, everyone knew what was *really* going down in that song. Pure. Carnal. Fu—

"*Come* here often?" A deep voice rumbled by my ear.

Jumping, I ripped out an earbud and whirled around.

Zane towered over me, sporting a long tan Burberry jacket with the collar popped. "Nice moves, by the way." He pointed at my hips.

"Are you stalking me?" In a huff, I shoved my earbuds into my jacket pocket.

"Someone thinks rather highly of themselves." He bobbed his brows at the illuminated walk sign.

With quick steps, I crossed the street.

Hopefully, he changed directions.

One glance over my shoulder made it abundantly clear. He still followed me.

"For your information—" Zane started, falling in stride beside me. "I live three blocks down."

You knew that, Keira.

"And you're *walking* there?" I slipped my gloves on.

"Why is that so hard for you to believe? You're doing the exact same thing *right* now."

The lust floating from him was like every man combined at a party in the Playboy mansion. My stomach did an unsettling flutter.

Biting the inside of my cheek, I ignored it, slipped the strap of my briefcase over one shoulder, and wrapped my arms around myself. "I have my reasons."

A woman with bouncing waves of auburn hair walked past us, plastering a sultry grin at Zane. She waved at him, and I caught a glimpse of him grinning like a fool at her. Rolling my eyes, I shoved my gloved hands into my pockets as we reached another stop light.

"I'm dying to know said reasons." Zane took a step closer to me.

Heat radiated from him like magma, and I fought every compulsion to wrap him around me like a blanket.

"I said I have them. Not that I was going to tell you what they were." My hot breath curled in the cool air like an angered dragon.

"Keira, Keira, Keira. Just because we're opposing counsel doesn't mean we can't be—" He bent forward, lowering his face to my level. "Friends." A spark ignited in his gaze.

The walk signal blazed, and I bolted forward. "No, Zane. That's precisely what it means. We'll say our arguments in the courtroom, I'll win, and after it's all over, hopefully, we'll *never* see each other again."

We neared our apartment buildings and Zane came to a pause, shaking his head at me but grinning. "Your confidence is astounding."

"And your ego is nauseating."

We locked gazes, and an electric current sizzled down my spine. I held back a breath that longed to escape my throat, my chest tightening.

"Okay, then. See you around." Peeling my eyes away from him, I turned to my building.

"Wait a minute. You live *here*?" He pointed a leather-covered hand and tipped his head to one side.

"Uh-huh. Have a good day." I wrapped my hand around the door's handle.

"Wait." He slapped a hand near mine but made no move to touch me. "There is absolutely no way I wouldn't have noticed you lived across from me for—how long have you been here?"

Grinding my teeth, I took a step back. "It's none of your business how long I've lived here, but if you must know, it's because I'm rarely home."

"You're a workaholic, aren't you?" He crossed his arms, a gleam in his sapphire eyes.

"Don't lawyers have to be?" I tightened my grip on the briefcase.

"Good ones, sure. But even dedicated lawyers have to come up for air, don't they?" He squinted at me.

Uncertainty. Longing. Frustration. It all fluttered from him, settling over my skin like static cling.

"Well, you don't have to worry about bumping into me. I practically live in my office." I scratched the back of my head, averting my gaze to a woman sitting at her window three floors up, reading a book.

"Do you do *everything* in your office?"

Gone were the real emotions—and back was the insatiable lust.

Snapping my gaze to his, I moved past him for the door handle. "Goodbye, Zane."

Stepping away from the door with a chuckle, he flew his palms up. "I'll be sure to leave my blinds open for you."

My insides clenched at the implication, my gloves creaking against the door as I gripped it. "Why the hell would you do that?"

He backed away with his hands in his pockets, his jacket flapping as he shrugged. "Guess you'll have to wait and find out." Smiling, he winked at me, that same spark flashing in his gaze.

I bolted inside without another word, another passing thought, or another betraying flip of my stomach. Zane played a game, unaware that I had an ace up my sleeve. There he was grinning at me from across the poker table with the four of a kind in his hands, waiting to lay the cards out and win. He didn't know being an empath gave me a royal fucking flush.

FIVE

ZEUS

WHAT WAS *WRONG* WITH this woman? Not only did she not so much as bat a fucking eyelash over my godly mojo, which, by the way, I'd been pumping out like a damn fire hose, but she also felt compelled to *challenge* me.

She couldn't have been mortal. A faerie, maybe? Nymph?

Rubbing my chin, I poured another scotch and leaned against the bar in my loft, absently scratching Levin's head as I stared into oblivion.

Hermes appeared in my living room in a flash of light and feathers, rubbing the back of his head and doing that Clint Eastwood squint of his. I'm sure women found it attractive. I, however, always felt compelled to ask him if he needed glasses.

"What did you find out?" I stood straight, resting the tumbler on the bar.

After the debacle that was the evidence meeting, I needed to know more about her. Any bit of dirt or information that could possibly explain why I didn't wake up with her in bed next to me *this* morning.

"Gee. Great to see you too, Dad. Can't you at least pour me a drink first?" Hermes smirked as he scratched the stubble on his chin and slid onto a stool.

Levin trotted over to him, and Hermes smiled as he scratched the dog behind both ears.

Tightening my jaw, I grabbed another glass and obliged him—this one time. I eyed the "flyboy" aviation jacket hanging over his frame as I slid the scotch toward him. "Still working the pilot cover, I see?"

"I like flying too much, and considering winged shoes aren't exactly discreet, modern technology is my calling." He grinned, forming those same creases in his cheeks as mine before taking a long swig of whiskey.

I tapped my pinky ring against the glass several times.

Hermes's gaze dropped to my hand before he lowered his tumbler. "Before I tell you what I found out, Pops, level with me here. Why the sudden keen interest in a mortal? I can count on one hand the number of times you asked me about one in the past century."

"So, she *is* mortal?" I pressed my fingertips into the marble.

Hermes blinked rapidly. "What else would she be without you knowing?"

Fuck. Me. Could any of this have been easy?

Pinching the bridge of my nose, I snarled. "Hera is no longer Queen."

"What? How? Is that—" Hermes slid from the stool and leaned his forearms on the bar. "That's possible?"

"Yes. And I let her leave." Staring at the swirling smoke patterns in the bar top, I curled my lip back before downing the rest of my drink.

"Wow, but—"

I cut a glare at my son. "Be careful with your next words, boy. I have a matter of days. *Days* to find a new Queen or risk losing not only the crown but part of my power as well."

Hermes nodded, taking a step back. "And this woman is a candidate? Why go through the trouble? You're King of the Gods, just force her to—"

Slamming the glass down, I pressed my palms against the bar. "What did you find out?"

"Alright, alright. Calm down. Last thing we need is a random lightning strike in New York City in the middle of winter." He snapped his brown leather jacket. "This'll probably make you feel better. She's a divorcée."

I balled my hands into fists. "How is her being previously married supposed to make me *feel* better?"

"Because that marriage was the only thing keeping her legal in the US." Hermes folded his arms.

Hope sprung eternal.

"Come again?"

"She's about to be an illegal alien. Canadian citizen, living in the US, practicing law. She passed the bar in New York while she was still married, but without the proper immigration status again, and fast, not only will she be kicked out but won't be able to practice here."

A grin tugged at my lips. "And with how wrapped up in her work she is, why would she remember a little thing like a deadline?"

"Sure. Clearly, you've been...investigating her on your own." A sly grin pulled at my son's lips, his fingers drumming on the bar.

Aggravation tugged at my spine. "Not as *thoroughly* as I would prefer."

Hermes's expression fell flat. "You mean you two haven't—"

"No," I growled.

He blinked once. "I don't know what to say to that."

"You say nothing. That's what."

Hermes whistled and drummed his fingers on the flat surface. "Man, this chick has done a number on you, hasn't she?"

The question made my blood boil. How *had* she worked under my skin? And *why* did I feel the need to pursue it?

"It's not anything I can't handle. She thinks she has some form of power over me." I dragged my knuckle under my bottom lip, electricity sparking in my palms. "She's sorely mistaken."

Hermes held his hands up, eyeing the lightning still circling my arms. "Ever stop to think *feeling* powerless with someone doesn't have to be the same as *being* powerless?"

Cutting my gaze to his, I shot a bolt at his tumbler, shattering it.

Hermes slapped the bar top. "Right. I know when I've overstayed my welcome."

Levin touched my leg with his paw, panting.

"Take Levin for a walk," I barked at Hermes.

He glared at me and scoffed. "I'm not your godsdamned errand boy."

I returned the glare. Only mine would've rattled Olympus's

foundation.

He gulped and hopped from his stool, whistling for Levin. "Right away, sir."

I had far more pressing matters to deal with…

I paused outside the courtroom. No doubt my presence would cause a stir, especially considering I hadn't done the "courteous" action of announcing my arrival via phone call. No. I needed to swoop in, discreetly work my magic, and get the Tartarus out of Dodge. I'd donned my dark blue suit with a matching necktie, knowing it made my eyes pop, slathered in extra hair gel, and as I entered, flashed a radiant-as-fuck grin.

The whispering and murmurs started as soon as my shoe touched the tan carpet leading into a barrage of cubicles. With one hand in my pants pocket, I used the other to give idle waves to those who chose to stare at me.

A random man walked up to me, puffing his chest, trying to make himself look taller. "Mr. Vronti, we uh—we weren't expecting you."

"Yes." I squinted, panning the heads peeking over cubicle walls, looking for one blonde in particular. "I was in the area and thought of something last minute to discuss with—I'm looking for Miss Bazin's paralegal, Olivia. Is she in?"

"Fuck me," an Aussie woman whispered nearby.

Smiling at the random man, I nudged my head in the voice's direction and swiveled on my heel. Resting my forearm on the cubicle wall, I leaned over. Olivia had her head crouched near her computer monitor, hands pressed against the desk and splayed open.

"Hello there," I said, dropping my voice an octave.

Olivia shot up, the phone headset nestled atop her head yanking off from lack of cord length. "Zane. Mr. Vronti." She cleared her throat and batted her bangs from her eyes before grabbing a tissue and dabbing between her tits with it. "Zane."

"Olivia." Stroking the wall with a single finger, I subtly chewed on my bottom lip.

Her eyes snapped to my finger, and she gulped before letting out a nervous laugh. "Is there uh—something I can help you with? Keira isn't uh—isn't here. She went to lunch."

"Perfect. Because I hoped to speak with *you*." I bent forward, finally managing to catch her gaze.

It was so much easier when they looked at me.

Her plump lips parted, and she absently dropped the tissue as she stuck out her chest. "Me?"

"Mmhm. Mind if I…*come* around?" I did a circle gesture with my hand, making my lightning power spark in my eyes.

"Come? Around?" She pushed her rolling desk chair back and opened her arms. "Have at it."

Keeping her gaze without blinking, I curved my lips into a grin, and walked around the corner of the cubicle with powerful, calculated steps. I stood in front of her, widening my stance.

Her chest heaved as she stared up at me, her hands gripping the seat of her chair on each side of her wide hips. "Hi."

"Hi," I whispered, sitting on the edge of her desk and crossing one ankle over the opposite knee. "Olivia, I need you to do me a favor."

Olivia halfway stood from her chair, glancing around the office with her fingers grazing her chest. "Here? In the middle of the office?"

"Olivia," I beckoned, making her look me in the eye again.

She slowly sat back down, rubbing her lips together as she devoured me with her gaze.

"Under other circumstances, I may have taken you up on such an enticing offer." I leaned forward, tilting my head, relishing in the whimper that escaped her throat. "But the favor I need involves your calendar."

"My—calendar?" She scrunched her nose.

Sitting back, I interlaced my fingers, letting them hang between my legs. "Particularly the one you keep for Keira?"

"Oh. Sure. What about it?" Olivia's gaze moved to her computer monitor as she rolled her chair to the desk and pulled up a digital calendar.

I was next to her in a swift move undetectable to the mortal eye, leaning on the desk.

Dipping my chin and lowering my voice, I laced every word with power only a god-king possessed. "Her paperwork deadline. The divorce. Her residency status situation. Erase it."

She stared up at me, sticking out her chest before letting out a moaning sigh.

Leaning forward, I moved close enough to let her smell the scent wafting from me that I'd explicitly conjured for her—eucalyptus, barbeque and…Vegemite. I would've chosen Aqua di Gio or even fucking vanilla and laundry, but no—this woman liked what she liked. "Olivia."

"Yup. Right. On it." Her hand worked the mouse, eyes wide

as she clicked onto the calendar, pulled up the instance…and hit the delete button with a single finger.

"Good girl." I rested my hands in my lap.

She let out a sensual groan, rolling her chair closer to me, puckering her lips, and closing her eyes. Scooping a folder from her desk into my hand, I lifted it between us, making her lips meet with it rather than my mouth. She fluttered her eyes open with an exaggerated pout.

"The entry never existed. In fact, blame it on a glitch if she asks. And I—" As I leaned forward, her chest swelled, and her eyes grew heavy. I bopped her on the nose with the folder. "—was never here."

Olivia's eyes closed again, and she moaned, gripping the armrests of her chair as her head fell back.

I stood, pulling on my shirt sleeves and scanning the other cubicles. Not a soul peeked. Just the way I'd willed it. Buttoning my suit jacket, I strolled from Olivia's cubicle and started to walk away.

Olivia gasped behind me. "I think—I just came and have no idea how."

Peeking a glance at her over my shoulder, I grinned at her fists thrusting into the air as she leapt from her chair.

"But I am *all* about phantom orgasms," she exclaimed.

Remember when I said it was far too easy?

I smirked to myself before exiting the building.

The first step was complete. The damsel would soon be in distress, and I could swoop in to save the day and make her an offer she couldn't refuse. Still, I needed more information. I'd only known Keira for a matter of days and she'd already managed to surprise me far too many times for comfort. A meddling god could not meddle properly without ammunition. And I knew precisely who to call on to provide me with an arsenal on our darling spitfire prosecutor.

I stood in my living room, waiting for the arrival of my enforcers, throwing a tennis ball for Levin. His ears flopped as he returned with it in the corner of his mouth. After dropping the ball at my feet, he bent forward with his butt in the air, tail wagging excitedly. Scooping the drool-covered ball into my palm, I threw it down the hall for the fourteenth time.

A side window flew open, the sound of feathers rustling echoing in my ears as Bia and Kratos flew into the room. Their brown wings fanned out as they landed, and Levin dropped the ball, growling at them with his lip curled back. I raised a hand to him, and on command, he sat with a whimper.

"Please tell me you both disguised yourselves before *flying* into my apartment on a bustling street in New York?" I flicked my wrist to shut the window behind them.

"We may not be on Earth often, but we do know the protocol, sir," Kratos said, his voice as deep as the Titans themselves. His tanned leather vest stood out in contrast to his umber skin, his bald head reflecting the overhead lights.

Bia bowed her head, her black hair shifting over the loose tunic top she wore. "*My liege.*"

Bia never spoke. Any communication she did was telepathically and only other gods could hear her.

"I have a task for you both." Spying Levin vibrating from the corner of my eye, I whistled at him, and he ran to my enforcers, circling them.

Bia lifted her hands, and folded her wings behind her as if Levin would chew on them.

"Interesting choice in enforcers, sir." Kratos crossed his massive arms, lowering one for the moment it took to pat Levin on the head.

"The last time you two worked together was Prometheus. I'd say you're due." Moving behind the bar, I poured myself a scotch, raising my brow at them as an offering.

They both shook their heads, and I shrugged.

"What would you have us do? A heist? Robbery, perhaps?" Kratos snapped his fingers. "Infiltration."

I sniggered at him over the rim of my tumbler. "You've been watching far too many movies, old friend."

Kratos's full lips tilted down in a deep frown.

"*What do you wish of us, my lord?*" Bia steepled her terracotta fingers, piercing me with hazel eyes. Her voice traveled over my brain like scattered whispers.

"I want you to follow someone. A mortal. I need to know absolutely everything about her." My grip tightened on the glass, making it squeak.

"A mortal? But wh—" Kratos started.

I pointed at him. "If one more god asks me *why*, one more time, I'm sincerely going to lose my shit. Since when am I questioned at every turn?"

"I meant no disrespect. We just need to know what we're looking for." Kratos interlaced his fingers behind his back and bowed his head.

"She's—different. I need to know why. What makes her tick, what makes her happy, how she spends her days. Be on her ass like a fly on shit. Get my drift?" I downed the whiskey.

"Yes, my lord," Kratos answered, flaring out his wings.

Levin yelped, his claws slipping against the floor as he scurried away.

"*Do you wish me to read her mind?*" Bia twisted her wrists as she canted her head to the side.

Bia's ability to read minds only extended to the mortal variety…thank Olympus.

"Yes. All of it. Any of it. Whatever it takes. You'll report in within twenty-four hours." Blowing out a breath, I leaned on the bar.

"A day? My liege, that's not a lot of time." The feathers in Kratos's wings rustled.

Tightening my jaw, I shook my head. "I don't *have* time. Currently, there is no queen." I cut my gaze to them. "Understand?"

Bia and Kratos exchanged bewildered glances before nodding.

"Good. Off you go." I jutted my head toward the window and waited for them to exit before slumping against the bar.

Holding my head in my hands, I let out a deep sigh. Levin's paw touched my thigh, and I smiled down at him, his pink tongue sprouting from the corner of his mouth, his brown eyes gleaming with happiness.

I patted him on the head and rubbed my temple. "I'm fine, boy. Just exhausted."

So. Incredibly. Spent.

SIX

The decorative border is between SIX and KEIRA.

KEIRA

"KEIRA." OLIVIA'S VOICE CALLED out.

My body jostled and I shot up, sucking in drool collecting at the corner of my mouth.

"What?" I grumbled, dragging my sleeve over my lips, wincing through a pair of dried eyes.

Olivia crossed her arms and tapped her foot. "You fell asleep at your desk again. Why don't you just go bloody home, Keir?"

My right cheek felt numb from lying on the hardwood, and I rubbed it. "I can't. I've got to go over this case file with a fine-toothed comb before the evidence hearing tomorrow."

"What would be the point of that? You don't want to bank on evidence we may not get to use. Go home." She moved behind me and jiggled the chair until I stood. "Take a hot shower, maybe flick the bean, and go to sleep in an actual bed, yeah?"

Moving hair stuck to my forehead out of my eyes, I squinted at her. "Flick the bean? Are you talking about masturbating?"

"What else would I be talking about?" She grabbed my pea coat and held it open, waiting for me to slip my arms through.

I frowned and let her dress me.

She shoved my briefcase into my chest and pointed at the door. "Go. I'll wrap things up here."

"Thank you, Ol—" I started, but she turned away from me, turning circles with a confused expression.

"What's that? Would that be the distant voice of a woman who should be halfway home by now with a hand in her undies?" She cupped a hand over her ear.

Rolling my eyes, I waved at her. "I'm gone. I'm gone."

"Love you, Keir Keir," she yelled to my back.

I made the same quizzical face she had while turning circles. "What's that? It sounds like a didgeridoo in the distance?"

Olivia burst out laughing and pointed at me.

"Love you too, Ollie." I blew her an air kiss before exiting to the sidewalk.

I'd taken the long way home, avoiding more people scurrying around holiday shopping and having lunch. Christmastime in New York City never failed to be magical, but it always left a pit in my stomach, knowing it also meant more tourists, more people, more crowds—more emotions. At times, it was enough to make me want to scream.

Once I reached the reprieve of my apartment building, I tripped over something resting on the ground in front of my door.

"What the hell?" Squatting, I scooped a box into my palms.

We had designated compartments for packages to pick up via assigned keys. This…was odd.

After walking into my apartment and locking the door behind me, I rested the mysterious parcel on my kitchen counter and stared at it. It wouldn't be the first time I'd received a nasty-gram from a disgruntled suspect's family that I'd put behind bars. I'd even been threatened in the past.

Would someone go so far as to send me a bomb that'd explode upon opening it?

I lowered my ear to the box. Silence.

"To hell with it." I ripped away the brown wrapping, opened the white box, and staring back at me were a pair of pink binoculars.

What. The actual. Fuck.

As I lifted the binoculars with two fingers, a folded piece of paper fell. Glaring at it, hoping it'd spontaneously combust from my stare, I opened it.

So you can get a better view. -Z

I turned my glare out the window, eyeing the penthouse suite in the adjacent building I knew belonged to Zane. Before yesterday, the blinds had always been drawn. And now, as he promised, a singular window was wide open.

Growling, I shoved the binoculars back into the box and pushed it away. "What a grade-A asshole, I swear."

A woman left his apartment building, adjusting her skintight dress once she reached the sidewalk. She flicked her dark brown hair, twisted on her heel, and gave his window the middle finger before hailing a cab. After rolling my eyes, I crossed the room and yanked on the cord to close my blinds.

I needed precisely what Olivia prescribed—a steaming hot shower.

I pressed my hands against the tiles, letting the hot water roll down the back of my head, my neck, my spine. It was absolute bliss when my mind had the chance to relax—to know the emotions I felt were entirely my own.

Zane's face shimmered through my mind. The electric blue eyes, the way they squinted when he smiled. His knuckle grazing his bottom lip. The way he moved around a room as if every crack in the floor, every pane of glass was his to own—to control. The man was a walking powerhouse, and I had no idea how he managed to make it leak from his very pores.

I traced my finger over my hip, trailing my stomach and dipping between my thighs. Zane Vronti was everything I hated in a man—a human being. Biting my lip, I fingered my folds. He was arrogant, boastful, overly confident…charismatic, powerful, and far too fucking attractive for his own good.

Sputtering water, I pressed my forearm against the wall, holding myself up and massaging my clit with two fingers.

I couldn't stand defense lawyers. Combining all of what Zane represented with the one job I despised most of all should make him my arch-nemesis. And yet, here I was, getting off at the thought of him—the idea of him, picturing his face as I did it.

There were fleeting emotions I'd gotten glimpses of from him. Feelings that didn't match up to the ones he brought to the surface. Was that what I held onto? The possibility that the first man to ever infiltrate my every thought, to make my insides twist simply from the smell of him, may be something more than an arrogant prick?

Because…he'd have to be. Or it'd make me all forms of backward. Deranged. Out of my right mind.

Whimpering, I cried out through my release, the euphoria circling through my stomach, making my spine tingle. I should've felt dirty—that of all the people I could have pictured, I chose to think of Zane. But I didn't feel dirty. He was merely a tool for my own pleasure—a plaything who would never get the satisfaction of giving me a climax himself. I *used* him the same way he used all of those women night after night.

After drying off and throwing on a camisole and shorts, I walked to my kitchen with the sole intention of making a bag of popcorn and watching something on Netflix. What possessed me to eyeball the box sitting on the counter with the binoculars—I couldn't say. What further possessed me to go to my window and part the blinds—eluded me. But what would eat at my brain for the unforeseeable future was the curiosity overcoming me to the point I raised the binoculars… and took a peek.

My throat dried, spying a fully nude Zane parading his apartment. His back was to me, giving me a clear view of his perfectly rounded, tanned, and muscular ass. The man was a Greek god statue in human form. He slowly turned— meticulously even, as if he knew I were watching. When he fully faced me, there it was. His. Dick. Before I could do the appropriate calculations in my mind, taking into account my distance from him and how far it fell against his thigh, I fumbled with and dropped the binoculars.

Probably for the better. I shouldn't have looked. What if he had seen me? He could hold the fact I spied on him over me. Possibly even use it against me in court. Slapping a hand over my face, I shoved the binoculars back in the box, stomped to my bedroom, and kicked it under my bed. Let it die there with the dust bunnies, lost pens, and paperclips.

Making my way back to the living room, I flopped onto my couch, sans popcorn, and clicked on the first movie that caught my eye. *Immortals*. Yes. Henry Cavill could cure anything. Nestling against the cushions, I rested my head on my hand and forced my concentration on a tale of Mount Olympus, Theseus, and the ruthless tyrant Hyperion. To say I hadn't thought of Zane's ass or other areas of him several times throughout the rest of the night—would've been a complete lie. And I hated myself for it.

I sat on a bench outside the courtroom, having arrived twenty minutes early to gather my thoughts and decompress. Pulling my pea coat tighter around my torso, I crossed my nylon-covered legs and bounced the top one. Closing my eyes, I concentrated on the steady hum of the fluorescent lights above me.

"Good morning," Zane's deep as sin voice sounded near me.

Opening one eye, followed by the other, I hugged myself tighter. He stood in front of me clothed in his usual suit attire and Burberry coat, but all I could see was what I had seen last night. It was as if I'd gained the ability of x-ray vision. A heavy lump formed in my throat, and I fought back the urge to gulp.

He squinted at me and cocked his head, pointing at me with his hand still in his coat pocket. "You alright there, counselor? You look a bit flushed."

My cheeks *did* feel warm. Shit.

"Perfectly fine. It's stuffy in here." I sat up straight, focusing all of my attention on his face to avoid the temptation to travel my gaze lower.

"And yet you still have your coat on." He rubbed his chin.

Grinding my molars, I glared at him. "I like stuffy."

"You don't say." After smirking, he sat next to me, leaving only a foot of space between us.

"I can't believe you're not only on time but early." Heat coiled from his leg, caressing my thigh. The usual lust and power flowed from him, but I also caught an overwhelming sense of exhaustion—so much it made me yawn.

"I have no issue making feisty prosecutors wait on me, but judges? I need them in my corner." His gaze dropped to my crossed legs, eyes roaming over my calves.

Part of my heel slipped, revealing half of my foot. His glance snapped to it, and I secured it back on, holding my breath. "And I'm sure you never fail to charm the pants off them."

Perhaps literally if it were a female judge.

"Level with me here—" He leaned his forearms on his knees, turning his face to look at me. "What is your beef with defense lawyers?"

I guffawed. "I should think that's fairly obvious, Zane."

"Maybe it is, maybe it isn't. But I want to hear from *your* lips." His gaze dropped to my mouth, the tip of his tongue skirting his bottom lip.

Did he imagine what I'd taste like?

Moving my attention to the light snow flurries stirring outside from the foyer windows, I took a deep breath. "You represent people who have done despicable deeds and fight to win their case despite knowing it."

"That hardly seems fair."

I snapped my focus back to him. "Fair? What isn't fair is when known murderers go free. Doesn't it bother you to know they'll more than likely do it again?"

"No, it doesn't. Justice was served, and they'll have something far worse to answer to at the end of it all." He circled his finger at the ground, pointing to hell itself.

He had a point, but it still didn't negate the fact that instead of rotting in a prison cell waiting to meet their maker, they were on the streets.

"I don't even know why I'm trying to debate this with a defense lawyer."

Confidence surged from him as he shifted on the bench, stretching his arms over the back of it. I stiffened when his jacket sleeve brushed my shoulder. "You better get used to it. You're about to debate with this lawyer on something far larger."

"You could've taken your skills elsewhere and done virtually anything else with them. Why a defense lawyer? Why?" I slapped my hand on my knee.

His eyes shot to my leg, acutely aware of every move they made. "Aren't there worse occupations out there? Pimps? Mafia bosses? I went to college for this career, built a legitimate and lawful reputation for myself."

Fuck. We weren't even in the courtroom yet, and this guy

was already debating me straight into a hole. And *why* was it so damn hot?

"The same could be said for heart surgeons." Turning my hips toward him by an inch, I tilted my head back.

His eyes roamed down again before panning to stare in front of him. "Are you trying to tell me prosecutors have never put innocent people in jail?"

I dug my nails into my ribs through the jacket with my arms still tightly wrapped around myself. "That's rare."

He leaned forward, his sandalwood scent dizzying me. "It still happens."

"Run out of arguments to plead your case, Zane?" I brought our faces closer, masking my expression from every neuron that sparked beneath my skin.

"I find it borderline amusing you think I have to explain myself at all to you, honestly." He stared at my lips, canting his head to one side.

We were a breath away from each other. He could've kissed me so easily—and I couldn't say that I would've stopped him.

Grimacing, I sat back, scooting away until my hip bumped the armrest. "Way to derail."

"Look, Keira. At the end of the day, remember that she, most of all, would disagree with your sentiments toward defense lawyers." Zane pointed to a painting hanging on the adjacent wall. A depiction of Lady Justice holding a scale and sporting her usual blindfold.

Justice is blind.

Satisfaction oozed from his pores, contrasting with the fury that shot down my spine.

"Fuck you," I whispered to him.

Zane drummed his fingers on the bench behind me as he looked around. "Well, we only have a few minutes, but I'm sure we could find a closet somewhere."

Heat rushed to my stomach, and I bit the inside of my cheek to keep from smiling at his somewhat humorous joke.

"Good morning, counselors," a woman's voice announced as she breezed through the foyer, shaking out her graying hair, ridding it of snowflakes.

A lady judge. Just. Perfect.

Under normal circumstances, I would've hoped to have an edge given the woman-to-woman stance I could take without even implying it. But with Zane, he could turn one notch of his charmgasms on, and she'd be putty in his hands.

"Sylvia, a pleasure to be working with you again." Zane stood with a handsome smile, bowing his head at her.

The woman grinned as she fixed her hair, smoothing it over her ears. "Mr. Vronti."

Zane held his hand out once the judge entered the courtroom, edging me to follow her.

I paused as I passed, glaring up at him. "Did you sleep with her?"

"Not relevant to the case, Miss Bazin." His hot breath curled over my skin as his lips hovered by my ear.

Sucking in a shaky breath, I stormed into the courtroom, regaining my composure once I'd taken off my coat and organized my paperwork, notepad, and pens.

Zane coolly took the seat at the table next to me, folding his coat over the back of his chair and buttoning all buttons on his suit jacket. He sat down and leaned back with such casualness you'd think we were about to discuss the weather and not the evidence leading toward a murder conviction.

The judge shuffled papers on her podium, and slid the squared reading glasses attached to a chain on her nose. "Confirming this is in regards to audio recording evidence in the Melissa Daniels case?"

"Yes, your honor," I answered, trying not to let the sight of nothing on the table in front of Zane bother me.

"Prosecution, please present your argument first as to why they should be included." The judge folded her hands, giving me her undivided attention.

I stood, feeling Zane's scorching eyes roaming over me. "Your honor, the recordings are relevant for establishing motive. It was clear from the defendant's tone she had immense hatred for her husband. She even stated it more than once."

"I object, your honor," Zane started before standing, towering over me. "Hatred toward a spouse isn't motive for murder. It could've easily been temporary feelings after a heated argument."

The judge turned her attention back to me. "Sustained. Counselor, was there anything more *specific* that you could directly relate to motive?"

"Yes. She said verbatim that she was going to kill him." I tapped my fingernails against the manila folder resting in front of me, keeping my gaze away from Zane.

"Your honor, with the number of voicemails there are, including *all* of them would only survive to unjustly bias the jury in favor of the prosecution. They were voicemails left in the heat of moments leading after an argument. It would be an unfair trial in direct violation of the tenets of which this country was founded upon."

My insides fluttered. Here I was, defending my argument for a case I wanted to win—to wipe the floor with the lawyer standing next to me, and yet the way he presented himself, the way he phrased things—he *was* good. Powerful. Commanding. I pinched my knees together.

"Counselor, do you argue for the inclusion of *all* voicemails?" The judge tapped her pen against her desk.

"Yes, your honor. All of them *are* relevant."

"The only reason to include all recordings as evidence is if the prosecution is unsure of my client's guilt and needs them to support a completely circumstantial case." His voice boomed like thunder right after a lightning strike.

I cut my eyes to him, and he'd already been eyeing me. We glared at each other.

"Are you doubting your own skills, counselor?"

Confidence. Lust. Satisfaction.

Emotions both from him—from me, mixing, swirling, and striking against my stomach.

"This has nothing to do with the uncertainty surrounding guilt, only the prosecution's desire to have every available piece of evidence pointing toward Mrs. Daniels' immense hatred for her husband, which could've been a direct factor in his death." I beat my fist against the table once, solidifying my final argument.

The judge nodded and peered at Zane over the rim of her glasses. "Anything else left to say for the defense?"

"No, your honor."

"Given the nature of the voicemails, I'm ruling that the only recording to be presented and used in court as evidence for the prosecution's case is the one stating she was going to kill him. All others will be dismissed." The judge slammed her gavel. "Adjourned."

My chest heaved as I turned to look at him. A sensuous, victorious smile pulled at his lips. I wanted to gouge his eyes out while also craving to ride his face. A battle of hate versus lust, despising versus respecting that had me whirling.

"No hard feelings?" He extended his hand.

I stared at it, struggling to keep my breaths even—to not outright pant in front of him. "Would you meet me outside?"

His cerulean eyes pierced me as he lowered his hand. No smirk. No frown. But a heat sparked in his gaze before I turned away, and he followed me out of the courtroom. All sensible rationalization had left my brain. I needed a release, a place for the swirling emotions—the overpowering feelings coursing through me to settle and hopefully…disappear.

Spotting a janitor's closet door cracked, I yanked it open and paused. Was I about to do this? When his sandalwood scent hit my nostrils, and I gazed at him over my shoulder, standing coolly with his hands folded in front of him, a challenging glint in his gaze—I'd made up my mind. Grabbing his arm, I pulled him into the closet and he let me, a newfound warmth radiating from him.

Shutting the door behind us and locking it, I slowly turned on my heel, coming face-to-face with Zane Vronti. Shelves of toilet paper, cleaning supplies, and a mop bucket surrounded us, leaving barely enough room to shift our stances. My heart raced, pounding in my ears. The lust coiling in the air between us, trapped in such a small space, had me quivering.

"You have me at your mercy, counselor." He held his palms up. "What are you going to do with me?"

He *wanted* to be controlled as much as he desired to *do* the controlling.

We locked eyes, and an urgency tugging at my brain had my fingers trailing up his jacket's lapels, not stopping until I reached his neck. I pressed my mouth to his lips, immediately slipping my tongue in, circling with his. Whimpering at the swirls, dips, and flips exploding in my stomach, I bunched my hands in his hair. Once his hands traced my lower back, I pushed off him, only so far away to make the tips of our noses brush.

"This is so fucked up," I whispered, keeping my gaze on his, drowning in the deep blue.

He chewed on his lip, chest heaving, his hands now raised at his sides. "It's only fucked up if you call it that. I've often lived under the principle of…if you want it—*take* it."

His eyes flashed with a beam of light I chalked up to my body and mind battling for control to the point of hallucination. I tightened my grip on his hair.

"I'm right here. Do you want it?"

One drop of my gaze to his tongue licking his bottom lip, my mouth covered that same lip, kissing him. No sooner had Zane been given the green light for the second time, his arm wrapped around my waist, and he turned us, shoving my back against one of the shelves, knocking a roll of toilet paper to the ground. I skirted my knee up his side, kissing him, devouring him, taking everything he'd give me. He pulled away, licking down my neck, biting it hard enough to make me gasp but not break the skin. His hand grabbed my ass, squeezing it, using it to pull me tighter against him—make me feel that cock I'd gotten a glimpse of last night.

Moaning, I grabbed his jacket and switched our positions, pushing him against the same shelves, crashing a sealed bottle of soap to the ground. Electric current pulsed over my skin, tantalizing it.

Surprise. Attraction.

A wicked grin pressed against my lips as I kissed him, sliding my hands into his jacket, feeling the hard muscle that made me whimper. Walking my fingers over the carved abs hiding beneath his shirt, I flicked his belt and cupped him. *All* of him. Hard as a fucking rock.

Jesus. Christ. What the hell was I doing?

I pushed away as far as the small room would let me and wiped the back of my hand over my mouth. "I—I got that out of my system. It's never happening again, Vronti. It can't."

He dragged a thumb over his bottom lip, smiling at me.

Frustration. Longing. But not surprised. Like he'd been expecting me to bail out.

"You made one small mistake, counselor." He took the singular step needed to bring us toe-to-toe, pressing his hands above my head on the door behind me, caging me. "Now you've had a taste." He pressed his lips to my ear. "You must've liked what you saw through my window last night, hm?"

"But how did you—" I stared up at him, trying to be angry

about it but felt more like laughing.

Pushing away, he adjusted his tie, did up the button of his jacket, and dragged his hand through hair that I'd ruffled. "You may want to wait five minutes before leaving after me. I can't imagine the scandalous rumors that'd fly if word got out of two opposing counselors exiting a broom closet in the courthouse together." That same flash blazed in his eyes.

I gripped the shelf behind me to keep myself upright, pressing my head against the cool metal.

He flicked the lock and placed his hand on the doorknob before resting his other hand on my hip. "Think about me tonight when you finish what you started, Miss Bazin." After slipping my earlobe between his teeth for a fraction of a second, he was gone.

Slapping my hands over my face, I slid down the shelves until my butt met with the ground. Glaring at the mop bucket in the corner, I kicked it with a growl. I'd been so unable to control myself, I resorted to pulling Zane into a fucking musty broom closet. Worst of all, I couldn't promise myself I wouldn't do it again. He was complicated, exuberant, and laced with so much sexual energy. That inner part of me I'd buried deep from past partners for fear they wouldn't understand poked at the surface, begging to be set free.

SEVEN

ZEUS

ON THE OUTSIDE, KEIRA was professional, orderly, put together. On the inside, she was broken, intriguing, and kept an absolute freak buried deep. And I fucking *dug* it. All of it. Yesterday convinced me of my worst fears—no other woman would do. It *had* to be her. Keira. My history spoke for itself— when the King of the Gods desired something or someone, it was rare it didn't come to fruition.

"Are we just going to sit here, or are we going to fuck? Is this really what you brought me up here for?" the raven-haired woman with topaz eyes asked, sitting in a frump in the chair across from me.

I sat with my forearms resting on my knees, hands steepled as I eyed my deluxe rotating Scrabble board, the faux ivory letters staring back at me, waiting for me to spell a damn word.

Did I think having Keira see a parade of women waltz from my apartment building every night would make her jealous? I hadn't a fucking clue what made that woman tick, but I'd pull every damn card I could.

Grabbing several letters, I placed them on the board without looking at her. "I told you I'd entertain you. If you misinterpreted my intentions, that's your business. PS – you don't spell penis with a 'z,' but nice try at triple points."

"I'm so out of here." She scoffed and rolled her eyes as she pushed from the chair and made for the door.

Glancing at my watch, I dug into my back pocket and slapped a hundred-dollar bill on the table. A woman like her would undoubtedly recognize the sound of cash, possibly even smell it from across the room. "Sit down. Finish the game. And you leave with a consolation prize."

She folded her arms and smacked her pink glossed lips together. "Make it two hundred, and I won't tell anyone that Zane Vronti invited me up here to play Scrabble." She did air quotes.

I ground my teeth together, narrowing my eyes at her from across the room. If only this woman knew who she was talking to—if only I could make a lightning strike singe the carpet between us. No.

Plucking another hundred from my pocket, I slapped it atop the other bill. "Only if when you walk out the door, you look—happy."

"Fine." She shrugged and moved back to her seat across from me, adjusting her faux fur jacket. "Oh, I'll be happy. Been eyeing these new Christian Louboutins, and you're about to give me the rest of what I need."

"Sure. Whatever," I grumbled.

Turning the board to face her, I bobbed a brow, insinuating it was her turn. The woman tapped her shoe against the hardwood floor, absently scratching her neck as she looked at the ceiling. She did everything except make an effort at spelling another word.

Sighing, I pinched the bridge of my nose. "You can go," I snapped, standing and shoving my hands in my pants pockets, jingling my keys as I waited for her to bounce her way out.

She clapped her hands before scooping the cash into her palm. After blowing me a kiss she said, "Well, at least you were nice to look at the past forty-five minutes." Winking, she swept out the door, not bothering to shut it behind her.

"You're welcome," I scoffed. With a flick of my wrist, I *whooshed* the door shut and let Levin out to run around the apartment. He'd spend the next ten minutes sniffing every inch the woman had touched, wagging his tail all the while.

Rubbing my temple, I walked to the window facing Keira's to see if she reacted to the woman leaving. Keira always seemed stone cold, but I knew she held back, especially after she shoved me in a closet and devoured me like a lioness in heat. Her taking control like that, having no idea she held a Greek god in her petite hands—fuck. Keira glanced out the window, but if she had any emotion, she didn't show it. Still, she took the time to look. That spoke volumes.

"*Are you alone, my liege?*" Bia's voice shuttered over my brain. "Yes."

Kratos and Bia materialized into the room versus *flying* through an unopened window as they had before.

Still spying Keira through her window in a dress shirt and

pencil skirt, but pacing barefoot with a folder in her hand, a tumbler of scotch in the other, I asked, "What did you find out?"

"This mortal is extremely job-oriented. From the moment she wakes up, she walks to work avoiding people at all costs—" Kratos started.

I snapped a gaze at him over my shoulder, finally looking away once Keira was out of view. "Avoiding people? Interesting."

"—yes. When she arrives at work, she breezes past everyone and sits in her office alone for an hour or more as if she's decompressing." Kratos folded his brown wings behind him, clasping his hands behind his back.

"I wonder why?" Rubbing my chin, I squatted as Levin approached me, scratching his head. "What else?"

"The only person she confides in is her paralegal, Olivia. She spends her day at work, most of the night and then walks home. Again, avoiding people even if it means taking a longer route home."

Work. Work. Work. It hit far too close to home.

"Bia, my dear. I'm *very* interested to hear your take."

"*Firstly, you know how I cannot read the minds of the gods?*" She took a seat on my leather lounge chair, adjusting her wings as not to sit on them.

I squinted at her, rising to my feet, despite Levin's groan. "Yes?"

"*It took extra effort on my part to get through to her. It was borderline exhausting.*"

"What does that mean? She's not a goddess. She's not even immortal." I pressed my palms against the bar top, glaring at it.

Levin forced himself between Kratos's legs, wiggling his ass to be scratched. "A demigod, perhaps?" Kratos obliged my dog, petting him with a wince.

"No. I would sense that. Anyway, go on, Bia."

"*She may not realize the lengths she's pulled toward it, but the woman is immensely drawn to power. Control.*"

"Her power? Her control?" Standing upright, I stepped closer to my lady enforcer.

Bia shook her head slowly.

A wicked grin tugged at my lips. "I *am* power."

"*Yes, my lord. And she's attracted to you—the power surging from you, the control you take, you demand. But she's confused why it's so intense from seemingly only you. She can't make sense of it.*"

And she says she hates me. Hardly.

"You could always tell her the truth. Imagine her reaction to power knowing who you really are." Kratos lifted his chin.

"It isn't that simple, Kratos. You both don't have interactions with mortals daily anymore. They think we don't exist. To flat out tell her would result in marriage proposal suicide. No. I have to work my way under her skin." I rubbed my neck, already feeling tension from the effort.

Bia stood, floating over to me, hovering at eye level. "*Out of all mortal women, you've chosen to pursue this one.*" She canted her head to the side. "*You're intrigued by her. Her work ethic. The ravenous desire she keeps hidden.*"

"I thought you couldn't read my mind." Rolling my shoulders back, I made myself taller despite her floating at my height.

"*I don't have to when female intuition plays a part.*"

Grimacing, I turned away from her and rubbed the back of my hand over my mouth. "Anything else I should know?"

"Her birthday falls on the winter solstice. I saw it on her calendar. It's as if she has to write it down to remember it." Kratos ruffled his wings, plucking a feather that had started to break off.

Or other vital deadlines…

Nodding, I glanced at Bia over my shoulder. "Bia?"

"*If you truly wish to pursue this woman as your future queen, I've felt her inner self, sir. She's a passionate woman who shifts it all to her job. She wishes to be the best at what she does but longs for more. Past mortals she's been with had issues occasionally being second best to the job.*"

I turned to face her, squinting. "Are you talking about her or me?"

Bia smiled. A rarity for her.

Kratos's lip twitched before he flared his wings. "Are we dismissed?"

I continued to stare at Bia, but she stayed quiet and sprung her wings. "Keep your eyes and ears open with her and inform me immediately of anything important. Dismissed."

As they both disappeared, I moved to the window and almost did a double-take. Keira stood with her back turned, her blonde waves falling over fully exposed skin. Her perky bare ass was in clear view, and as she squinted over her shoulder, showing only a hint of her nose and mouth, she gave a peek at the side of her breast, the nipple in shadow.

Fuck. Me.

Arousal dipped into possessive irritation, knowing anyone else in this building could see the same show. She could lie through her teeth any which way from Sunday, but I knew this display was for *me*. The rest of them be damned. I dragged a hand down my face, staring at how sexy she looked, the table lamp near her accentuating her curves, giving her hair a golden hue. She reached for the lamp, and with one last smirk over her shoulder, she wrapped her gorgeous body in a cloak of darkness.

I'd waited until I knew Keira would be exiting her apartment to walk to the courthouse, meeting her on the sidewalk with a smug grin.

"You've got to be kidding me. You *never* walk to work this early," she spat, the chilled air making her breath fog the space between us.

"Not sure if you heard, but I'm working on this high-profile case. Figured I'd get a few early mornings in." I winked at her, rubbing my leather gloves together and flipping the lapel of my jacket around my neck.

She pointed at me, squinting those bright blue eyes. "I'm onto you, Vronti."

"I wish you would be." I dropped my tone an octave and leaned toward her, making my power hover like an invisible shield.

My gaze dropped to her throat, watching it bob.

She bit her lips, no doubt holding back a smile. "You're a pig."

"Well, if you'd only give me a chance—I'm certain I could make you squeal."

She dropped her jaw, suppressing a grin again, and swatted

my arm.

Her touch ignited a spark over my skin, even through layers of cloth.

Clearing my throat, I shoved my hands in my pockets and walked beside her. "Nice weather last night, wouldn't you say? Extra…nippy?"

She slipped her briefcase over one shoulder and tugged the coat tight around her chest. "I *knew* you could see me."

"Very true. And so could *all* the neighbors." I rose a brow at her, turning my head enough to eye her sidelong.

She clucked her tongue against her teeth. "They couldn't see my face."

"That's what you're concerned about?" I asked, chuckling through my words.

"If you got it, flaunt it?" She shrugged, still not looking at me.

There went that irritating jealous pang in my gut again, making my lip bounce.

"Was that your idea of torturing me? Punishment, perhaps?" Discreetly, I got close enough to her our elbows *almost* brushed.

"Absolutely. Showing you something you'll never have." She lifted her chin, the tip of her nose rosy red, and she sniffled.

I side-stepped in front of her, walking backward. "Well, I've been a naughty, *naughty* boy. You should punish me further but maybe in a bedroom this time instead of a closet? Hell, I'll even settle for one of our offices." Flashing a confident grin, I watched her neck flush.

She stopped walking, stomping her foot for extra emphasis. "I've already told you that was a momentary lapse in judgment.

You're attractive. So, sue me."

I morphed the most panty-melting smolder I could muster. "Bold words to say to the best lawyer in New York City."

She idly sucked on her bottom lip before snapping it out of her mouth and bouncing on her heels. "*One* of the best. I've earned that title too."

And why would she want to give it away for some petty thing like being deported when she had options?

"Did you do what I asked last night?" I dropped my gaze to her hips before lifting my eyes back to hers. "Finish what you started?"

"Why yes, I did. I had company last night." She sniffled again, rubbing her wool glove under her nose.

"No, you didn't."

She guffawed, the skin between her eyes creasing. "You don't see everything that goes on in my apartment. And besides, I'm not like you with a new bang every other night."

Bingo. It *did* bother her.

"I wouldn't have to see a thing."

"What the hell does that mean?" She blinked her baby blues, the gray hues in the sky from an impending snowfall making them brighter.

"I could smell him on you."

She scrunched her nose and leaned back. "What are you? A wolf or something?"

"Much better. I don't have fleas."

She let out a single laugh and brushed past me, continuing to walk.

"Is there a reason you insist on walking to work over public transportation? Especially in a skirt? Even Jack Frost's balls would freeze out here." I pretended to shiver.

"It's a good thing I don't have balls then, huh?" She stopped at the crosswalk, bouncing on her heels.

"Prove it," I whispered in her ear from behind her.

She loosed a breath and peered at me over her shoulder, our lips almost brushing. "You never give up, do you?"

"And you won't ever admit you *like* being chased, will you?"

She remained silent, simply staring up at me with doe-like eyes.

Yanking one of my gloves off with my teeth, I touched her cheek. Ice cold. "For fuck's sake, Keira. You feel like death. Let me call you a damn cab. Stop being so stubborn." I walked to the sidewalk's edge, holding an arm up.

She grabbed it and yanked it down. "No. I don't want a cab."

"*Why?*"

"Because."

Getting more pissed off by the minute, I deepened my tone. "Because. Why?"

"I don't like being around people, alright? Cabs give me the creeps being trapped with a stranger in a small space—and a bus or train?" She sighed. "Claustrophobic."

She was only telling half the truth, and it boiled my irritation even more.

Snapping her eyes to mine, staring at me for a beat, she made a tsking sound with her teeth. "Goddammit. Do you want to—grab a coffee to drink on the way? It'll warm me up." She couldn't make eye contact with me, her eyes falling to the concrete beneath us.

And so it began.

I half-grinned and pointed to a cart across the street. "I'll even buy."

"Wow. The fancy lawyer man wearing the Burberry jacket will spring for a whole four bucks worth of coffee. I'm a lucky gal."

Shaking my head, I dug in my pocket, producing a money clip. "Smartass. Want me to ask if he'll throw in a shot of whiskey? I'm sure he has a flask hidden somewhere." I smirked, holding out the cash to the attendant. "Black and—"

Keira cleared her throat. "Black."

"Two blacks."

The attendant adjusted the New York Yankees beanie on his head before grumbling and pouring the coffee. Sliding them toward us with his fingerless gloves, he mumbled some form of having a good day as I handed Keira the second cup. I moved to the nearest trashcan to remove my lid and toss it. Keira stepped beside me, performing the same action, and we both locked eyes.

"I uh—" She wrapped her hands tightly around the cup and dipped her face over it. "I like to feel the steam on my nose." Discreetly, she shoved several sugar packets into her jacket pocket, but didn't put any in her coffee.

She continued to pleasantly surprise me at each and every turn.

Fucking Olympus. I really was in trouble.

"I, on the other hand, find the covers to be for pussies. If I'm going to burn my mouth, well, that's my own damn fault, isn't it?" I squinted at her as I took a tiny sip, pretending to burn my lip and sputter. "Shit. See?"

She laughed and grabbed a creamer from the vendor, tossing it at my chest. "You know these street vendors make it hot enough to melt a tire."

"You're right. I should sue them like McDonald's." I winked at her, sipping on the small container of creamer.

"Hey. She had a case. They had a corporate policy to serve it at a temperature that could cause serious burns in seconds. She wasn't the only one who got injured, just the first one to take it to the next level." Her eyes beamed at me as she sipped on her coffee, lifting her shoulders as the warmth coursed down her throat.

"I agree, but I would've gotten her triple the settlement. Easily." Smiling, I tossed the empty container in the trash and we continued walking.

"What are we doing, Zane?" She looked straight ahead, drinking her coffee.

"We're walking, I believe."

She rolled her eyes, and for the first time, when she smiled, I noticed the small dimple that formed in her left cheek. "We can't be friends. At some point we're going to be at each other's throats on this Daniels case in front of a jury. That can't end anywhere but uglytown."

"Have you ever had a relationship with another lawyer, sexual or otherwise?" I raised my brow at her, leaning forward in an attempt to catch her gaze.

"No." She frowned.

"Then how would you know?"

Her jaw tightened, and she stared into her cup before briskly shaking her head. "I can't. I just can't. Look, I appreciate you walking with me and buying me coffee, but I need you to let me walk on my own from here on out, alright?"

Tartarus. This woman was wound tighter than the Fates' spindle.

"Sure, but Keira—" I bumped her elbow.

She paused and tossed me a glare over her shoulder.

"You look good smiling. You should try it more often." I shrugged before backpedaling away with a lopsided grin, heading in the opposite direction.

Again, she bit back a smile and shook her head before walking.

I'd laid the foundation. *Knew* she was into me. And next… I'd offer her a solution to the problem she didn't think she had.

EIGHT

AS SOON AS I passed Olivia's desk, I motioned for her to follow me, making her smile turn into a frown. "My office. Now."

Tossing my briefcase onto my chair, I dragged my hands over my face, pacing and not bothering to take my coat off.

"Am I in trouble? Because I do feel like I was supposed to remind you about something, and I can't for the bloody life of me remember what it is." Gazing skyward, she tapped her finger against her plump lip.

"What? No. And isn't that client wedding soon?"

She pointed at me with a broad smile. "That's it. Yes. The wedding. Whew." She slapped a hand on her chest. "And I'm so proud you remembered that."

"Can you please close the door?" I flicked my hand at the entrance.

Olivia's eyebrows rose before she slowly closed the door and locked it. "Okay. Something is clearly up. What's going on,

89

boss?"

I sat on the corner of my desk with a groan. "You never call me boss. Why are you calling me that now?"

"It felt appropriate at the moment?" She steepled her fingers before tugging my coat down my arms.

"First, you dressed me the other day. Now you're undressing me," I mumbled, staring numbly at the floor.

"Well, I'm stopping at your coat." She dipped her face into mine. "Unless you're into that kind of thing, then I'm probably game to try."

I tossed her an exasperated glare.

"Right. I was kidding. Mostly." She tossed my coat over my chair.

"It's probably a good thing I'll be leaving the country for a bit. Will be good to…get away, you know?" I chewed on my thumbnail.

"Woah. Seriously, what is going on?" She grabbed my shoulders. "You've never been game for even leaving the state in the middle of a case, let alone the country."

"I kissed him, Ollie."

She gasped and grinned, punching me in the shoulder. "Who? That cute intern bloke in cubicle B?"

I looked from left to right. "Milo? *You* kissed that guy."

She snorted. "Oh, right."

"Zane, Ollie." I pushed to my feet and paced. "Zane fucking Vronti."

"What?" She yelled.

I widened my eyes at her, twirling my finger above my head in a circle, referencing the entire office could hear us.

She crouched, holding her hands at her sides. "What?" She repeated in a loud whisper.

"I seriously don't know what gotten into me." I stared at my hands, remembering how they felt wrapped in Zane's hair.

"Well, that's easy. You're—the 'h' word. Rhymes with corny?" She raised her brows. "How'd it happen anyway? Where? Did you use tongue?"

I cupped my hands on my forehead, circling through events that led to the incident on a loop in my brain as if it were a case I prepared to argue in court. "We were in the midst of the evidence trial, and the way he talked, the way he presented himself—he's good, Ollie." Unbuttoning my top two shirt buttons, I shot my gaze to hers. "Real good."

"No bloody shit. He's Zane Vronti. What were you expecting? Mediocre?"

No. But I wasn't expecting to be pulled in by his prowess like he was a black hole.

"I became so swept up in his skill, Ollie, that I actually dragged him into the first broom closet I saw, shoved him against the shelves, and *kissed* him." Between my legs pulsed, and I sat down, pinching my knees together.

Olivia grinned and bounced. "Holy hell. That's *hot*."

It was. It really, really was.

I undid another button on my blouse. "It was stupid, is what it was. What if someone had seen us go in there? What if someone had snapped a photo with their phone when we left?"

"It was you acting on impulse because you wanted something. It's bloody hot. End of story." She stomped her foot.

"I don't understand why I wanted it at all. I hate everything that man represents. Do you have any idea how many women's tongues have been in that man's mouth? I see women parading out of his apartment building practically every night." I grimaced. "And I stuck my tongue in there."

"Bugger me. You know how to take the fun out of a situation." Olivia sighed and sat beside me. "Hate and love are blurred lines, for one. For two, most blokes who are stallions in the sack, have, and this is shocking, slept with a few women."

Hate and love are blurred lines.

"That isn't the point. I have absolutely no intention of screwing him." Standing in a huff, I turned to face her.

"Whatever you say, Starshine. But I can tell you exactly why you're so into Mr. Hotshot Lawyer Man." She drummed her fingers on the desk's edge, stretching her legs out in front of her and crossing them at the ankle.

Folding my arms, I glared at her. "And why would that be?"

"Much like your job entails, you like a challenge. Tyler was an incredibly nice bloke, but he was simple and to the point."

A lump sprouted in my throat. "Do you have to bring up Tyler?"

"Yes. Because it's how I intend on proving my point. You and Tyler were smitten from what, the first two dates? All batty-eyed and puppy love. He had a good job, worshipped the ground you walked on, and at the end of the day came home and did you in the missionary position." She bounced her top foot, making the ballet flat fall from her heel.

Ugh. Her bringing up Tyler only brought back the depressing memories of what happened between us. He *was* a nice guy.

"But he wasn't what you, Keira Bazin, needed." Olivia stood

and interlaced her fingers behind her back.

"And how the hell would you—"

Olivia raised a finger to silence me. "You are a strong woman with arguing skills that rival a master debater." She snorted, cleared her throat, and waved a hand over her face, morphing it back to neutral. "You need someone who can match you point for point, challenge you. Someone who is as passionate about their career as you—to *understand*. And maybe at the end of the day…fuck you from behind against a wall."

My brain betrayed me, dipping into thoughts of Zane behind me, my palms pressed against my office door, sweat beading my forehead.

I shook my head and moved away from the door, closing my eyes with a wince. "I get what you're saying, Ollie. But I can find that elsewhere. Zane isn't the only man in existence who has those traits."

"Yeah? You're in your mid-thirties, Keir. You find him yet?" She threw her arms out at her sides and let them flop back down.

Ouch.

"Maybe I was meant to go it alone. Ever think about that?" I crossed my arms again in a huff.

"I don't buy it. You wouldn't have ever gotten married in the first place if you were okay with being alone." Olivia frowned, crossing the room to rest a hand on my shoulder. "How did you feel during that kiss, huh?"

Alive. Reborn. Ravenous.

"It doesn't matter. It's not happening again, and that's final."

I'd also not felt overwhelmed by his emotions as I normally

did in sexual situations. It was as if everything equalized between us the moment our skin touched.

"I'm going to say one last thing, and then I'm done playing the role of the best friend who makes you see through the bullshit...for now." Olivia took a dramatic deep breath. "You can be into something else besides your job and still be good at it. It's part of being human, mate." She patted my arm.

"I'll keep it in mind," I mumbled.

The day wore on, and I spent most of it daydreaming about the swirl of emotions passed between Zane and me during that walk to the office. Flirtatious. Lust. Happiness. The occasional bout of irritation. And I could *not* get him out of my mind. Sighing, I pinched the bridge of my nose, forcing my brain back into work mode.

Olivia knocked on my open door. "It's well after five. You heading home?"

Home. My apartment building. Zane's apartment building.

"No. I'll probably stay the night here going over paperwork." I moved behind my desk, shifting papers from left to right as if I were organizing them.

"You're going to avoid him now, aren't you?"

After that kiss? After the alarmingly normal moment walking to work this morning? Bet your ass I was.

"No. I just want to go over the files more." I kept my gaze down, avoiding eye contact.

"You're an amazing liar when you want to be, Keira, but I

know you well enough to know that is precisely what you're doing." Olivia grabbed my coat and threw it at me. "Come on. I'll sleep at your place tonight. He won't try to sweep you off your feet if I'm there to cockblock him."

"I think you underestimate him," I muttered, slipping the coat over my arms and grabbing my briefcase.

She paused, blinking. "*That* good, huh?"

Pulling my hair from the jacket collar, I fished for my gloves. "Broom closet, Ollie. Broom. Closet."

Olivia grinned and stared at the ceiling as if trying to conjure the image of Zane and me making out. "Still so hot."

Olivia came over as promised, grimacing at my boxes littering the living room floor. "You seriously haven't finished unpacking?"

"Essentials, sure. Those boxes are just full of junk mostly. Haven't had time." I shrugged, playing with the seam of my pajama bottoms.

"And you also didn't have time to at least stack them against a wall?"

I narrowed my eyes at her. "Did you come over to chastise me about cleanliness or to distract me?"

"It's only—how are we to have a dance party with these boxes strewn about? Hm?" Olivia kicked a box with her foot, making whatever was inside clank.

"Dance party?" My stomach gurgled.

"Uh, yeah. Didn't you do that in college? Dance parties and drinking?" She rushed past me to the kitchen, rummaging through my cabinets.

"I think you know the answer to your own question, Ollie. College for me was pulling all-nighters studying law until my eyes bulged from my skull."

"Right." She ducked and returned with a bottle in her hand. "Maybe we should invite Johnnie Walker to the party. Is this really all you have? Should've stopped at the bottle-o on the way over."

"Yes. It's all I have. It's all I ever drink, and it's only to help clear my head at times."

She grabbed two glass tumblers from the cabinet in front of her, sliding them across the counter. "It'll have to do then. Even though I think it tastes like arse."

Stealing a peek over my shoulder, I squinted through the slit in the blinds to see if Zane's light was on. It wasn't. I frowned.

"What you lookin' at?" Olivia asked, appearing at my side with a scotch in hand.

I jumped and snatched the glass from her grasp. "The moon."

"You're quick, Bazin. And good too because you're not technically lying, are you?" She grinned and took a sip of her drink, scrunching her face like she drank gasoline.

"What? It *is* a full moon." I gulped the scotch, sighing as the delicious smoky taste coated my tongue. A full moon always revitalized me.

"You want to catch a glimpse at a full moon, alright, but *not* the one in the sky." She snorted before bolting toward the windows.

"What are you doing?" I sipped more scotch, fighting the urge to down it.

She parted the blinds with about as much covert ability as a wolverine. "Which apartment is his?"

In an attempt to change the subject, I asked, "How was your date with uh—what was his name? Blake?"

"Eh. He was good for a night."

"You sound bummed about that. Doesn't sound like your usual self. What's up?"

Sighing, she let the blinds close with a loud *fwap*. "I just—I guess I need someone more…adventurous?"

"Adventurous? You? No offense, but I never took you for the type."

She blew her bangs from her eyes. "I haven't done much since moving to New York, so that's fair. But back in Australia?" She bit her lower lip, smiling, staring into space. "I did all kinds of shit."

"Seriously?" I grinned and nudged her arm.

"Yeah. Even scuba diving."

I cocked my head to the side, attempting to imagine her in a snorkel. "No kidding. Huh."

Olivia sighed and moved her gaze to the swig of alcohol left in her drink. "I miss it sometimes. The motherland."

Melancholy. Homesickness.

"Do you ever think about going back, Ollie?" I rubbed her shoulder.

"Hell no. My family and friends are here, and I *love* it here. Mum passed away when I was a kid, I followed dad when he moved here for a job, and then—there's you." She smiled and bumped my shoulder with hers. "You're like a sister to me."

The momentary sadness swarming through her floated away

as quickly as it arrived.

"You know what? You and I should go on vacation sometime—to Australia. I've never been."

Olivia's eyes widened, and she squished each of my cheeks. "Woah. Are you a doppelganger? Keira Bazin speaking of *vacations*?"

"Maybe I've seen the light. Maybe it's the alcohol. Either way, I want you to hold me to it. Deal?" I lifted my glass.

"That—" We clanked our tumblers. "I can do." Olivia tilted her head back and finished the drink.

"Did I tell you he gave me binoculars?" I dipped my pinky in the scotch and traced it over my bottom lip—the image of that muscular ass of his etched into my brain.

She sputtered and wiped the back of her hand over her mouth. "Um, no?"

"The bastard left them in a box on my doorstep with a note saying, 'So you can get a better view.'" Rolling my eyes, I stuck my nose back in the glass, slurping more elixir.

She squeezed her glass with both hands, beaming. "You looked. Didn't you?"

"Maybe." I tapped my fingernail against the tumbler.

"Good *on* ya, mate. What'd you see? Tell me." She made a hurry-up gesture with her free hand as she made her way to the kitchen, pouring herself another drink.

"His ass." I couldn't think about his dick. I just couldn't.

She squealed and did a spin before grabbing onto the countertop to steady herself.

Smiling at her extra enthusiasm and mixed with the speed I sipped my scotch over usual, I added, "There's more."

She leaned on her elbow, resting her chin on her hand, staring at me from the kitchen unblinking. With every sip of scotch, she'd wince and gag.

"I may have teased him back with—" I dragged my hand over my body.

Gasping, she ran back to me and playfully shoved my shoulder. "You did not. Who *are* you?"

"It was completely inappropriate and out of line, wasn't it?" I downed the rest of my scotch.

"Who cares if it was? What is life if not occasionally being inappropriate? Boring. That's what." She threw her arm around my shoulders, pulling me to her side. "I like this side of you."

"More Johnnie?" I pointed to the bottle with a grin.

After finishing what she'd just poured, making less of a disgusted face this time, she held her glass out. "Definitely. The bloke's warming up to me."

Pouring doubles this time, I hopped onto a stool near the counter.

Despite the company and the drinking, I still couldn't help thinking about the case. The nerves that bubbled every time it crossed my mind—going up against Zane. For the first time in my career, I actually *feared* losing.

"Do you remember the Johnson, Ekols, and Mirand case? The one where we convicted those three young guys for the drowning of the little girl?"

Olivia did one slow-motion blink. "Well, that was out of absolutely nowhere, but, yes. Why the bloody hell are you bringing that up *now* while we're trying to get our buzz on?"

"I can't help it." I rubbed my glass, making it squeak. "It

always eats away at my brain the investigators couldn't find DNA that matched later on, and they were released from prison on an Adams plea. They served thirteen years in prison and may have never even done it."

Olivia gave an exaggerated head roll, and bumped her finger under my tumbler, encouraging me to drink more. "And they very well could have. It's all speculation. The prosecution had plenty of evidence to convict them."

"I haven't lost a case, and yet, technically, I won that one, but they were released."

Olivia gasped. "A light just went on in the apartment on the top floor. Is that his? He seems like the type to live in a penthouse."

Excited jitters fluttered in my stomach. "Yes."

"Where are those binos?" Olivia spun around, flicking her head left to right, making her bangs fall into her eyes.

"I threw them away." Sipping on my drink, I kept my back to the windows.

Don't look, Keira. Do. Not. Look.

"Yeah, right." She whizzed past me, heading straight for my bedroom.

I chased after her, holding the glass above my head, trying to keep it level as I ran. "Ollie, don't."

Her ass was in the air on her hands and knees, bent forward, and rummaging under my bed. She sat up with the box in her hand, holding it above her head like the Holy Grail. Ignoring my continued protests, she scurried past me, removing the binoculars as she went, and tossing the box to the floor.

Rubbing my thumb between my eyes and sipping on my

scotch, I shuffled down the hall, groaning at her as she peered out the window through the blinds.

"Bugger, I don't see anything." She frowned at me over her shoulder.

Shaking my head, I sat on the sofa, and curled my feet underneath me. "I highly doubt he'll do it twice."

I gulped more scotch, my cheeks warming.

"Fuck me dead," Olivia said.

The warmth in my cheeks traveled down my neck, settling in my chest. "What?"

"I just—" Olivia walked over, the binoculars limp in her hands. "I just saw his donga."

"You did?" I leaped up, snatching the binoculars from her. As I neared the window, giggles followed me.

Zane was nowhere to be found in the lit room across the street.

"I knew it." Olivia pointed at me.

"You didn't actually see it did you?" I rolled my eyes at her before shoving the binoculars into her chest.

"Nope. But you sure as hell want to." She chuckled and did a little dance.

Oh, I had. And *felt* it against me.

Sitting back down, I leaned forward and absently traced my finger around the rim of my glass. "The kiss *was* hot, Ollie. So fucking hot."

"You should tell him that." She flopped next to me, giggling as she fell sideways against the cushions.

"Please. As if the man needs any more of an ego boost." I sipped more of my drink.

"Who cares? Besides, you've got an ego too." She elbowed me.

I snapped my gaze to her. "I do not."

"Yes. You do. It's part of the reason you're a confident, good lawyer." She crawled to the nightstand, grabbed my phone, and shoved it at me. "Text him. Tell him."

"Do you really think I have the defense lawyer in our case's personal phone number?"

She stuck her bottom lip out to the middle of her chin. "True. But you *do* have his e-mail." She wiggled the phone until I snatched it.

With the alcohol bubbling in my brain, lulling me into a wistful intoxication, I shrugged. "Why the hell not. It'll torture him even more."

"That's the spirit," Olivia shouted, spinning until she lay on her back with her head in my lap.

Pulling up a new e-mail, I worked my thumb across the touch screen.

To: Zane Vronti

From: Keira Bazin

Subject: Expletive Content

Now that I have your attention, I just wanted to say...I really, really really, REALLY enjoyed that kiss.

All the best,

Keira

Send.

If I'd stayed awake long enough, my mortification may have been a distant memory by the time I woke up the following day. But at three in the morning, still on the couch, and squinting into the darkness, the blinking blue notification light caught my attention.

A work e-mail? This early?

Groggily pulling it up, all my limbs froze, seeing it was an e-mail *reply* from Zane.

Oh my god. Had I actually sent that? *Why* would I send that? With a shaky thumb, I selected it.

To: Keira Bazin

From: Zane Vronti

Subject: RE: Expletive Content

You did, did you? Maybe you should try me again sometime. ;)

Always ready for more,

Zane

Dropping the phone in my lap, I slapped my hands over my eyes. I'd been avoiding him for a reason, and now there was no way in hell I could face him after this. Jumping to my feet, I sprinted to my bedroom to change. If I hurried, I could start my walk to work before Zane conveniently met me on the sidewalk.

"Why are you making so much noise?" Olivia whined from the couch.

"I'm getting ready to go in for work." After getting dressed, I quickly pulled a brush through my hair.

"At three in the bloody morning?"

Trotting back to the living room, hopping on one foot while I slipped on a heel, I handed her my spare key. "I know it's early, but if I go now, I'll avoid Zane. Here's my extra key so you can lock up after you leave."

She groaned and snatched it from me, slamming it on the coffee table in front of the sofa. "You realize doing this is only delaying the inevitable, right?"

I thinned my lips and grabbed my coat. "I'll see you later, Ollie."

Maybe it would, or maybe it wouldn't, but I knew whatever may have been bound to happen between Zane and me—I wasn't ready for it. But would I ever be?

NINE

ZEUS

THIS WOMAN WAS GOING to be the divine death of me. I was sure of it. Hot and cold. Back and forth. She shoves me into a broom closet to have her way with me. Then basically tells me to fuck off. And now? This damn e-mail. *What* was her angle?

I sat on a bench in Central Park, letting Levin run freely with the other canines left off-leash. Glancing at the calendar on my phone, I growled at the time I had left to wrap up this arrangement. One of three scenarios was bound to happen with Keira. The most likely being she'd ask for some time to think it over. Least likely? Saying yes without a passing thought. Wouldn't *that* be delightful?

One thing was certain—I needed to bring it up, and I needed to do it now. I managed to make an impression on her, but now using her deportation as leverage? It was bound to piss her the fuck off, and I needed time for her to cool her jets about it and realize...it was a solid deal.

"Oh, my God," a woman screeched. "Is this your lab?" She knelt by the bench where Levin sat next to me, moving her hands toward his head.

"Don't touch him." I snapped my gaze to the curly-haired woman sporting bright purple spandex pants and a matching long-sleeved shirt.

She froze and looked up at me, confused. "I'm sorry?"

"Don't touch him. I don't know where you've been."

She snapped her hands away and shot to her feet with a glare. "Jesus. I just wanted to pet your dog. You don't have to be a prick about it."

I flashed a spark of lightning in my eyes, waiting for the fear to pour over her face before continuing her jog.

A little over the top? Maybe. But Keira Bazin had me so fucking on edge I wanted to roast every tree in the damn park.

Scratching behind Levin's ears, I rose and shortened his leash. "Come on, boy. We've got a Queen to nab."

I stood outside of Keira's apartment, leaning casually on the doorframe, waiting for her to answer the door. Her feet brushed the carpet, and a faint "shit" fluttered into my godly ears. I'd bet my left nut she was going to pretend she wasn't home. And judging by the fact I'd been standing here for a solid thirty seconds, knowing she already spied me through the peephole, it's precisely what she was doing.

"I know you're home, Keira. Come on. Being an ass isn't your jurisdiction. That's mine." I patted my hand on the doorframe and grinned once I heard the chain lock being removed.

She whipped open the door with such force it sent her hair flying. "What do you want, Zane?"

"You—" I bopped her nose with a single finger. "Have been avoiding me."

"Wow. Did you deduce that all by yourself, counselor?"

Smirking, I pushed off the door, standing straight and gleaming down at her. "Why?"

"The usual reason someone avoids someone else. I don't want to see you." She crossed her arms over her grey t-shirt, a pair of jeans clinging to her legs.

I rubbed a hand over my chin. "Even though you really, really, really, *really* enjoyed it?"

Her cheeks turned rosy. "People say a lot of things when they're tipsy."

"It's been proven that alcohol brings out your true self."

She dug her bare feet into the carpet. "And what sources do you have to support this claim?"

Damn, I loved when she talked like that.

Chuckling, I shook my head. "I've got to talk with you. Mind going for a walk?"

"It's about to get dark."

I slid forward, my toes inches over the threshold. "I could always come inside?"

She pressed her hand on my chest. Just as before, despite layers of clothing, the touch still managed to ignite my nerves. She gulped and took in a quick breath in an attempt to hide the reaction I could sense from her a mile away.

"Stay *right* there. I'll grab my coat."

I went to take a step forward to wait in her apartment, but the door slammed in my face.

Such a minx.

Grinning, I leaned on the opposite wall, watching the darkness starting to overtake the sky.

"This better be about the case," Keira said as she locked her door behind her and slipped a bright red wool hat over her head.

"Oh, it is."

Considering her distaste for crowds and the conversation we were about to have, I led us away from downtown. Sounds of tires screeching, people whistling for cabs, and random shouts from food vendors drifted away—replaced with the faint hum of traffic lights and melting snow emptying into storm drains.

"I enjoyed it too, by the way. In case your declaration was founded, and you're too embarrassed to admit it." I grinned down at her, giving her a sidelong glance as we walked side-by-side.

"I'm not embarrassed. I just didn't want to ignite your ego." She huffed, focusing her attention forward.

"If we men aren't complimented, though, how else can we please you?" My power surged through my veins, and I choked it back.

The lack of Keira's heat near my arm gave me pause, realizing I was several feet ahead of her. Turning on my heel with my hands in my pockets, I spied her standing motionless like a statue.

"Keira?" I closed the distance between us with steady steps.

She closed her eyes so tightly it pinched her entire face. "Do it again."

My power swelled, striking through my fingertips. I balled my hands into fists within my jacket, squelching it. "Do what again, Keira?" I whispered the words, and stepped closer.

"Kiss me," she breathed out, tilting her chin to gaze up at me, her chest rising and falling.

Hot and cold.

I'd take the hot whenever she offered it.

Removing one glove, I grasped her chin, lowered my lips to hers, and kissed her. Thrusting my tongue between her lips, not bothering with an invitation, I swirled it into her mouth and curled my other arm around her waist. Grabbing her ass, kneading it, I backed her up until she bumped into a nearby pole, pinning her against it and grinding into her stomach.

Testing the limits on what she'd let me do, what she *wanted* me to do, I traced my gloveless hand over her chest, grabbing one breast through the thickness of her coat, making her whimper. Continuing my test, I trailed my hand down her stomach and continued until I reached that convenient seam in her jeans, using it to rub her clit.

She whimpered and I drowned it by deepening the kiss, hiding her body with mine from anyone who might pass by. I sent a tantalizing sizzle of electricity through our joined lips, coursing it through her chest and down to the spot I sensually tortured with my fingers. It didn't take long for her to shudder in my arms, her knees buckling as she moaned into my mouth. Holding an arm around her to keep her standing, I slowly peeled away and grinned wickedly at her.

"What the *fuck* just happened?" She whispered, gazing up at me with a mixture of ecstasy and confusion.

Pressing my cock bulging through my pants against her hip, I lowered my lips to her ear. "I believe I made you come in public with all your clothes on."

"Jesus, Zane. I just wanted you to kiss me." She gulped and let out a sensual sigh, her gaze as she looked up at me suggesting she was almost ready to let me take her right here on the street corner.

"Well, things escalated. And you didn't stop me." I brushed our lips.

She breathed against me, sweet smells I couldn't decipher floating from her neck—her hair. "No, I didn't."

"We really need to talk, Keira." Adjusting myself with a tug at my belt, I stepped back, slipping my glove back on.

Getting a complete look at her made my gut twist. She was gorgeous before, but fuck, if she didn't look even better satiated. A radiant glow and color in her cheeks, her eyes slightly groggy—and that tiny smile tugging at her reddened lips. I held my hand out to her, and to my surprise, she took it after only one moment of hesitation.

We continued to walk, and after a moment to psych up, don the mask of the mighty god-king, I took the plunge.

"I know something about you that you don't think I know." I tightened my grip on her hand.

"Alright, Riddler. Care to speak English to me now?"

Licking my lips, I cut my gaze to her. "You're Canadian."

She gasped, pressing a hand to her chest. "A Canadian in New York? That's shocking."

Do or die.

"And about to be deported." Cut and dry.

She stopped walking and yanked her hand away.

Here we go.

"What did you just say?" Her cheeks were still rosy from when she came but now, they flamed.

I interlaced my fingers in front of me and widened my stance. "You're about to be an illegal resident of the US because your resident status was through your American husband. Your ex-husband. And you forgot to file the necessary paperwork on time."

"I—what? This can't be. How the hell do you even know this?" She fumed, pacing a small square on the sidewalk in front of me.

"I told you, Keira." I tightened my jaw, keeping my strong demeanor firm. "I always research my opponents."

Her lips slowly parted, her chest rising as she took a deep breath. "You're going to use this against me, aren't you? To get me off the case." She let out a feminine growl and turned away from me. "I should've known all of this—everything you've been doing was to distract me."

Standing firm, I watched her pace. "I don't plan to use it against you. I plan to offer you a solution."

"A solution? Oh, you're just going to help me out of the goodness of your black heart?" She clenched her fists at her sides.

"No."

She stormed forward, tapping her toes against mine and glaring up at me. "Why don't you just come out and fucking say it, Vronti?"

How the woman managed to make me hard despite the

conversation was beyond me.

"The solution would also benefit—me." I pointed to myself and leaned forward, bringing our lips closer.

She sneered at me and turned away. "Of course, it would."

"Marry me."

She whirled around, her eyes cutting into me, tearing at my flesh. "Excuse me?"

Even having been proposed to before, I didn't imagine this is how she pictured future ones.

"Marrying an American citizen is your fastest and only way to become legal and still work the Daniels case."

"And what would *you* be getting out of this?" The scowl forming on her brow could make Cerberus whimper away.

Think fast here, King of the Gods. You can't tell her the truth, but it also has to make sense.

"I recently came upon an inheritance. To receive it, the will clearly states I need to be married." I chewed on my lip, still cementing my feet to the sidewalk.

Her eyes blinked with the speed of a jackhammer. "You have *got* to be fucking kidding me." She stormed up to me again, poking me in the chest. "I'd be doing this to save my livelihood, and you are doing it for goddamned money?"

More like eternal power and maintaining the kingdom and only livelihood I know.

"That about sums it up, yes."

She turned away in a huff, the fury building in her so strongly it was almost as if I could *feel* it carving into my bones. It was enough to make me roll my shoulders, attempting to shrug it away.

"How exactly did you picture this going, Zane? You'd ask me, I'd give you a big hug, thanking you for saving my career, and we'd be off to a justice of the peace?" Her top lip curled in a snarl.

"No. But I at least expected you to say you'd think about it. You don't have a lot of choices here. And you could do a lot worse for a husband." I held my arms out at my sides, displaying myself like a prized stallion.

"I do have another choice. Suck it up and march my ass back to Canada with my head held high."

I lowered my hands. "You hate me that much, you'd be willing to give up the career you built for yourself here?"

"I can still practice law in Canada." She gulped, and by the way her eyes glistened it looked like she was about to cry.

Fuck.

"Yeah? How many high-profile cases are there for you in Saskatchewan? Hm?" I slid forward.

She stepped back and pointed at me. "It's not about the high-profile cases. Law is the law. I'd still be helping people."

"High profile cases *made* you into the lawyer you are now." Cautiously, I moved closer again. This time, she let me. "Take some time and think about this, Keira. You're not going to find a better offer anywhere else."

Her knee bounced, and she rubbed her forehead. "I wasn't sure if what I felt toward you was hate or just resentment over defense lawyers as a whole, but it is crystal clear to me now, Zane."

We were arguing—fuming at each other. I'd just dropped a bomb, and yet the arousal in her stare was plain as day.

We're both officially fucked in the head.

"Tell me you'll think about it."

Her lips were still slightly red from our kiss, and she pursed them. "Fine. But you need to stay away from me."

"Why's that?" I breached her invisible shield again, looming over her, igniting my scent tenfold into the air around us—sandalwood and cologne.

Lust flashed in her gaze as she stared up at me, anger still tightening her jaw. "You could have asked any woman to do this. Why me?"

"You—intrigue me." I trailed the tip of my nose over her cheek.

She pushed me back. "I *intrigue* you? And that's enough to be roped into this with me for the rest of your life?"

It was so much more than that, and I couldn't even explain it to myself.

"Also, I mean—look at you." I referenced her face, her body.

She rolled her eyes. "Stay. Away. Zane. I'll reach out when I've made up my mind."

Squinting at her, I took a step back and watched her make her way down the street until she disappeared around the corner.

I sure as hell had no plans to stay away. The need to *show* her what could be hers ran far too deep to ignore.

"Trouble in paradise, Pops?" Hermes slunk from the shadows with a snarky grin.

Pointing a stern finger, I took one last glance in the direction Keira had stormed off, hoping like some damned fool she'd have come running back. "I'm not in the mood, Herm."

"I have some information on your darling girlfriend you

might like to hear." He peered at his cuticles before rubbing them against the collar of his aviation jacket.

"Out with it," I growled.

"I saw her name on the flight passenger list for tomorrow. She's going to Argentina."

My mind raced with possibilities. "In the middle of the case? What the hell for?"

"I did some more digging, and apparently, it's for a former client's wedding."

A feral grin played over my lips.

"Make sure you're a pilot on that flight. Keep an eye on her. Let me know when you land and where she is so I can port there."

Hermes snapped his fingers, slipping his Aviator sunglasses on despite it being nighttime. "One step ahead of you. Consider it done."

A wedding in a romantic setting like Argentina. I planned to charm the ever-loving shit out of her and leave her begging for more.

TEN

KEIRA

THE TRIP TO ARGENTINA could not have come at a better time. I was still fuming over Zane backing me into a corner like that. A corner I demanded to be backed into, but I just couldn't get over how I felt around him. Whenever we touched, all the swirling emotions settled over my skin, comforted me. It was surreal to simply *feel* something I *wanted* to feel instead of trying to wade through it and organize.

"Miss, would you please mind grabbing your belongings?" A male TSA agent said to me, pointing at the bin of items I'd put through the scanner.

I jolted to attention and grabbed it. "Sorry, I was daydreaming."

"Must've been some dream." He raised one brow and turned his attention to the next person.

Sulking on the nearest bench to put my shoes and watch back on, I scowled at the floor. How could I have possibly forgotten about my residence paperwork? And I couldn't blame Olivia. It wasn't her responsibility. She was my paralegal. My friend. Not a damn servant.

In fact, I should be giving her the benefit of the doubt.

Fishing my phone from the front pocket of my briefcase, I called Olivia as I rolled my carry-on suitcase through the terminal.

"G'day?"

She never failed to make me smile. "G'day? Really?"

"I bet it put a grin on that pretty face of yours, though, didn't it?"

"Guilty. Hey, I had a quick question for you, and if you didn't, I'm *not* mad at you. I just need to know."

She went silent for a beat.

"Ollie?"

"I'm here. Just sweating my tits off, wondering what you're about to ask."

I licked my lips as I stopped in front of my gate. "My residence permit paperwork. Did you have a reminder in your calendar or anything?"

"I—" Typing on a keyboard and frantic clicks of the mouse sounded from the other line. "Keira, I know I put it on the calendar. I have no idea what happened. Shit. Fuck. Shit. Did it lapse?"

I closed my eyes and sighed. A small part of me hoped she'd tell me I still had time, but I knew around my birthday was when we'd gotten divorced, however long ago it was. And here we were in December already. "Yes. But I'll figure it out. No worries."

"No bloody worries? Keir, you're going to be kicked out of the country. You're my lawyer. I can't be one half of the Blonde Bulldogs by myself." She sniffled.

"It's going to be fine. Worst case scenario, I go back to Canada, get it straightened out, and come back."

"Oh, yeah? How many years later?"

I pinched the bridge of my nose. "I know, I know. Like I said, I'll figure it out. This quick trip should be a good time to clear my head."

"Enjoy the hell out of yourself, alright? No thoughts of dudes in acid, evidence trials, or defense lawyers. Or *do* think about defense lawyers." I could tell she smiled at that last part from the inflection in her voice.

I pinched my thighs together, recalling the exploding orgasm I had on a damn street corner simply from Zane rubbing me *through* my jeans.

"I'm not going to think about anything except how beautiful Argentina looks this time of year."

"Good on ya, Keir. Have a safe flight. Kisses."

"Bye, Ollie."

The boarding process started not too soon after I hung up with Olivia. I stood in line, waiting in the terminal tunnel leading to the airplane door, still marveling how many passengers were on the red-eye flight. As we neared the cockpit, one of the pilots stood near the entrance, casually leaning against the doorframe and greeting passengers.

When his blue eyes fell on me, his smile brightened, creasing his cheeks and giving his gaze a sort of Eastwood-like squint to them. He was pretty damn sexy.

"Good morning, miss. Enjoy your flight." He winked at me, a sparkle in his gaze as he kept me in his sights.

"Well, that's entirely up to you, isn't it?" I smiled, feeling confidence floating from him and the same plain arrogance Zane exuded.

"I suppose you're right. I'll be sure to take real good care of you." With a dimpled grin, he nodded at me.

Finally getting to my row, I couldn't stuff my bags in the overhead compartments fast enough. As soon as my butt hit the seat and I put on the buckle, slipped the sleeping mask over my eyes, popped in my earbuds, and readied to sleep for the longest number of hours I had in *years*.

"Sit on my face, Keira," Zane whispered in my ear.

I let out a harsh breath. "What?"

"Sit. On. My. Face," he commanded, pulling my hips to straddle him, both of us naked.

Doing as he asked, I slid forward on my knees until my pussy hovered over his lips, my breathing going erratic.

"Now ride me like I'm your damn pony." Zane's sapphire stare gleamed at me from between my legs, his tongue lapping over my folds…

"Miss. Miss." A woman's voice said, shaking my shoulder.

I jumped awake, the song *Pony* by Ginuwine blasting through my earbuds. Groggily slipping the mask off, I squinted up at her.

"Sorry, miss, but I need you to put your seat in the upright position for landing?"

Smacking my lips together, I sat up, wiping the back of my hand over my mouth. "Sorry. Of course."

After I pushed the button, raising my seat, the flight attendant gave a kind smile and continued her routine through the aisle.

The dream came back to me as the song played, and I rubbed between my eyes. Ride me like a damn pony. Jesus. I couldn't even *not* think about him if I tried.

I took a taxi from the Ezeiza International Airport in Buenos Aires to the closest hotel I could find to Rivadavia Park, where the wedding ceremony and reception would take place. I had no intention of spending the night and planned on going straight to the airport after the festivities were over to fly back to New York, but I wanted the room to store my luggage and relax before dealing with a wedding crowd.

Once in the comfort of my room for the next several hours, I slipped into my silver sparkly dress, sticking my leg out to the side from the slit gliding up my right thigh. The design exposed most of my back, and it had a swooping neckline. I'd owned this dress for years, having bought it on a whim when I saw it in a shop window, but never had an excuse to wear it. After styling my hair into loose, long waves, I slipped into a pair of silver heels and breezed out the door with a deep inhale.

As my heels met the concrete sidewalk outside the hotel, an onslaught of murmured conversations in Spanish, children laughing, car horns blaring, and every emotion possible flooded me like a monsoon. I winced, curling my arms around myself as I walked, concentrating on the sounds of my heels clicking on the hard surface beneath me. It didn't take long to reach one of nine entrances into the park, and I took a hard turn, letting out a roiling sigh once I found an area flourishing with palm trees.

The sight of the wedding was evident given the lights hanging in a circle around a central space in the park near the Simon Bolivar monument. A concrete walkway widened at the center, leading to the statue while several smaller paths darted in all directions, park benches every few feet and trees of varying width and height. Magnolia arrangements, as well as a flowered arch, stood at the end of the walkway. Dozens of white folding chairs were intricately placed in parallel rows, facing the arch and they'd hung lit lanterns from some of the lower hanging tree branches.

"Holy shit. Keira?" A man's voice said behind me.

Whirling on my heel, I spied Todd, my former client, standing on the other side of the walkway with his jaw dropped.

"Todd, long time no see." I walked close enough to outstretch my hand. "Congratulations, by the way."

He wore black tuxedo pants, a white jacket, and a pastel pink bow tie. "I honestly didn't think you'd show up." His eyes glistened like he was about to cry as he eagerly shook my hand, making my whole body rattle.

Fear. Anxiety. Suffocation.

Not exactly the best emotions to be exuding on one's wedding day.

"I wouldn't have missed it for the world." Offering a warm smile, I cocked my head to the side. "Are you alright? You seem nervous. More than the usual jitters."

A knife twisted in my gut, remembering how I'd felt the day I married Tyler. I hadn't been nervous per se, but it was as if I had an out-of-body experience, watching myself marry one of the nicest men in the world. Any woman would've killed to be in my position, and I was happy, I was—but that whole saying of the love of your life feeling like your other half? I'd still felt like a lone half.

"I—" He lightly touched my elbow and led me off the path near a large tree. "I don't think Cynthia wants to actually marry me." Frowning, he wrung his hands together.

"Why would you say that?"

Fear. Mortification. Self-Consciousness.

"She's been extremely distant the past month leading up to the wedding, and when we have talked, she's been *so* spiteful."

Poor guy.

"Think it could just be wedding nerves? They made an entire show about Bridezillas, you know?"

A flutter of amusement.

"I don't know. I do know I have this deep-rooted fear of being ditched at the altar, though."

Oof.

"Todd, I'm sure you're getting in your own head about this. Look at this beautiful setting you're in. And dozens of people have flown from all over the globe for it." I squeezed his shoulder.

When I decided to come to Argentina for this and…relax, the last thing I expected was to play therapist to my former client.

"Would you talk to her?" His brown eyes widened, his palms pressing together in prayer.

I pressed a finger on the bridge of my nose. "Oh, I don't know. I don't want to get in the middle of—"

"Please. You can read people so well with your profession.

It'd really ease my mind." He pushed his hands together so tightly they turned white.

Desperation.

"Fine. Where is she?"

He hopped, and before I could stop him, hugged me. With the five inches I had on him in heels, his ear pressed near my cleavage. "Thank you. She's in the bridal suite in that hotel there on the corner."

I patted his back with a sigh. "Does she remember me?"

"Are you kidding? It's hard to forget the woman who proved someone you love's innocence."

After giving his shoulder a last squeeze and shoving every thought away about this being a bad idea, I ventured to the bridal suite.

I shouldn't be here. The bridal suite was a place for the mothers, the bridesmaids, friends. Not former prosecutors who represented the groom-to-be.

Crying—no, sobbing, flowed from the other side of the door.

Fear. Anxiety. The *same* emotions as Todd.

I raised my fist and grimaced before lightly knocking. "Cynthia?"

Through several sniffles, she replied, "Who's there?"

"It's Keira Bazin. I'm not sure if you—"

The door flew open and the same fiery red-head I'd remembered sitting in the courtroom during Todd's trial threw her arms around me, dressed in an ivory mermaid wedding gown.

These people acted like we were all best friends. I'd seen

them for half a year on and off and said goodbye over a year ago when the trial was over.

Shh, Keira. Since when were you so impatient? Zane must be rubbing off on you.

Rubbing.

"You're crying on your wedding day?" I patted the part of her back covered by cloth.

She pushed back, a wad of tissues in her hand, her mascara partially running down her face. "I don't think Todd wants to marry me."

For fuck's sake.

I loved helping people with my gift. I did. But sometimes, it was a matter of two people simply *talking* to each other to clear the air.

"Funny. He said the exact same thing about you." I grabbed a fresh tissue and started to dab the mascara away from her pretty bridal face.

Had the make-up artist not heard of waterproof mascara?

"What? How could he possibly think that?" The curled ringlets of her up-do hairstyle bobbed as she shook her head.

"Have you been distant? Maybe a little…snappy?"

She sniffled again, turning to look at herself in the mirror. "Maybe? I've been so busy with the last-minute plans for the wedding. If I ever did this again—which I hope I never have to—I'm *not* doing a destination wedding. It's been a logistical nightmare."

Ugh. I hoped I'd never had to do it again either. And my second husband could very well end up being an arrogant asshole lawyer with a killer ass.

"Plain and simple. You took out your stress on him, and he backed off because he didn't want to stress you out more, which made you both distant." I tugged on the tulle veil falling down her back. "It's your wedding day. You have a man who loves you, waiting to marry you. Smile. Be happy. And most of all, stop worrying."

There weren't many positive things happening in my life lately, but I tried nonetheless to push as much positivity out of me, offering it to her.

"You're right, Keira. Thank you, sincerely. You've always been so good with people. I know lawyers sort of need to be, but you—you have a gift." She took both my hands and squeezed them.

If she only knew the half of it..

"It's really no problem at all. And you look beautiful."

She guffawed. "Me? Look at *you*, you smokeshow."

My cheeks blushed, and I ran a finger under the hem hanging over my chest. "Well, thank you. I'll see you after the ceremony."

She bounced as she turned back to the mirror, smiling wide and giggling as several bridesmaids barged into the room.

Jealousy. Excitement. Resentment.

Yet each of them smiled radiantly as if they had no other thought other than the bride's happiness.

Slipping past them, I made my way back to a nervously waiting Todd. I held the train of my dress as I passed and waved. "It's a go, lover boy. Everything's fine. Go get hitched."

"Oh my—really? Keira, you're a goddess. A living, breathing goddess." He blew several kisses at me before jogging off.

Smiling, I shook my head and took a seat on one of the folding chairs. The ceremony was beautiful, and the setting sun in the background added to the scenery. Fortunately, the ceremony was also of the shorter variety. I'd been to some that lasted damn near an hour.

I now sat at one of several rounded tables under a canopy in the park, trying desperately not to glance at the time every five minutes. Sipping on champagne, I poked at my wedding cake, not feeling up to consuming sugar. A live band played in the corner, and there were two dance floors. The one that called to me the most was the one outside underneath the moon and stars. Not to mention, it had far fewer people crowding it. A small smile tugged at my lips as I watched Cynthia and Todd dancing on the floor beneath the canopy, the happiness swelling from them so pronounced, I could feel it from this distance.

"Excuse me, miss?" A deep voice laced with an Argentinian accent said.

I looked up at a tall man with a thin face and chocolate-brown hair. "Yes?"

When he smiled, it was lopsided, curving higher on the left side of his face, and tiny creases formed under his pale blue eyes. "I was hoping I could ask you to dance?"

My throat tightened as I stared up at him and his chiseled jawline with a scattering of dark stubble. After downing my drink, I stood. "Sure."

He held his hand out, keeping the drool-worthy smile plastered over his thin lips. I took it, and he led me out of the canopy and to the stone dance floor. Wrapping an arm around my lower back, he pulled me closer.

Lust. Lust. And more lust.

There was no doubt in my mind this man's number one objective tonight was to feed off the romantic vibe women felt from weddings. I'd dance with him because I was bored, but he'd better think again if he thought there'd be more.

"The name's Rodrigo, by the way," he whispered, his Argentinian accent making my toes curl. I'd give him that much.

"Keira."

His hand explored further, dipping near the lowest exposed part of my back. "Do you know how to tango, Keira?"

The callused bumps on his palms slid across my skin, giving me goosebumps. Unlike someone else I knew, Rodrigo's touch failed to suppress the emotions floating around us from other couples dancing. It was so fucking distracting.

"I'm a bit rusty, but I think I can manage."

He pulled me tighter with a sultry grin.

"Move," a baritone voice barked.

Rodrigo glared over my shoulder, not dropping his arm from my waist. "I believe the lady and I are dancing."

Zane appeared beside us, his eyes feral. "Move. Now." A flash in his gaze was followed by a random crackle of lightning streaking the sky.

Rodrigo threw his palms up and backed away. "Me chupa un huevo. She's all yours."

Fury shot down my spine as I turned to face Zane. The sight of him made my mouth dry. Tall. Imposing. His white linen shirt flapped in the breeze, while enough buttons were undone to show his tanned, muscular chest. And those blue eyes I'd repeatedly drowned in countless times trailed over my body before he pulled me against him.

"What the hell are you doing here, Zane? How did you even know I was here?" I pushed against him, but he held firm.

"I'm on vacation," he said through a snarl.

"Bull. Shit." I tried to pull away again, but he took my other hand in his.

Staring up at him made my chest pulse—our emotions swirling together like paints in water until eventually blending. "I'll make a scene."

"No. You won't." He dipped his nose near my neck, inhaling me.

"You're so sure of yourself." I forced myself not to close my eyes as his lips traced over my jawline.

"At least one of us is." He lifted his gaze back to mine, probing me with it. "If you don't want my hands all over you right now, push me away again. I'll let you."

My heart pounded against my chest, the exposed leg from the slit in my dress pressing to his thigh. "Bastard." I kneed him in the stomach, making him grunt.

He snapped me to attention, moving the hand on my back to my ass, squeezing it. A light shock zapped through it, causing me to yelp. "Tease."

What the hell? I'd have thought it static shock—if we were on carpet.

The band played a tango, the fluttering of the guitar melody matching the swirls in my stomach. We started circling each other with my hand pressed against his chest, his fingers grazing my forearm. He spun me, and I slid one leg behind me, dipping into a lunge. He pulled me to him, and I raised that same knee to his hip, staring at him. My feet moved of their own accord, my mind focused on the movements and the man in front of me.

"You drive me batshit crazy. I'm jealous over a woman who isn't even *mine*," he said, ending his last word with a conquering growl.

He spun us with my leg wrapped around his waist and paused, dipping me backward with his arm curled against my lower back.

When he pulled me up, I pressed our foreheads together. "Aw. Is the criminal defense lawyer mad he's not getting his way?"

We crisscrossed our feet, moving in a circle with our foreheads still connected, glaring at each other.

"How much longer are we going to play this game? Hm?" Zane pulled me against him, my breasts pushing against his chest.

I turned my back to him, and with one of his hands on my hip, the other holding our arms out, we danced to the side, my ass bumping against his already hard impression. "I haven't the foggiest idea what you're talking about."

He spun me out and away from him and at the last moment, grabbed my hand, stopping me. Turning his back to me, he peered over his shoulder, waiting for me to approach. With the sultry grin of a tigress, I stepped forward, wrapping my arms around him from behind, but instead of pressing my palms to his chest, I dug my nails into his exposed skin, smooshing my breasts against his back and grinding my hips against his ass. He growled but let me claw him. I traced my leg up his side, and as soon as his hand landed on my thigh, I pushed away, backpedaling.

He stormed forward and in pure tango fashion, I dropped to one knee, gazing up at him with an arousal dancing in my eyes. He pulled me up to him, spinning me around and shoving his chest against my back.

His hands dragged over my stomach as we swayed. "You know exactly what I'm talking about." He kissed my neck. "The mind games. The fleeting touches, stares, the verbal fucking we've been doing." He squeezed one breast, kneading my hip with his other hand, his teeth nipping my earlobe.

I took several steps forward, and he grabbed onto both my forearms, halting me, urging me to come back to him. Spinning back into his arms, I grew dizzy, not from twirling but from that look in his gaze.

Need. Lust. Possession—the glow of the moon and stars above us blanketing me like night-lit velvet.

I kissed him, still swaying my hips to the rhythm of the tango music. He dipped his fingers into the hem at the back of my dress, drumming them against one ass cheek before grabbing it, kissing me back with nips, licks, and raw energy.

He pulled away, pressing his cheek to mine, turning us in circles. "This could be yours *every* night, Keira."

Letting out a moaning sigh, I wrapped my arm around the back of his neck, and he dipped me backward. Thunder boomed, followed by a sudden torrential downpour that sent the other dancers scurrying for the canopy. I moved to stand, to follow them to shelter, but Zane held me tight, dragging his hand between my breasts as the rain soaked us. When he pulled me up, lightning flashed across the darkened sky, reflecting in his eyes.

"Why do you have to be so stubborn about this?" He searched my face, his jaw tightening.

Impatience. Confusion.

"You like when I'm stubborn. Why do *you* need to be an asshole?"

His white shirt clung to his body, reminding me of what lay beneath the shield of his clothes. Even drenched with rain, his hair still looked sexy as hell, falling in tendrils over his forehead.

"No, I'm a dick. Assholes and pussies get fucked." He pulled me tight against him again, making the water spray from our soaked clothes. "Besides, you get *wet* whenever I'm a dick." He trailed a hand down the side of my face, running his thumb over my bottom lip and slipping it into my mouth.

With a grin, I bit it.

He smiled back and hoisted my knee up, encouraging me to wrap it around him. With one hand on my ass, the other curled under my knee, he trailed his touch down my thigh, torturously slow.

"I play games because—" I dipped a hand into his soaked shirt, scraping my nails against one of his pecs. "I don't know what else to do with you."

Lightning sizzled across the sky, and a tingle coursed through my inner thigh. I fell against him with a gasp, holding onto him with my arms curved around his neck.

"There's *so* much you can do with me." His fingers inched closer, skirting up the inside of my thigh.

A haggard breath escaped my lungs, fluttering over his lips, water beads collecting on my eyelashes. Lightning crackled behind him and a surge pulsed down my leg, circling my clit and making me cry out. He crashed his mouth over mine and hoisted me up, wrapping both of my legs around his waist. I flicked my hair back, sending a spray of water, and gazed down at him, panting. He walked with me curled around him, his hands on my ass, my fingers grabbing his hair.

My back hit against a tree trunk in the shadows away from the crowds at the reception. He ground against me, dry humping me with his hard-as-sin cock bulging against his soaked pants. He lifted me, throwing my legs over his shoulders and burying his face between my thighs. His nose brushed my folds through the fabric of my panties and he smiled against my leg before lowering me to the ground.

I was aroused, confused, and ready to throw him to the ground and reenact my dream from the plane. I parted wet hair from my face and stared up at him.

He snapped his head back, flicking water from his hair and face, and pushed against me. With a thumb teasing one nipple through my dress, circling it, he whispered, "I'm going to be the one to walk away this time, Keira. And it's going to drive you *mad*."

I shuddered a breath, blinking away water as he slowly backed away. "Zane. Zane, wait." Pushing off the tree, I trotted forward, reaching.

He grinned at me as he walked and a flash of lightning crashed above us, blinding me. When I opened my eyes...he was gone.

ELEVEN

ZEUS

"I DON'T KNOW WHAT else to throw at this woman. She was ready to fuck against a tree trunk, but has she called? Texted? E-mailed saying 'marry me now, you bastard'? The answer is no, Levin." I sighed, looking over at my dog, who cocked his head back and forth at me.

Levin yipped and scurried away as Kratos appeared with his wings splayed wide, Bia following him.

"We have some interesting news that you'll definitely want to hear, my liege." Kratos stood tall with his hands folded in front of him.

Bia had a conniving grin on her face, and she flicked her fingernails together.

"Let's hear it." I leaned on the bar.

"Your hopeful bride-to-be is, in fact…a demigod." Kratos's jaw tightened.

Shaking my head, I worked my pinky finger in and out of

my ear as if Kratos had just told me Aphrodite was celibate. "That isn't possible. I would've smelled it from miles away."

"*It* is *possible if her mother put a spell on her*," Bia chimed in.

I gripped the edge of the bar, lightning sparking down my arms. "A spell? Who the Tartarus is her mother?"

"Oizys."

I stood straight. "Oizys? She's still active? Haven't heard about her in eons."

"*She is not on Earth anymore. But for a time, she fell in love with a mortal man, thus producing Keira*." Bia floated to stand in front of me, canting her head to one side.

"I kind of gathered that, Bia. It *is* how pregnancy works. I should know." I ground my teeth together.

"She spends her time in Tartarus now, assisting Hades and using her powers of misery to torture the condemned."

I scratched the back of my head, growing more impatient by the minute. "Oh, good, I'm glad she's keeping busy—would you two get to the point?"

"We 'coerced' the information out of her, sir. She did not wish Keira to grow up dealing with the gods and politics of Olympus. She left her with a mortal couple and put a shielding spell so that no other god could detect her blood. Not even you." Kratos clenched his fists as if preparing for my backlash.

How much more complicated could this possibly get?

Kratos shifted his stance. "Oizys also told us that her father had a message for you."

"Erebus? What does that 'ray of sunshine' want?"

"He said you should stop by to his new 'operation' in Chicago." The skin above Kratos's eyes wrinkled as he lifted a brow.

"Operation?"

"Apparently, he's running a highly organized crime ring."

A chuckle escaped my lips after pausing mid-sip. "He *must* be joking. I can't show this face mixed into that bullshit."

"He always *has* had a bit of dark humor, sir." A gleam formed in Kratos's eyes, which was the closest one would get to witness him smile.

Downing the rest of my drink, I shook my head. "He knows the deal. I don't fuck with them, and they don't fuck with us."

When I became king, I struck a bargain with the primordials. There'd be no interference both on their part or the Olympian gods so long as they played nice. And it would stay that way, otherwise, I'd need to banish them the same way I did another group of rather large bullies.

"Is there anything else about *Keira* I should know?" I looked between my two enforcers.

"*We also believe she's your—fated bond.*" Bia brought our faces closer and grinned.

I glared at her. "That's impossible. What are you trying to say? The Fates made me wait for thousands of years?"

"*Do you think, sir, it is a coincidence that Hera, after thousands of years of marriage, left you right before you and Keira crossed paths?*"

"Fuck," I said under my breath.

Kratos crossed the room, standing beside Bia as if they were about to have a united front. "Forgive the insubordination, sir, but you really need to tell her who and what you are."

"Fuck if I will." I shoved away from the bar, turning my back on them and raking my hands through my hair. "I'm *this* close to snaring her."

"If you want any chance of a relationship beyond what you and Hera had, a partnership, she needs to know what she's getting into so she can make that choice for herself. Meddling won't solve this one—my liege." Kratos pounded his fist against his chest and bowed.

"What makes you think I care if I have anything beyond what I had with Hera?" I spoke to the mirror behind the bar, my reflection partially skewed from hanging wine glasses.

"*You do care.*" Bia leaned to the side, peering at me through the mirror, still grinning.

The lightning pulsed over my skin, swirling over my arms and sparking in my eyes. "Out. Both of you. Now," I roared.

A fated bond? Me? Not. Possible.

And she's a demigod?

I leaned against the wall, my head heavy, tiredness pulling at my bones, begging for rest. Maybe just for a moment. Moving to my leather chaise lounge, I slowly sat with a deep sigh, closing my eyes.

My phone buzzed on the counter.

"You've got to be fucking kidding me." Groaning, I pushed to my feet and swiped the phone screen.

Melissa Daniels wished to speak to me. With the first day of the trial tomorrow, it didn't surprise me in the slightest, but the last thing I wanted to deal with was her acid husband-dunking ass. Not to mention the irritation of the hope that'd idiotically bubbled in my stomach that the message would've been from Keira. Rage shot down my spine, and a blast of lightning shot through my arm, shattering the scotch decanter resting on the corner of the bar.

Levin had creeped his way out from his hiding spot after Kratos and Bia left, only to yelp and scamper away again.

"Shit." Waving my hand to make the shattered glass disappear, I rubbed my temple and walked to Levin's room.

He cowered in a corner, shaking.

And now I *was* an asshole.

Sinking to my knees, I patted my leg and spoke softly. "Come here, boy. I'm sorry."

Levin didn't budge at first, and I sat on my ass with a sigh, holding my head between my knees. Eventually, a tongue lapped my knuckles and a furry head pushed against my palm. I lifted my chin, and petted Levin's head with heavy eyes.

"Sorry, boy." I opened my arms to him, and he scooted closer, resting his head on my chest. I hugged him and rested my cheek against the fur on his back.

It would've been so easy to fall asleep like this—listening to the dog's steady heartbeat, the softness against my skin. So. Fucking. Tired.

My phone buzzed again—another notification about the meeting with Daniels.

"Fucking Olympus. Fine, fine." I scratched Levin's chest before forcing myself to my feet.

I sat across from a more well-presented Melissa Daniels, having had her hair cut and styled. Twirling a pen on the table, I eyed her hands wringing in her lap.

"You seem nervous, Mrs. Daniels. Something you want to tell me?" I pointed at her busy hands.

"The trial starts tomorrow."

"Yes, it does."

She shifted forward, slamming her shackled arms on the table. "I covered my tracks, I'm sure of it, but—what if—what if they find the check written to the storage facility?"

Clicking the pen, I pressed it to the notepad. "The storage facility where they found the barrel?"

"Yes. I had to fucking pay for it somehow, didn't I?" She yelled, her top lip bouncing.

"When you say you covered your tracks, how exactly?" I scribbled, but it had nothing to do with what she was saying. I just wanted to look busy.

What? A Greek god keeping notes? Please.

"It'd been processed through Quickbooks, and I changed them all around, shredded the original check, so it never showed."

"Smart thinking. So, what's the issue?"

Her light eyes widened. "The issue? What if they discover it? They search computers and junk, don't they?"

"Mrs. Daniels, there's always the possibility of them finding anything. We can argue that it's the only storage facility in the immediate area. Doesn't mean you stored a decomposing body."

She rubbed her upper lip, sweat collecting on it. "Okay. Okay. But what about the barrel? I *did* purchase it, and they know that."

"You're a biochemist. Why wouldn't you need barrels for the lab?" Drawing circles now on the notepad, I rose a brow at her.

She blinked once. "Damn. You are good."

"If I had a dinar for every woman who told me that…"

"What?" She scrunched her broad nose.

"Nothing."

She thinks of you, sir. Thinks of how she…needs you.

Bia's voice trickled over my brain.

A feral grin tugged at my lips, and I snapped my gaze to the killer across from me who was keeping me away from my horny future Queen.

"If you have no further concerns, Mrs. Daniels, I'll see you in court tomorrow." I stood and shoved the notepad under my arm.

"Wait, I—" Melissa held her hands up, stammering.

I slipped a hand over her shoulder. "You look tired."

She slumped in her chair, sleeping and snoring.

"Where is she, Bia?" I adjusted my tie, waiting.

Her office.

My grin turned downright villainous.

Once I was near the courthouse, I made myself invisible so no one would see me walk into her office. I could be an outright bastard, but she'd never forgive me if I sullied her reputation. Still hidden from everyone else's view but Keira's, I slowly opened her office door, only to find her sitting on the front of her desk, leaning back, her knees ever so slightly apart, peeking out from her pencil skirt. She slowly turned her head to look at me, surprise traveling over her face like melting wax.

"I got this peculiar feeling that you—" I closed the door with an audible click but didn't lock it, showing her she was free to go at any point. "—needed something from me." I'd made my voice extra husky.

"How could you possibly know that?" She unbuttoned two buttons of her dress shirt and pinched her knees together, sliding her heels back.

She didn't deny she needed me. Mm.

"Intuition? Magic?" I took several steps forward, testing if she'd stop me or run away. "Does it matter?"

She shook her head, her chest rising and falling with quickened breaths the closer I got.

"So, what do you need then, Keira? Hm?" A step forward. "Sustenance? Legal advice?"

She kept quiet, simply shaking her head, and as I stood a breath away from her, her bottom lip quivered.

I cocked my head to the side, standing in front of her but careful not to touch—not even a brush. "That dance in Argentina? I'd go so far as to say if you didn't 'hate' me, we might've fucked in the nearest stone alley."

She gripped the desk with both hands, but I kept my gaze focused on her. "After the stunt you pulled regarding my deportation, you're lucky it even got that far. Look. You're attractive, you know it. That doesn't mean I'll spread my legs for you."

Mm. Or was that precisely the reason why.

I let my gaze drop to her lap before slowly panning it back to her face.

"Not to mention we're opposing counselors, as I've said many, many times." Her grip tightened on the wood, knees pressing so hard together they turned red.

Mm. Mm.

The rabbit was wound so tightly in my snare.

"True. True. Doesn't mean we have to—" I took a small step forward, enough to brush my pant leg against her bare knees. "—go full tilt. So many other options."

A breath caught in her throat, and goosebumps littered her skin.

I nudged my knee between hers, testing her again, seeing if she'd deny me.

"You say, 'stop,' and I will." I willed her gaze to mine, further clarifying I meant what I said. "But something tells me—this is precisely what you need."

Her throat bobbed as she yet again remained silent.

I traced a hand over her knee, traveling to the top of her thigh, waiting, waiting for her to say, "no," or, "don't." But to my fucking sheer delight…she kept quiet, only making enough noise to let out a shaky breath. Her knees spread an inch, inviting me.

Moving my fingers to her inner thigh, I coaxed her legs wider, trailing my hand until I felt the lace of her panties against my fingertips. Flicking at them with a single finger, I raised my brows, waiting for the signal to retreat.

Instead, she didn't say a word and leaned back with a moan.

I parted the cloth with one quick swipe and plunged a finger into her.

Fuck. Me. Already so wet.

She gasped, and her neck craned back.

Pumping in and out of her, I watched her every reaction and wanted to make damn sure she knew what she'd been missing the entire time we've played games—what more she could *have*.

"I *crave* consent because it gives us both power to devour each other." I thrust a second finger in, and her thighs tightened on my waist. "And you repeatedly keep giving it to me without so much as a whispered word. The way your thighs pull me closer, the whimper escaping your throat." Dropping my face near her neck, I dragged my lips over her skin and paused at her ear. "The fact you're so wet right now you'd damn well slip off the desk if I weren't grabbing your ass."

She moaned, not caring if it was loud enough for surrounding offices to hear. Not that they could, I made sure of it.

"I could bend you over the desk right now, and you'd let me, wouldn't you?" I whispered, coating it with gravel.

She thinned her lips and craned her neck back. "Currently, I'm physically incapable of saying I wouldn't." A sigh escaped her lungs as her eyes panned down to watch what I was doing to her.

"But I won't."

Her gaze snapped to mine, distance and arousal playing in her stare.

"I want you to be able to scream without fear of someone hearing. To become unbridled. Because that's what you truly *need*, isn't it, Keira? No burdens. Freedom." I curled my finger inside her, probing her spot and making her whimper.

"I didn't know I needed it until I met you, Zane." She wrapped a hand around my tie, pulling me closer. "Why is that?"

Slipping out of her, I dragged the juices collected on my fingers over her lips, locking our gazes again.

My dick had gotten hard the moment I knew she wasn't going to stop me and it fucking throbbed at the sight of her licking herself from her lips.

I leaned in. "See you in court tomorrow—counselor." And I left her with nothing but the memory of me inside her.

I'd be the first to say this method would be bound to have me exploding, but that's what I needed her to be…a volcanic eruption of need and want for the King of the Gods. Mainly because I knew Kratos and Bia were right. I *did* have to tell her, or I'd surely lose her. We'd get through the first day of the trial, she would get to see me at work, *really* at work, not some damn trivial evidence trial, and when she was coiling with admiration—I'd strike. Still, there was the unsettling notion how I knew what she needed. And it's because…I needed the same damn thing.

TWELVE

KEIRA

NOT ONLY WAS THE trial weighing heavy on my mind, but the possibility of being deported and the only two solutions I had were as well. One would destroy the career I'd built for myself in New York. The other might destroy my dignity. Possibly. I didn't even really know this guy, minus what I could feel from him and what he shared about himself thus far, which wasn't a lot. Not to mention how *he* made me feel. It wasn't as if my first marriage ended all that well—maybe love wasn't the key. Part of me wanted to tell him no, simply so he didn't get his way. Petty? Childish? Maybe.

I wanted to be angry at him, not only for using my misfortune as leverage but the repeated confusing moments of sexual encounters. But try as I might, the fury would dissipate, and I'd be ravenously curious and hungry for him all over again. What held me there? What kept me coming back for more? Like freshly wiped glass, I could see straight through to his true nature. Something ate at him, made him leak desperation from his pores, made him smell hopeful, and I wanted to know why. I'd kept opening myself to him, but he did the exact same thing for me. *Why?*

Olivia snapped in front of my face. "Thinking about Argentina still?"

Argentina. The broom closet kiss. Yesterday in my office…

"That one couple I caught watching is certainly still thinking about Argentina," I grumbled, sulking in the back seat of the cab as it whisked us to the courthouse.

When Zane had stranded me in the middle of pouring rain after nearly driving me to orgasm, an older couple under a nearby canopy had gasped, staring at me wide-eyed. It unsettled me that their watching wasn't what bothered me. It was them witnessing Zane bailing on me. I'd waved at them, offered a small smile, and returned to the reception. The couple was nowhere to be seen for the rest of the night, so lord only knows what they'd gone off to do.

Olivia scrolled through her phone, frowning. "You would think with all the phones in existence, one person would've recorded it."

"Did you seriously Google that? To see me grinding on Zane?"

Glancing up from her screen for a millisecond, she shrugged. "So, what? You're both hot. I did, however find this smoking dance number from Magic Mike Live." She shoved the phone in my face. "Lookie, here."

It was a video recorded by a screaming group of women audience members—a tall man with long dark hair danced provocatively with a blonde woman on an elevated clear stage, rain pouring over them throughout the dance.

Gently, I pushed the phone back to her. "Last thing I need right now is my mojo going into overdrive. I need my head clear."

After watching the video for several more seconds, Olivia tossed her phone in her pocket. "So you almost had sex in public, big bloody deal. Do you have any idea how many times I have?"

"Seriously?"

"The beach, in the back of a car in a Macy's parking garage, the bottle-o," she counted on her fingers as she recalled.

"Wait. You had sex in a liquor store?" I bit back a smile.

"Yeah. It *was* out of the view of security cameras." Her tone suggested she'd been mildly insulted I was surprised.

"Oh, then that makes all the difference." Grinning, I shook my head, and turned my face toward the window, groaning at the standstill traffic.

"Here's what I don't understand. Why haven't you two fucked already?" Olivia leaned toward me, her arms slapping on my lap.

I shot a look at the driver in the rear-view mirror, hoping he'd pretend he couldn't hear our conversation. The arousal ebbing from him suggested otherwise.

"It's some sincerely screwed up game we're playing. A tug for power, if you ask me." My groin pulsed, thinking about Zane's fingers inside it. I pinched my thigh.

Focus on the case.

"It sounds like you're losing this battle, Keir Keir. You may as well lower the wall and get something good out of it."

A man with dark hair and a tan Burberry jacket whizzed past the cab, hurriedly talking on his cell phone and running to a coffee vendor on the corner. My stomach fluttered and then deflated when the man turned around, showing his face. Not Zane.

"Maybe." But I needed to know more about him. And after the trial today, he was going to tell me whether he liked it or not.

When we walked into the courthouse, Zane paced the foyer, talking to someone on his cell phone. As if sensing my presence or something, his gaze snapped over his shoulder when I entered his proximity, and he grinned.

"Just get it done," he said before hitting his thumb on the screen and slipping it into his pocket. "Well, you look spry this morning." His eyes panned to my lips before snapping back up.

One look from this goddamned man and everything he did to me in my office yesterday flooded my brain, making a small whimper in the back of my throat.

"I'll uh—I'm going to meet you in the courtroom, Keir. Yeah?" Olivia patted my arm before walking away.

I'd absently nodded at her, only half hearing what she said.

"What the hell were you even doing at the courthouse yesterday, Zane? How many people saw you walk in and out of there?" A sudden panic twisted my gut.

After scanning the area, he pressed a hand between my shoulder blades and led me to a vacant corner. "No one saw me. I assure you."

"How is that possible? Did you crawl through a damn

window or something?" I crossed my arms in a huff, glaring up at him, ignoring the continued pulse between my legs.

He shook his head as he narrowed his eyes. "Why don't you save all the questions for the trial, hm?"

"You aggravate me to no end."

He bit his lip. "You keep telling yourself that, counselor." His mouth lowered to my ear. "Because you didn't seem mad in the slightest with my fingers inside you."

His scent. How close he was. The sizzle that tantalized my skin. All of it was enough to have me moaning in the hallway.

I put a hand on his chest, which was—a horrible idea. Instead of pushing him immediately away as planned, tingles coursed over my palm, radiating from his skin through the shirt. "How did you know how to dance like that?"

"Been around. Learned a thing or two." He didn't step away from my touch.

And I didn't pull my hand back. "I've never danced like that before."

"Well—" He slid forward, pressing my hand between our almost touching chests. "—when given the opportunity, I can be an *amazing* lead."

I gulped. There was no hiding it.

"Don't let dirty thoughts distract you too much, Miss Bazin. I expect the 'Bulldog' to challenge me in there." He stepped away, catching my hand in his when it fell from his chest.

Anger. Lust. Determination.

With a final smirk, he let go of my hand and whisked into the courtroom.

After composing myself and slapping my face several times

to float back down to planet Earth, I readied for the fight of my life.

The trial ran smoothly at first, with Zane not throwing any curveballs or surprises as I'd expected. The usual questioning and presenting of evidence—receipts, digital evidence captured from computers, things of that nature. It was when we started to call in witnesses that he began his usual Zane bullshit.

I'd just finished questioning the accused's hairdresser, confirming they talked about how much Melissa wanted to kill her husband and that she could get away with it. When I passed the table, allowing Zane to rise for his turn with the witness, he slid a piece of paper to the corner and bobbed his brow.

Too curious to ignore, I bit the bait and read to myself:

Tell me the truth. Are you thinking about it right now?

He drew two boxes: One with a yes next to it, the other—also a yes.

Grinding my teeth, I snatched the pen as he brushed past me. He adjusted his tie with a smug grin. I drew my own "no" box and circled it several times, adding: Because I'm a professional.

"Miss Nichols, how well did you know my client?" Zane asked the hairdresser witness, slipping one hand in his pants pocket.

"Pretty well, I'd say. We talked a lot, and she came in for her hair every six weeks."

Where was Zane going with this?

"Right. So, you're saying gossip and rumors never *ever* happen in a hair salon?" He flashed a charming grin to the women sitting on the jury stand.

They all wanted to smile, everyone could see it, but they held back by either adjusting in their seats or covering their mouths with a hand.

"I mean, it's possible?" Miss Nichols answered, shrugging.

Zane walked toward the jury, his debonair swagger plain as day. "So, it *is* possible my client was simply venting about trouble at home and not actually planning her husband's demise, as you so eloquently put it?"

Fuck.

Miss Nichols gulped and looked first at me, then the judge, as if hoping I'd object to the question. How could I?

"Please answer the question, Miss Nichols," the judge said, nodding.

"Yes, it's possible."

Zane smiled and patted the corner of the stand before turning on his heel. "No further questions, your honor." He sauntered back to the table, sliding the paper I'd written on with two fingers toward him, a light chuckle fluttering from his chest.

I folded my arms and crossed my legs, forcing my attention in front of me. Out of the corner of my eye, I spied him writing again and risked craning my neck to look. Like a third grader guarding anyone copying his work, he lowered his shoulder to block the paper.

"Miss Bazin," the judge's voice boomed.

Jolting in my chair, I snapped my attention to her. "Yes, your honor?"

"I asked if you have any further witnesses to present?"

Olivia snickered at my side and nudged me under the table.

"Yes, your honor. I do have one final witness." Rising, I flattened my jacket. "The prosecution calls Miguel Huarez to the stand."

Surprise. Anger. Fear.

The emotions swirling through the courtroom often had my head spinning, which made for complete exhaustion at the end of every day of trial. Between squelching the feelings in the air and the mental mind game of being a good lawyer, it took every ounce of gasoline in me, including reserves. But I couldn't see myself doing anything else.

As I shimmied past the table, Miguel made his way to the witness stand, and I caught Zane's intrigued grin. Miguel was a family friend who'd known Mr. and Mrs. Daniels for over a decade, which I had him confirm from my first few questions. I then had him confirm Melissa's sudden change in behavior leading up to the time of the incident, how good of a dad her late husband was to their children, and how her husband was the type to avoid confrontation at any cost. Once satisfied I'd pulled at the jury's heartstrings, making them sympathize for the unsuspecting *dead* husband, I concluded.

Zane slid a paper to me again as I passed, and I yanked it toward me with more force than last time.

It read: *Do you like me?* With two boxes again, yes and no.

His gaze caught mine, making my stomach clench, my throat drying as I thought back to that kiss, the feral look in his eyes as he walked toward me in my office. Grinding my molars, I wrote "hell" above "no" and checked the box several times.

Chuckling, he balled the paper as he stood and re-did his top jacket button. After tossing the paper into the closest wire wastebasket he spun to face Miguel.

"Mr. Huarez, you were very close with the Daniels. And it sounds like you were at their house often, is that correct?"

Miguel squinted at Zane. "Yeah. That's right. Me and Larry were tight. Watched sports, talked politics, sometimes smoked cigars."

I caught Melissa rolling her eyes from the table next to ours.

"So, you would know about Larry and Melissa's sex life, correct?"

Slapping my palms on the table, I stood. "Objection, your honor. Their sex life has no relevance to the motive."

Sex. Sex. Sex. That's all this man ever thought about.

"Sustained. Mr. Vronti, please reword your question or specifically address the relevance?" The judge adjusted her glasses.

"Absolutely, your honor. I'm merely attempting to have the jury consider the possibility of the emotions that can stir when a marriage is unsatisfactory in the bedroom."

Fucking. Fuck. Who *was* this guy?

The judge tapped her finger on her podium before nodding. "Overruled. Mr. Huarez, please answer the question."

Fuming, I slowly sat back down.

Olivia leaned over, gulping. "Holy balls. He *is* good."

Zane flashed me a villainous grin over his shoulder before he continued his questioning. I knew from the moment he breezed into the meeting room that first day this wouldn't be easy. But what I hadn't realized was not only would it be difficult to fight him in the courtroom, it proved increasingly difficult to fight my growing attraction for him.

The trial lasted for several hours before the judge dismissed us for the day. Zane hadn't slid me any further notes, but the smugness and arrogance never ceased. What irritated me to no end, however was his arrogance was somewhat warranted. The man knew what he was doing and could work the courtroom like a surgeon with precise, unwavering movements.

Once everyone filed out, I shoved my paperwork into my briefcase before turning to Olivia. "I'm going to grab some dinner and head home. Meet up with you tomorrow?"

"Yup. Probably going to grab some gyros myself. That cucumber sauce is calling my name." She rubbed her tummy before frolicking away.

My elbow brushed with Zane's as we turned for the walkway at the same time, glaring at each other as we walked pace for pace to the doors exiting the courtroom.

"Zane, we need to talk. And we need to talk now," I barked once we were alone in the hallway.

Zane did a quick glance at our surroundings and gently grabbed me by the crook of the arm. "I couldn't agree more."

"What?"

He pulled me into a nearby holding cell and locked the door behind us.

THIRTEEN

ZEUS

I'D TAKEN A RISK locking her in the cell with me, but I knew she'd protest about it at first only to give in to the idea, maybe even enjoy it. It was as if I *knew* her without knowing her. Knew what she needed versus wanted. Knew how to hand her Olympus itself but not knowing—if she wanted it.

Without dampening the power as I'd been doing since we met, I flashed lightning in my palm, frying the surrounding cameras and blanketing us in darkness. Red washed over our skin as the single emergency light sprung to life in the corner of the room.

She slammed her palm on the door, the only lock available from the other side. "Zane, what the hell are you doing?"

I stepped forward, pressing my forearms to the door on each side of her head, smiling down at her. "We really need to stop meeting like this."

"Zane." She pressed a hand on my chest, sending a surge

down my arms that had nothing to do with my lightning power.

Any other woman would've flown into a panic being locked in a room with a man she claimed to hate. Any other woman may have even slapped me. But not Keira. No. Because this was yet another segment in our game, and she was ever the willing participant. And it's what kept me coming back time and time again.

"You're right. We need to talk. And what I need to tell you can't be seen or heard by anyone else." I rolled my bottom lip past my teeth.

Keira ducked under my arm and walked to the opposite side of the room—standing her ground, open to what I had to say, but showing me, she wasn't going to make it easy.

I'd be disappointed if she did.

"Well? It's not as if I'm going anywhere. What do you have to tell me?" She folded her arms.

Might as well come right out and say it.

Clasping my hands in front of me, I locked gazes with her, the emergency light giving her cheeks crimson shadows. "My name isn't Zane Vronti. It's a name I use as a cover along with the lawyer job." I took a step forward. "My real name is Zeus. And I'm King of the Greek gods." Another step.

She didn't say anything at first, pressing her ass against the wall behind her, her eyes searching my face…and then she burst out laughing.

"Fuck, Zane. I've heard a lot of ego complexes, but this has to take the cake." She flicked her wrist. "You think you're a *god*, now? And not just any god but a god-*king*?"

"I am, Keira." The lightning sparked over my arms, circling

them.

Just believe so we can move on from this.

I'd never been so close to begging in my immortal life as I was at this very moment.

She gasped and shook her head, her gaze falling to the electricity coiling around me. "No. No, this must be some kind of trick. Zane, how dare you—"

We *don't* have time for this.

Growling, I ported across the room, appearing in front of her. Taking her face in my hand, I gently forced her gaze to mine, sending a series of tingles from the lightning rolling over my knuckles into her cheek. "I. Am." The lightning took over my eyes, pulsing in them, making me see in black and white. "I could port us to Mount Olympus, right *now*, if I wanted, and *fuck* you on my throne."

Her bottom lip trembled as she looked up at me, a mixture of fear and lust washing over her features. "But you won't."

My power fizzled, and I blinked, recoiling an inch. "Excuse me?"

"You're so used to getting your way, to everyone and everything around you doing your bidding without hardly flinching. You *want* me to ask." She tightened her jaw.

The lightning pulsed again, reacting from the sheer confidence and balls this woman had.

"Where is this coming from?" I narrowed my glowing eyes at her.

Most importantly, I needed to know because…she was right.

"No. You finish explaining this first." She rested her hand on my forearm, my power reflecting in her light eyes as she stared at me. "How?"

Scraping my callused fingertip over her skin, I kept her gaze. "You're having a hard time *not* believing it, aren't you? There's a reason for that too, Keira."

Silence.

She licked her lips as her gaze dropped to my mouth. It was one thing to feel my power when she thought I was a mere mortal, but now to see it? Feel it? Have it standing right in front of her?

"You're part goddess." I hovered my mouth near hers but made no move to kiss her.

"What?" She spat, her forehead crinkling.

"Did your parents ever tell you, you were adopted?"

She gripped the sleeve of my jacket, wrinkling it, pulling it taut over my arm. "Yes, but—they were older. They've been gone for years now." She frowned, letting herself slump against the wall.

"Your birth mother is a goddess." I cupped her chin, lifting her bewildered gaze to meet mine.

She balled her hands into fists and beat them against my shoulders. "This doesn't make any sense."

Her expression suggested otherwise. It was as if my words were the most sense she'd heard in some time but couldn't process why.

"Her name is Oizys. She's a goddess of specific emotions— misery, depression, anxiety." I kept my hand on her face, caressing her cheeks with my thumbs.

Her gaze dropped, and she palmed her forehead. "Please step back, I need to—this is all too much."

As she requested, I slid away, willing my power to dissipate.

Anger suddenly flushed her face. "Wait a minute. How long were you going to wait to tell me this? You were just going to let me marry you without knowing it meant signing up to be a Queen or a goddess or whatever the hell this entails?" Her chest pumped, her breaths increasing.

"I figured telling you too soon would have you running for the hills. Doesn't this make your decision easier?"

Frustration twisted at my gut.

"What?" She growled, dragging her hands through her hair and shaking her head. "You cannot be this dense, Zane."

"I'm not sure what the hell you have to be angry about. You thought you were marrying into an inheritance when it's more than that. A queendom. Godhood." I ran a hand over my beard, trying to hide the irritation and confusion punching through my veins, the lightning sizzling under my skin. "*Immortality*, Keira."

Her eyes widened, lips parting ever so slightly. "I honestly can't believe you. I just found out you're Zeus. *The* Zeus. And I'm part goddess, and you expect me to what—say hell yeah, let's do this?"

I scratched the back of my head, wincing like I'd been mentally slapped. "It would be preferable?"

"Oh my—" She turned her back on me, pressing her forehead against the door with a stifled scream.

"I don't know what you expect from me. This—I'm not used to this." King of the Gods—reduced to a stammering fool. Bile would've worked up my throat if my body were capable.

This is what I got for having mortals eating out of the palm of my hand for nearly my entire life. Especially. Women.

She whirled around. "Doing what? Holding a civil conversation? One that doesn't involve innuendo and jabs?"

Ouch. I adjusted myself, feeling like I'd been kicked in the nuts with her foot never leaving the ground.

"Trying to convince a woman to be with me. To not only explain what I could offer but show her." I clenched my fists, reining in my power. It wanted to light up the whole fucking room.

She dropped her hands at her sides. "And there we have it. It always circles back to you."

I opened my mouth, and for the first time in my unnatural life…nothing came out.

"Open the door," she huffed, pointing behind her and keeping her gaze fixed on the floor.

"Keira, we don't have a lot of ti—" I started, crossing the room to her, the anger scraping my spine, puncturing it.

The corners of her jaw bobbed, her eyes glistening. "Open the goddamned door, Zane."

"Fine," I growled, waving my hand at the door, making the metal slab slide.

Without another word from either of us, she stormed to the hallway.

What the actual fuck just happened? The polar opposite of what I thought would, that's for damn sure. I offered the woman a kingdom, the chance to be an immortal goddess and she says it's about more than that? What the Tartarus else is there?

Sitting on the edge of the metal table, I dropped my face in my hands. Tiredness tugged at my brain again, and I glanced at my watch, sighing at the time left until my kingly demise. Rounds. I hadn't done rounds in weeks. Sparking life back into the room—the lights and cameras—I ported to a live concert being held in Buffalo, New York. Walking amidst the crowds of people in stadium seating, I remained invisible to all mortals and immortals alike.

My son, Apollo, blazed onto the stage, fronting himself as the lead singer of the band Apollo's Suns. He definitely inherited his cunning and ego from me. In all the years he'd been performing, I'd only watched him once. He did exactly what I expected him to—danced shirtless, focused on the women, and used his Fates-given gifts to inspire the masses. At least he was doing his job.

He strutted out on stage with his guitar strapped to his back, asking the audience how they were doing, referring them all to the city name itself. But unlike the last time I'd watched him, he stretched his hand behind him and welcomed someone else on stage. A blonde woman in ballet attire with one of the most radiant smiles I'd ever seen. His goddess and newly appointed leader of the muses, Laurel.

Observing the two of them, I rubbed my chin. Overseeing the muses had always been Apollo's favorite part of his duties. He'd been focused on himself since he was a teenager and the little ass drove me mad. And one run-in with this woman…changed everything. They didn't even have a fated bond—plopped into each other's paths, both missing a part of themselves they hadn't known they'd lost.

Huh.

Apollo curled Laurel against him, kissing first the side of her head, followed by a practical make out session for all eyes to see. Grimacing, I snapped my gaze away, peeking now and again to ensure they weren't licking each other's faces any longer before I continued to watch. I'd seen my son happy, but never like this—slaying the Python, the victory at Troy, after Eros lifted that idiotic spell, so Apollo was no longer in love with a damn tree. He had countless women he pursued, but all ended in tragedy. If I had to take a step back and look at the bigger picture—his experiences could've been entirely my fault. Who else did he have to emulate? Who else did he have to admire? Rubbing the back of my neck, I tore my eyes away from the stage.

The crowd roared with applause as Laurel spun in circles on her toes, and Apollo danced around her, playing guitar. Something told me I'd never need to worry about these two slacking on their godly jobs. There was so much inspiration floating in the air, it almost had *me* spinning damn circles. But my son performed one of the most selfless acts for this once mortal woman, gave up his leadership for her to make it her own.

I wasn't my son. And my leadership wasn't one I could give up. It had to be supported. Understood.

Snarling, I ported to the next location. Los Angeles, California. My daughter, Aphrodite, sat in front of a vanity, staring at herself in the mirror. She lifted her hands, conjuring her powers in her palms, but it resulted in crackles and pops versus its full force.

"I don't understand it," she snapped, throwing a hairbrush

into the mirror, cracking it.

Shit. I'd *never* seen her this angry.

A woman swept through the door with wide eyes once she spotted Aphrodite's chest heaving at the broken mirror. "Ma'am. Sorry to disturb you, but you have a visitor?"

"Who?" A scowl morphed over Aphrodite's face, an anguished one.

The woman remained in the doorway, using the door as a makeshift shield. "All he said was to tell you it's Heph."

My daughter's face softened, brightened even, before she wiped an invisible slate over it, ridding it of all emotion.

"Tell him I'll be right out."

"Yes, ma'am." The woman quickly retreated.

Aphrodite swirled an arm around her, appearing in a tight light pink dress. After fanning her hand at the mirror, repairing it, she leaned forward and primped herself. I cast my eyes away as she adjusted her cleavage. A smile tugged at her lips before she scurried out the door, her demeanor changed on a whim.

Heph as in Hephaistos? Seriously? That dopey oaf? Did not. See. That coming.

I hesitated at first before snapping my fingers, and porting to Pensacola, Florida. Hera whisked through an apartment living room, walking back and forth from the bedroom to the kitchen and back again as if flustered. Observing her, I folded my arms.

She suddenly halted near me, squinting, her finger aimlessly searching the air. "Do you think after all this time I couldn't sense you and your little invisibility trick?"

Fuck.

Making myself visible to her, I kept leaning on the counter with crossed arms. "Hi, Hera."

"Zeus." She lifted her chin, standing regal and posh as ever. "If you came here to—"

I lifted a hand and shook my head. "No. You deserve to be happy. And clearly, that wasn't with me."

Her jaw fell open, and she slow-blinked like I'd blindsided her. "I—I mean, we could have been. You realize that, right?"

"I honestly don't think so, my dear." Rubbing my chin, my eyes heavy, I lifted my gaze to hers. "We were never right for each other. Just convenient at the time."

"Olympus. You look like shit, Zeus."

"I've got a lot on my mind. You kind of left me in a situation." I smirked and adjusted my cufflinks.

"Situation? You haven't picked a new Qu—" She stopped short and placed a hand over her opened mouth. "Did you *meet* someone?"

The last thing I wanted to do was talk about Keira. I decided to go on rounds to distract myself from the entire fucking thing.

"Take care of yourself, Hera. And if you need anything, all you have to do is ask." I pushed off the counter and slid a hand in my pocket. "You'll always have a spot on the Olympian Council. Whatever the shit good it does in the modern age, but it's still yours."

"I—" Hera pressed a hand to her chest. "Thank you."

Grimacing, I ported outside. I didn't know where I intended to go next, but I couldn't stay there anymore. This whole new dynamic I suddenly decided to try on myself already had my asshole hurting.

Sighing, I ported to Denver, Colorado. The Bulldog gym, to be exact. My son Ares sparred with his also newly formed goddess wife, Harmony. I was still bitter he didn't ask me to turn her and went behind my back to Hades instead. But could I really blame him? And even still, when I first met Harmony, I had to lay down the law. I was her leader, and she had to realize there were consequences for pussy-footing around. She wasn't only good for my son, she was good amongst the war gods, period.

Ares leaped from the mat with a snarl. "I still can't believe what that maláka said to you. He's lucky I didn't bash his teeth in on the spot."

And he hadn't?

"Ares," Harmony started, curling her hand over his bicep. "Breathe. We've talked about this, remember?"

Ares's lip bounced, and he wrapped a hand around the back of her neck, pulling her to him. "You're right. What would I fucking do without you, gatáki?"

"We're in this together, war god." She cupped his face and kissed him.

The kiss soon turned ravenous, and they dropped to the mats. Smirking to myself, I let my gaze fall to my feet.

My one legitimate child was the only god who could ever overthrow me if they tried and also…the most like me.

Against my better judgment, I appeared in Keira's apartment. The room was pitch black save for the light beaming from a computer monitor. Keira sat at the desk with her nose inches from the screen, chin resting on her hand.

I could've done this at any moment—appeared invisible and

watched her. So, why did I send my enforcers to do it?

Bia could read minds. Yes. That was the obvious reason. Yeah.

Peeking over her shoulder, I spotted several windows and tabs open in her browser, her hand feverishly working the mouse as she bookmarked websites, jotted notes, and scanned endless text.

And what had she typed repeatedly into her Google search bar?

Zeus.

She…was Googling me. It was ego-boosting yet altogether nauseating at the same time. The internet was an absolute rabbit hole of hell when it came to information about me.

Grimacing, I turned away from her. This was wrong—spying on her, invading her privacy because I *could*. It was as if I were cheating in this elaborate game we'd created between the two of us. I winced, the realization hitting me like a thunderclap.

Fuck. Me.

I held my head low as a slight grin pulled at the corner of my lips.

All this time, and she was the one who ensnared *me*. And I hadn't a fucking clue how she did it.

After placing a single kiss against her head, one that'd feel only like a passing breeze to her, I whispered, "This is it, Keira. It's either you or no one. And it's completely your choice."

And with that mind-boggling revelation…I disappeared.

FOURTEEN

KEIRA

"HE TRANSFORMED HIMSELF INTO a shower of gold?" Staring at my computer screen with a scrunched face, I slapped my hand over my forehead. "How does one even fuck a shower of gold?"

I'd been researching myths about Zeus for the past several hours and grabbed my third can of Red Bull, swigging more of the energy elixir down my throat. Adjusting my clear framed blue screen glasses, I eyed the open internet tab I'd yet to have the guts to look at: Oizys. He said she was my biological mother. A goddess. Which made me—no. It just couldn't be real. But not one ounce of deceit flooded from his emotions. He'd spoken with the same conviction as when he declared himself Zeus.

It sparked so many more questions. What was my birth mother like? Why didn't she want me? Who was the mortal man she spent her time with? Did he know I existed? Was she still alive? *Could* gods die in some specific way, like vampires or werewolves? Is she the reason for my empathic abilities?

A phantom breeze blew through my hair, making me shiver. Furrowing my brow, I glanced at the windows behind me, knowing full well I'd never leave them open in the dead of winter, but where else would a draft come from?

With a groan, I snatched the can again, tilting my head back to take a swig and frowning when I realized it was empty. Resting the glasses on top of my keyboard and rubbing my eyes, I pushed from the desk, heading for the kitchen for another energy drink. My phone buzzed on the counter, and I swiped it into my hand as I popped the can.

"Hey, Olivia."

"I'm coming over."

I made a slurping sound, nearly choking on my drink. "Now? Why? It's two in the morning."

"When has the dead of the night ever stopped me? And what do you bloody mean *why*? I'm bored."

Throwing a silent temper tantrum by kicking my feet and beating my phone against my forehead, I held back a sigh. I'd planned to spend the better part of the night into the wee hours of the morning inundating myself with information on a would-be suitor. The King of the Gods. It seemed crazy, outrageous, positively bonkers, but he wasn't lying. The lightning—the sight of it, the feel of it—was undeniable. And the desperation steaming from him as he almost begged me to believe him…that did me in.

"I'm kind of in the middle of something, Ollie. Can we hang out tomorrow?"

"Nope. I'm outside your door. Answer it, hoe bag." She knocked on my door.

Groaning, I flopped the cell phone back to the counter and shuffled to the door. Olivia waved at me from the other side of it and whisked past before I had a chance to close it.

"What in the hell are you doing? It's pitch black in here except for the computer—" She gasped and turned on her heel with a wide grin. "Were you watching porn?"

I rolled my eyes and took a swig of my drink before moving back to my desk. "No. I wasn't. I'm doing research."

Before I could minimize the window, Olivia darted in front of me. "Research? On Greek mythology?" She clicked through the thirty-two tabs I had open, her eyes widening with each passing website. "And these are all on Zeus. What does this have to do with the case?"

Nothing. Absolutely nothing.

"Ollie, it's tough to explain." The can crinkled in my hand as my grip tightened on it.

Olivia stood straight as she raised a thin brow and circled me. "What are you hiding, Miss Bazin?"

"Are you seriously trying to lawyer me?"

She tapped a finger over her lips. "And now you're sidestepping the question."

I didn't have time for this.

"For fuck's sake. Come here." I motioned with my head toward the couch, sitting with one leg propped. Zane's penthouse light came on across the street, and like a moth to a flame, my eyes darted straight to it.

"You're acting far stranger than normal, Keir." Olivia slowly sat down with her palms pressed against her thighs.

"Zane isn't really Zane. He's Zeus, King of the Gods. And I'm apparently the daughter of a goddess, making me a demigod."

Could I have done that more eloquently? Definitely, but not only was it two in the morning I was also downing my fourth Red Bull.

Olivia squinted at me before snatching the can from my grasp with lightning speed. She sniffed the mouthpiece, still eyeing me. "Hm. I don't smell vodka."

"You would barely smell it anyway."

Not tearing her gaze from mine, she took a sip and gagged. "Nope. No vodka. Just arse."

I yanked it back. "Do you think everything tastes like ass?"

"If it doesn't taste any bloody good? Yeah."

Repeatedly flicking the tab of the can, I spied Zane's shadow waltzing back and forth in his apartment. One singular shadow. A peculiar wave of relief washed over me.

"Keira, are you being serious?" Olivia threw her hands at her sides, shrugging.

"Yes," I said, the word barely escaping my throat, my gaze still drawn to Zane's window.

Olivia's palms slapped her thighs as she dropped them. "Huh. I would never under any circumstance call you crazy, but this is all a bit wonky sounding, don't you think?"

How had I expected this conversation to go?

The only reason I somehow managed to believe it so quickly was because I had ties to their world—my mind, my body, my very bones all sang to me that it was all real. Not to mention my ability to know whether he lied or not.

My ability.

I turned to her, dropping my foot to the floor and resting the can on the coffee table between us. "I've never told you this—well, I've never told anyone this, but I have special abilities. And until yesterday, I thought it a weird quirk, but apparently…it's because of my lineage."

She leaned forward. "What abilities?"

"I'm an empath. A heightened, specialized, empath." I steepled my fingers. "It's why I walk to work. Why you always see me in my office alone after I get there. It's to give myself a break from the surge of emotions that flood this city."

Olivia's eyes shifted from left to right. "So, at any point in time, you can tell how I feel, even if I'm saying otherwise?"

"Yes. But I'm around you so often I've been able to drown most of yours out. It feels intrusive otherwise."

She thinned her lips and lifted her chin. "What am I feeling right now, then?"

I rolled my shoulders back, opening my mind to her emotions again—a feat I hadn't done in years. With her vibrant personality, her emotions tickled over my skin. Holding back a smile, I answered, "Skeptical. And horny. Very very horny."

How shocking.

She gasped and pointed at me. "You're good."

With her emotions open to me like a floodgate again, I let out a roiling sigh and sulked into the couch cushions. "You don't believe a lick of what I'm saying, do you?"

She gave a half chuckle. "Come on, Keir. I'm trying here. I really am. But—Greek gods? We all know they were mythology made up by 'Thosecles' and 'Homeboy,' or whatever their names were."

I could've corrected her, but what would've been the point?

Grinding my teeth, I pushed off the couch and grabbed my coat.

"Where are you going?" Olivia leaped to her feet.

"For a walk. I need to clear my head." It came out far more gruffly than I'd intended.

Olivia crossed the room, grabbing my elbow as I slipped the coat over my arms. "Keira, come on. Be reasonable. It's three in the bloody morning in New York City."

"It's not as if I've never walked around here this early before." I plucked her fingers from my arm and slipped the jacket on the rest of the way. "This apartment suddenly feels suffocating, and I need fresh, cold air."

"Keir, I'm sorry, I—" Her large green eyes blinked.

Remorse. Guilt. Sadness.

I patted her shoulder. "I know you are. And I don't blame you a bit. I'll be right back, okay? You have my key if you want to leave. Lock yourself in, alright?"

As she stared at me wide-eyed, I gave her one last pat and exited, heading down the stairs and to the quiet sidewalk outside.

Popping my earbuds in, I cued up a random Spotify playlist and hit shuffle. I started walking in the direction toward work, shoving my hands in my pockets and ignoring the loud chatter my teeth made.

Fuck the cold. I needed its harshness to ground me—to numb me.

The song *Hail to the King* by Avenged Sevenfold blasted in

my ears, making me pause. I gazed up at the sky, the moon peeking through the dark wispy clouds that'd rolled in. Zane was a king. And not just any king…a godly, immortal one that could control lightning. The realization struck fear and lust, mixing, molding together until an ache pooled between my legs. Snarling, I started walking again, this time faster. The song continued to play, and I timed my steps with the rhythm, my gaze glued to the sidewalk.

What would it even mean to be Queen? What would it entail?

I stopped at a crosswalk and shook my head, diving through my mental bank of factoids I'd researched the past several hours. "And wait a fucking minute. Why would Zeus be looking for a wife? Whatever happened to Hera?"

Thank Christ it was early morning, or my out loud thinking may have turned a few heads, even if it *was* New York City. The walk sign illuminated, and I continued my brisk pace, paying no mind to my knees shaking beneath my thin yoga pants.

No. It all made absolutely no sense.

Maybe he was good at hiding when he lied. He was a damn good lawyer, and I'd heard about people who could fool lie detector tests by controlling their heartbeats. It was as reasonable an explanation as any. And yet—every other emotion I felt from him wasn't fabricated.

A car door from a parked car suddenly swung open. Someone dressed in all black, sporting a ski mask, grabbed my shoulders and shoved me into the nearby alley with such force it jostled the earbuds from my ears. Fear wrenched down my spine with such ferocity my throat forgot how to scream.

Fear. Anger. Confusion.

The masked person faced me, and I lifted my knee, ready to strike them in the gut, but they grabbed my shoulders and shoved my chest against the stone wall. Cool metal pressed against the back of my head, and my breaths grew shaky, knees numbing—the wall my fingernails clawed was the only thing keeping me upright.

"Don't scream. Don't move, or I *will* shoot you," the man growled near my ear, the heat from his breath leaking through the mask.

"Alright. Alright," I managed to blurt out.

I'd gotten several threats since practicing in New York, and one had been severe enough I started to carry pepper spray with me everywhere. Not once had I ever needed to use it. I picked a bad day to forget.

"You put my little brother behind bars, you prosecuting bitch," the man snarled, shoving the point of the gun harder against my skull, making it ache.

Wincing, I sucked in a breath to keep my voice from sounding as petrified as I felt. "Who's your brother?"

"Mark Valesco. You remember him? Or do you just ruin lives and dust them under a rug?" He pushed between my shoulder blades, causing my cheek to scrape against the bricks.

Valesco. Murdered three innocent people. One of them was a ten-year-old boy. And all because they happened to be in the wrong place at the wrong time when he was fleeing the scene of a bank robbery. I *never* forgot a case.

"Yeah, I remember Mark. He *murdered* three innocents." I gritted my teeth. Stupid. Stupid. Don't bait this guy.

The gun dug further into the back of my head, and I bit the inside of my cheek to keep from whimpering.

"The judge could've given him twenty, thirty years. But no. Because of you, he got life without parole. We'll never see him outside that damn place anymore, and neither will his baby girl."

A knot formed in my throat. "I'm sorry."

I wasn't sorry for putting a murderer behind bars for the rest of his life, but I *was* sorry a girl had to grow up without her father because he chose poorly.

"Yeah. You're going to be." He shoved his mouth near my ear again. "Hope you've made peace with your maker."

The sound of the gun cocking flashed through my head.

Fear. Indecision.

This guy was just as terrified as I was. I pushed as much of my own fear as I could toward him, hoping it would overwhelm him and make him stop.

"You shoot me in an alley in the middle of downtown, and you don't think anyone will hear?" I controlled my breathing, slowing my erratic heartbeat.

Hesitation. Questioning.

He blew out two harsh breaths and ran the back of his hand under his nose. "Makes no difference to me. Cops can kill me for all I care. At least I'll die knowing *you're* dead."

Shit. He was too far gone to allow my ability to seep through. I closed my eyes, wincing, saying a silent prayer to whatever deities existed in the world to do something—anything—to stop what was about to happen.

A sizzle of lightning blazed through the alleyway in a

blinding flash, sparks flying. The pressure from the man's hand and gun disappeared. Darkness spilled over the alley, not one single street lamp lit. Slowly, I turned.

Zane stood at the opposite wall, the man in his grasp, booted feet scraping the asphalt as his hands clawed at the one Zane had wrapped around his throat. Lightning curled around Zane's chest and arms. I side stepped until I stood next to Zane laser-focused on the man in his grasp. Zane's eyes glowed bright white, the lightning crackling within them. His expression was cold, predatory—deadly.

Anger. Distaste. Absolute fury.

"Zane, don't." I lifted a hand to touch his arm but snapped it back when the lightning hissed, swirling around his body faster.

"He was going to *kill* you."

The man gagged and gurgled within his grip, what little pale skin that showed through the mask, reddening.

Licking my lips, I stepped closer. "But he didn't. You stopped him. You can't do this."

"Watch me," he snarled.

"I know you *can*, but you shouldn't. There are security cameras everywhere." My chest heaved, and I moved so close, I could feel the heat from the lightning coursing over him—feel the hairs on my arms standing on end.

"I fried them upon arrival." Zane's lip bounced, and he gripped harder around the man's neck.

The man's feet kicked harder, and his arms fell limp at his sides.

"Zane, stop," I yelled.

Silence.

I stared at the man dying with each passing second.

"Zane," I yelled again, raising my fingers to his shoulder but wincing as the lightning flicked at my skin.

Still such utter silence.

"Zeus," I said quietly, ignoring the sting from the lightning as I slid a hand over his shoulder. "Please. Stop."

He rapidly blinked, those brightened lightning eyes turning to look down at me. The lightning curling around his arms fizzled away, and all that remained was the bit ignited in his gaze.

Confused. Shocked. Still angry, though.

Zane lowered the man and loosened his grip but didn't fully let go. Dipping his face closer, he said, "The only reason you're still breathing is that I'm trying to get in this woman's good graces. Remember that the next time you're seeking petty revenge against a woman who was just doing her job." He let go of the man's neck, moving his hand to his shoulder, and making him slump to the ground unconscious.

Anger. Fear. Lust.

I stared up at him as he turned to face me, his blue eyes back to normal. A deep crease formed in his brow, his eyes heavy and sullen as if he were exhausted. He wiped it away as he lifted his chin, not tearing his gaze away from me—waiting to see what I'd do, what I'd say.

I leaped against his chest, curling my arms around his neck and kissing him. He wrapped his arms around my waist, kissing me back, his hands roaming up and down.

That was so fucking hot but so, so fucking *stupid* on his part.

Angrily I pushed away, beating one fist against his chest before I stepped back. "Why do I always want to punch you and fuck you all at the same time?"

His lazy gaze took me in, his tongue licking his bottom lip, tasting me. "You—" He pointed at me with a wicked glint in his eye. "Called me Zeus."

I picked at flecks of wood in the doorframe, focusing on it. "You wouldn't answer to Zane. You were about to kill him. What else was I supposed to do?"

After what I'd just seen, the display he'd given…there was no denying he was who he said.

"How did it feel? Saying my real name? Feeling the lightning sizzle against your skin when you touched me?"

Powerful.

I poked his chest and tightened my jaw. "We need to talk. Now. And you're going to answer every damn question I have."

He batted my finger away with a smirk before pulling me against him. The world whizzed past us in a vibrant blur, and within seconds, we stood in the middle of…his penthouse apartment.

FIFTEEN

ZEUS

DON'T GET ME WRONG. I was ecstatic she was curious enough to ask questions. It meant she was actually considering my proposal, but fuck me if it wasn't going to be as painful as an ass full of razor blades. Since the age of mortals worshipping and believing in the gods, let's just say the modern era had never painted me in the best light? I may as well have been the poster boy for everything everyone should hate.

Keira stood in the middle of the living room, her coat still on, hands wrapped around herself. Creases formed in her forehead as she turned circles, almost as if she were afraid the place was booby-trapped and one false move would cause a door in the floor to open.

"I promise you nothing will happen beyond talking—" I flashed her a grin. "—unless you want it to." Moving behind the bar, I grabbed the decanter and two tumblers. "I brought us here because it's soundproof."

"If it's soundproof, then why didn't you bring us here before instead of yanking me into a damn holding cell?" Her shoulders relaxed, and she shrugged off her coat, making sure to fold it before draping it delicately over the chaise lounge in the corner.

"Ah, yes." I poured scotch into one glass. "Bringing you to my lair would've made the 'Greek gods are real' conversation far easier." Offering her a small smile, I lifted the bottle.

She scratched the back of her head. "Point taken."

I shook the bottle. "Scotch? Could help. Trust me. This is going to be a strange conversation."

"You're right. Make it a double. No ice." She leaned against the bar, tapping her fingernails on the marble as she scanned my place.

Levin came barreling around the corner, his tongue flopped out the side of his mouth.

I stopped mid-pour, slamming the bottle to the bar top. "Shit. I forgot I hadn't put him up. Sort of well, left in a—" Stopping short as I rounded the corner, I paused at the sight of Keira squatting with my dog between her knees. He licked every dry spot on her face as she laughed and scratched behind his ears.

"You have a dog?"

A warm smile pulled at my lips, and I folded my arms, watching them. "You sound surprised."

"I guess I am. You didn't seem the dog type. How come I've never seen you walk him?" She cooed at Levin, scrunching his face within her hands. He repeatedly lifted his paw to her knee every time she dared to stop.

"I don't tend to walk him at four o'clock in the morning usually." Canting my head to the side, I marveled at Levin's behavior. He never acted like that around anyone else but me. "He…likes you."

"Now *you* sound surprised." She cut her gaze to me as she sucked her lips into her mouth to avoid Levin's slobber getting on them as he licked under her chin.

Scratching the back of my head, annoyed at the continuing confusion plaguing my every damn thought as of late, I said, "I suppose I shouldn't be. I just don't normally like too many people touching him on account of his past, but with you—" I trailed off and shook my head, returning to the scotch.

She stood and moved in front of me with the bar top between us. "I, what? Finish your sentence."

"It's nothing, Keira." After pouring her scotch, I slid it across the bar to her.

"Every. Damn. Question." The corner of one of her thin brows quirked.

I ran my teeth over my bottom lip, eyeing the way her chest swelled whenever she challenged me. She pushed past my lightning in that alleyway, despite the fear of death prickling her skin, despite the fear that I was about to kill that man— and I would have. She stopped me. It was enough to make me want to bend her over a barstool and fuck her brains out, but—a promise is a promise.

"I don't mind seeing him with you. In fact, I enjoy watching you with him." I tapped the glass, encouraging her to drink.

She took a sip, not moving her gaze from my face. "You're a peculiar man."

"That's because I'm not one, my dear."

We both drank, taking each other in, undressing one another with our eyes alone.

Levin rested his head on her lap, giving her his best puppy dog stare, begging for attention. She obliged him and scratched his head with a small smile.

"You have questions, Keira." My shoulders tensed, mentally preparing for what I knew she would ask.

She took a deep breath and curled both hands around her glass. "The women."

Here we fucking go.

It took every bit of strength in me not to roll my eyes. She couldn't know the truth. How could she? Cool it.

"What about them?" I downed the rest of my drink and poured another, highly considering switching to ambrosia wine to obtain an actual buzz.

"I read some pretty crazy shit, Zane. Animals? A fucking cloud?"

I ground my teeth together and leaned on the bar top to bring our faces closer. She didn't back away. "Alright, look. Let me make something perfectly clear. The myths were written by a bunch of horny old men who lived vicariously through the stories they created."

"Uh-huh. So, you didn't sleep with a bunch of women?" She raised a thin brow before finishing her drink.

"I never said that. I love women. I love sex. But I never had to turn myself into something other than what I am to seduce them. Give me a little credit here." I poured her another double, and she immediately scooped it into her hand. "And before you ask…I don't force myself on *anyone*. Besides the fact I find it wrong, it's far sexier when they want it—ask for it."

"Alright. So, a lot of it was made up. But why? What good did that do for them?" She shrugged, her bright blue eyes searching my face.

"A lot more than you think. It gave them excuses for their misdeeds, their taboos. It gave rhyme and reason for everything." Holding back a grimace, I rubbed my beard. "If the King of the Gods did it himself, surely it's okay. Right?"

"Shit. I never even thought about it that way." Her gaze bored into me.

I hadn't seen that look in a very long time—understanding. It damn near made my chest tighten.

"Most don't. You see, as more and more towns throughout Greece began to worship me, they molded me into the version of myself that best suited their needs."

She scooted forward on her stool, bringing our hands a breath apart. "And you just let them?"

"Of course, I did. And still do." I chuckled, closing the distance between our skin, brushing our knuckles. She didn't budge. "What am I supposed to do? Smite them?"

"No, but it doesn't bother you? The way people think about you if it's not accurate?" She canted her head to the side, a slight frown pulling at her lips.

"You have to understand something about a divine leader, Keira. It's not my job to be liked. It's to give the people what they need to thrive—to survive. And if putting me in a certain light is what does it? So be it." I clenched my jaw as I traced my pinky finger over her skin.

She gulped, her gaze falling to our hands touching. "But you still cheated on your wife countless times."

Fuck me sideways.

"In the eyes of the sanctity of marriage, yes. But with our agreement we made? No."

Look at me, Keira. Please look at me.

Her eyes lifted, and she blinked. "Agreement?"

"Hera and I were an arranged marriage of convenience. For politics' sake. We tried to make it work. We really did. Had Ares together. But at the end of the day, it just didn't work out between us." I leaned back and took a large gulp of my drink. "We decided to stay together and perform our duties, but anything outside of that? We'd seek elsewhere. She too had lovers."

Keira's head snapped back. "And that didn't bother you? Your wife sleeping with other people?"

I traced my fingers over the hair above my upper lip, mulling it over. "No. It didn't."

"But the possibility of anyone in your apartment building seeing me naked when you didn't even know if they had…that bothered you?" She narrowed her eyes at me, rechallenging me with a heated stare.

The sight of her naked ass from her apartment window sparked in my mind, the thought of another man, any of my neighbors seeing it, infuriating me. "Yes," I answered simply.

"You sound like a werewolf with its mate in a paranormal romance novel right now. You know that, right?" A fluttery laugh bubbled from her chest.

I didn't smile. It jarred me how spot on the nose the

statement was.

"Zane. What?" Her grin faded, and she flattened her palms on the bar.

Not like this. I did not want to tell her like this.

"Nothing, Keira. Ask another question. I know you have to have more."

She stood on the rung of her stool, gaining height on me. "I do. What the hell was that look on your face after I made the werewolf comment?"

She had one thing right. I *did* like her stubbornness. And it was so ass-backward.

Glaring up at her, I leaned forward, my chin in line with her collarbone. "I don't want to tell you like this. Not right now. I don't want it influencing your decision one way or the other."

"Tough. Shit. Tell me." She dug her nails into the marble, her neck turning pink.

"We have what's called a fated bond."

Her entire demeanor changed, the expression on her face resembling someone who'd been punched in the gut. She slowly lowered herself back to sitting, silent and staring behind me.

"It's rare amongst our kind, but I confirmed it. I didn't fucking believe it myself at first." I pressed my palms to the bar's edge, turning my gaze away from her.

"What does it mean?" She whispered in a voice that sounded like a little girl.

Sucking air through my nose, I played with my lightning bolt cufflink. "It means—our destinies are intertwined. No matter if we part ways and never see each other again, they always will be."

The thought pained me more than I was ready to admit. I sucked on my teeth to keep my expression neutral.

"So—" She slouched as she looked at her palms, studying the lines in her skin as if they held the answers. "I don't have a choice. It *has* to be you."

"No, Keira. You do have a choice." I hunched forward, dipping my face to look at her, to urge her to look at me. "I told you I won't force anyone into doing anything. Coerce. Meddle. Perhaps. But at the end of the day, it boils down to *them*."

Her eyes finally lifted back to mine, exhaustion settling into them. "Is there a grain of truth to anything I read? Are you as ruthless as some of the myths describe?"

Rubbing the back of my neck, I came around from the bar, sat next to her, and turned her to face me. She didn't fight me on it.

I'd trade places with Prometheus if it meant I could avoid having this conversation, but—she deserved the truth.

"There is some truth to it. Yes, Keira." Resting one elbow on the bar top, I leaned the other on my thigh, dangling my scotch glass with two fingers.

She folded her hands in her lap, piercing me again with her gaze, carving me a new asshole. "Then speak some truths."

"Before I do, tell me—are you the same woman you were at age ten? Seventeen? Twenty-five?"

"Of course not."

"Keep that in mind with what I'm about to tell you, and remember that I am *thousands* of years old." I guzzled some of my scotch, focusing on her throat bobbing when I mentioned my age.

"I keep forgetting somehow, despite you sitting right in front of me." She forced a small laugh.

With one swift thought, I pulsed my power over my arms, lightning swirling and crackling. "Does that help?"

Her fingers wiggled on the bar as if she wanted to touch the electricity again, and she nodded.

"When I initially became king, I was hungry for power. I couldn't get enough of it. I was young. Naïve. And well, pig-headed."

Half of her lips grinned. "You? Never."

I squeezed her knee with a smirk, retreating my hand back to the bar.

Her eyes snapped to the spot on her skin I'd touched before lazily rising back to my face.

"I *did* rescue my brothers from our beloved dad's stomach, trapped the Titans, bestowed my brothers their kingdoms, and took the Olympus throne for myself. I'd earned it." I shrugged, still believing I was the best of us for the job to this day.

She dragged a finger over the exposed flesh on her chest, listening to me intently.

"Did I order some ruthless punishments? Yes. Did they all deserve it? Some of them, yes. Did I do some fucked up things I regret?" I clicked my teeth together. "At the time I did them, I would've said no. And continue to deny it for a decade later. But now? I guess I can say I do."

"And is that what you most regret?"

The question jarred me, making the back of my head throb. Rubbing my skull, I tapped my finger on the glass. "No."

"Then what do you regret most, King of the Gods?" She

slid forward on her stool, resting a hand on my knee and staring at me with those sky-blue eyes I wanted looking at me while taking her from every angle and on every surface of this apartment.

"Ares," I said gruffly.

She leaned back. "Having him?"

"Olympus, no. He's the only legitimate child I have." I drained my scotch and tossed it to the bar with a sigh. "I regret being so harsh with him. He needed it, and it shaped him the way he was meant to be, but I ruined any possibility of ever having a relationship with him."

"Are you joking?" Keira snickered, slipping her hand to my thigh.

I frowned. "No. You asked me the question, and I gave you a damn answer. And now you're mocking me?"

"I'm not mocking you. You just make it sound like all hope is lost. It's called an apology."

I shook my head and turned my gaze to the eagle statue above my bed. "No. I can't do that."

"It's easy." She grabbed my chin and turned my face to look at her. "Ares, I'm sorry. See how easy that was?"

Gently taking her hand, I moved it back to my knee. "It's not that simple, Keira. You don't understand what position a role like mine puts me in."

"Fine. Explain it to me. You're asking me to put everything aside to be Queen, and now you make it sound like a burden."

It partially was. It really was.

I placed a hand on each of her shoulders and pushed down with enough pressure to make it uncomfortable but not hurt her. "Imagine this is a portion of the universe resting on your shoulders. It never lessens, never disappears, and if anything, backing down for a moment could make it even heavier."

Keira winced and rolled her shoulders after I removed my grip. "Don't you ever take breaks?"

"Do you?"

She slipped her hands under her ass. "I mean, I—"

"You don't. Because you want to be the best, as do I—the best leader I can be. This means there is no backing down, no breaks, constantly on at a hundred plus at all times. Such are the sacrifices we make, right?" I tightened my jaw, clenching my hand into a fist on the bar.

"You're right, but there are too many times to count I've done this and it makes me the opposite of what I seek to be." Her eyes grew heavy.

Olympus. We were so much alike.

"You have a hard time sleeping, don't you?" I pressed a knuckle under her chin, lifting it.

She nodded. "Half the time, I feel guilty when I'm sleeping. Isn't that the craziest thing you've ever heard?"

Not in the slightest.

"What my people don't see, Keira, is that I'm exhausted. My tank has been running on vapors for quite some time, but not only can't I afford to rest, I also can't let them see me tired." My entire body tensed. I'd never told a soul what I just told this woman. Not a soul.

Her eyes lifted to mine and she slid from her stool, slipping between my legs and taking my face in her hands. With a tenderness only a woman could give, she kissed me—sweet and light.

After she pulled away, I rested my hands on her hips. "I reveal a weakness, and you kiss me?"

"It's precisely why I kissed you—" She brushed her lips against mine again. "—Zeus."

It was only the second damn time she said my real name, and just as the first, the sound of it made my dick hard.

I rubbed the back of my neck. "There's also—Eris."

"Eris?" She canted her head to the side and touched my forearm.

Dropping my gaze to the floorboards, I sighed. "Goddess of discord. My daughter I created in the hopes of balancing chaos. I should've learned with Athena. I'd created her with the intention of balancing war, to balance Ares, but all those two did was argue."

Her grip tightened on my arm, but she remained silent.

"At least Athena turned out to be a righteous war goddess. Instead of balancing chaos, Eris *caused* it." I beat my fist against my knee.

"Couldn't you, I don't know how it works, but simply tell her *not* to do it?"

Tracing a finger between her knuckles, I let out a roiling sigh. "I can't stop a god from performing their purpose. There was no way to predict that's what hers would've become." I lifted my gaze to Keira's. "Evil exists in the universe to shed light on the good. I only regret that I lent a small piece to it."

Keira frowned and wrapped her arms around me. She rested her head on my shoulder and hugged me tight.

An embrace from a woman that had nothing to do with sex.

I never knew how much I wanted it—needed it. Until Keira gave it to me.

Zeus. King of the Gods liked *hugs* now. Fucking Olympus.

"Wait." She slapped a hand over her forehead as she pushed back. "If Greek mythology is real, does that mean Celtic is? Egyptian?" She gasped, and her eyes widened as she dropped her hands at her sides. "Holy shit. Is *Thor* real?"

If I could get through one more lifetime without hearing that asshole's name once, I'd be a delighted god-king.

"Fuck Thor. He can do his little lightning tricks, but at the end of the day, *I'm* the one with the true power." I pointed at myself and stood.

She blinked, and her lips slowly parted. "So, it *is* all real." Her eyes panned to the floor as she went silent before snapping her gaze back to me and crossing her arms. "You sound jealous."

"Of Thunder Nuts? Please." I bent forward, lowering my face to hers and brushing our lips. "I'll gladly compare *bolts* with him any day of the week. You can even set up the meeting."

Keira gulped as she trailed my tie through her petite fingers and stared up at me. "The uh—trial is in two hours. I should go home and try to get *some* sleep."

Clearing my throat, I squeezed her hip. "You're right. I need you to be in top form. Give me a challenge tomorrow." Winking at her, I took a step back.

"Oh, don't you worry, Vronti. I've won plenty of cases on zero sleep, let alone an hour." She winked back.

Walking her to the door, my hand on the small of her back, Levin trotted behind us, waiting for his goodbye pettings.

Keira chuckled and scratched behind Levin's ears, his chest, and under his chin. "Thank you for being honest with me."

"You're welcome." I opened the door and stared down at her.

Every fiber in my being told me to pull her toward me, kiss her, and slam the door shut as we tore each other's clothes off during our trek to the bed. But no. She would be the one to make this happen. And when it did…

She bit her lip, baiting me, enticing me. "See you tomorrow." With one last smile and a pat to Levin's head, she whisked out the door.

After she was down the hallway, I let the door shut and pressed my forehead against it with a deep sigh.

Two more days, and I could very well be crownless.

SIXTEEN

KEIRA

I SAT OUTSIDE THE courtroom, my legs crossed, the nylons brushing against each other causing static. My mind should've been focused on nothing else but the trial ahead. The trial I was only minutes away from walking into and fighting against Zeus, the King of the fucking Gods. And he is precisely who I couldn't get out of my head long enough to concentrate on my standing arguments. The conversation we had earlier this morning. The conviction in his voice with each passing word. His confession to me. Me. I'd gotten the sinking feeling he hadn't told anyone else before either, so why me?

"You ready for this, bulldog?" Olivia asked, looming over me with several folders cradled in her arm.

Gulping, I rose and smoothed out my suit jacket, tugging the hem of it. "Always."

Zeus was already there when we entered the courtroom, sitting at the table with Daniels at his side. He leaned over, whispering something to her, and she remained stone cold and expressionless as usual. We reached our table, and Zeus slowly turned his head to catch my gaze over his shoulder.

When our eyes locked, a twinge rocketed through my stomach. After the trial—I was going to fuck him. I knew it from the moment I'd left his apartment this morning when I wanted to do it right then and there. If it weren't for this trial today…I probably would have. Even with dozens of people surrounding us in the busy courtroom—media, audience, the jury, security guards. His lust, his power, his growing need, stood out, settling over my skin like warm silken drops.

Those deep blue eyes gave a subtle squint. He knew it too. Tonight would be the night I fucked a Greek god. The thought should've terrified me—or at the very least bubbled my nerves, but instead, I felt determined and antsy.

The trial started, and we each did the usual song and dance—bringing in witnesses, questioning them. Presenting evidence, correlating it to the case whether it proved her guilt or innocence. We'd locked gazes several times and sent so many secret signals to each other, I'd already gotten wet.

It was when I pulled my wildcard, signaling to the custodian to bring in the large blue barrel into the courtroom, that I'd gotten the stare from Zeus I'd been craving all day. As the custodian wheeled the barrel down the middle aisle on a dolly, Zeus slowly turned his head toward me, the lust and admiration pulsing from him so profusely it almost knocked me out of my chair. The custodian displayed the barrel—a replica to what Daniels used when filling it with both acid and her husband—in the corner I'd instructed him to in clear view of the jury. It would serve as a constant reminder every remaining day of the trial of the gruesome act this woman carried out.

A small smile tugged at Zeus's lips, one he only let me see before hiding it with his hand, his other hand drumming fingers on the table. Daniels whispered something to him, and he shook his head, flicking his wrist at the barrel and cutting his gaze to me sidelong as he spoke to her.

The trial went on for another three hours, and by that point, I was ready to tear the clothes from Zeus's body and throw him to the hallway floor as soon as we exited the goddamned courtroom.

No sooner had the judge thrown the gavel down, dismissing everyone, I stood. "I'm out of here, Ollie. See you tomorrow?"

"You—" Olivia looked around her, palming the table, the folders, her chest. "Already? Where the hell are you going?"

"I uh—out. On a date." Wincing, I shoved the paperwork in my briefcase, and stole several glances at Zeus, who looked just as hurried, waiting for them to retrieve his client and cart her back to her holding hole.

"A date? Seriously?" Olivia tugged my jacket sleeve. "With who?"

I wanted to tell her. I did. But we were in a courtroom with dozens of ears. Any one of them catching the mention of Zane from my lips could turn the situation sour. "I promise I'll fill you in tomorrow, okay?" After squeezing her hand, leaving her standing there slack-jawed, I made a beeline for the aisle.

Once in the foyer, I rounded a vacant corner, holding my briefcase by its handle with two hands. The crowd filed out, soon fading into only several stragglers.

"Call me crazy, but I have the feeling you need something from me again." Zeus's voice sent tremors of warmth and ecstasy vibrating through my chest and down to my toes.

Closing my eyes, I took a deep inhale, dizzying myself with his masculine scent. His body hovered behind me, his crotch inches from my ass.

"What do you *need*, Miss Bazin?" He whispered.

I whirled around, my heart racing, pounding, punching at my chest. "Take us somewhere. Anywhere but here."

A knowing, wicked grin curled over his lips, and he pulled me to him, into the shadows and away from prying eyes. We appeared a blink later in his penthouse apartment—his lair, as he called it. I splayed my hand, dropping my briefcase without caring where it landed. We stared at each other before letting our eyes wander over one another's lips, our chests…

His mouth crashed against mine, and he pushed me against the nearest wall, his hands slamming on each side of my head. I bunched my hands on the lapels of his jacket, yanking it off his shoulders.

He pulled away, dragging his thumb over my bottom lip, waiting for me to open my eyes. "You didn't answer my question."

"What?" The question pushed from my throat like a moaning whisper.

He pressed his cock still hidden within his pants against my stomach. "What. Do you. Want, Vasílissa?"

He wanted me to ask for it. To crave it. And he wanted to hear me say it.

"I want you to fuck me." With a firm grip, I took his face in one hand. "Zeus."

Lightning flashed in his eyes, and he snarled, kissing me again, hoisting me up with the wall as leverage behind me. I wrapped my arms around his shoulders, my back arching as he shoved the pencil skirt up my legs, bunching it at my hips.

His fingers brushed the nylons between my legs and panties, and he paused, his gaze lingering downward. "I don't recall a shield before?" He turned his head to one side.

"I only wear them for trials," I said, breathy. "Get rid of them."

He met my gaze and, with a harsh tug, ripped a hole. He could've used his powers, I was sure of it, but instead, he chose the feral route.

I gasped and grinned at him, my hands greedily fishing for his belt and zipper, undoing them until his pants fell to his ankles. After tugging his black boxers, they too fell to the ground, and the thick, long cock I'd spied that night made another appearance. Binoculars could do it no justice in the slightest.

I felt my panties disappear, and before I could even process another thought, he plunged into me—filling me, shoving me hard against the wall. Stifling a scream, I dug my nails into his shoulders, every muscle in my body tightening.

"Remember, the walls are soundproof." He sucked on my earlobe, biting it. "Absolute. Freedom."

As he pumped inside of me, swelling with each stroke, I cried out loud. "Holy fuck."

We were both still in our lawyer attire save for the lower half, not bothering with the pesky tasks of removing all clothes before having each other. It made it all the more erotic, and with my legs wrapped around his waist, I dug one of my spiked heels into his ass cheek.

He growled and kept one hand on my ass, holding me, while the other hand bunched in my hair, yanking my head back. He kissed me as he fucked me—deep and rough, his beard scraping my chin, reddening it.

"How long have you wanted to do this, Keira?" He rolled his hips, shoving into me with such rhythmic timing it had my eyes rolling back in my head. "And don't you dare fucking lie to me."

I gulped, gyrating my hips in time with his now, meeting him stroke for stroke. Locking his gaze, I bit my lower lip. "Since the moment I heard that deep voice on the other side of the door. Before I ever even saw your sexy as hell face."

His nostrils flared, and his eyes glowed bright white. "Fuck," he breathed out before covering my mouth with his, his fist punching against the wall near my head.

He brushed the spot inside me with every thrust and pump, the swirls and familiar tightening in my stomach soaring. Gripping his hair, whimpering into his mouth, he pulled away, letting me scream through my release, shuddering around him.

When I opened my eyes, we took each other in, both panting, and he slowly lowered me to the ground. He waved his hand in front of him with a wry grin, making my clothes disappear, save for the heels.

I stood in front of him naked, and as he lifted his hand again to himself, I snatched his wrist. "Wait. Not this." Loosening his tie, I slipped it over his head.

He raised a brow, that wry grin sliding into a villainous one. Once the tie was safely in my hands, he stood nude, tanned, and muscular in front of me. Fucking immaculate. The mere sight of him made me soaking wet all over again. Letting my bottom lip roll past my teeth, I guided his arms behind him, testing to see if he'd let me. I knew at any moment he could overpower me if he desired. Obliging, he didn't fight against me, that same smile plastered on his lips.

Holding his gaze with mine, I slid the tie over his wrists, pulling it tight. I kept the tie in my hand, forbidding him from touching me as I sank to my knees. Not taking my eyes away from him, I licked the tip of his cock, teasing it with short wet flicks of my tongue. It pulsed from my touch, and Zeus's head fell back with a moan before returning to watch me. Licking my lips, I slid my mouth over him, inch by inch, taking him all in until I could feel it hitting the back of my throat.

He groaned, his arms twitching within the confines of the tie. I held it tighter, pulling his arms against the back of his legs. Working in tandem with my hand, I stroked, sucked, licked, my stomach fluttering from the groans, moans, and growls pouring from the god-king's throat.

He blew out a breath. "Come here, Keira."

Dabbing the corners of my mouth with my thumb, I rose, letting go of the tie with a grin.

He snapped the tie away and, with a carnal gaze, lifted me into his arms. "Let me remind you who you're fucking."

My heart raced at his words as he crossed the room to his bed, the eagle statue above it bearing the same feral look in its eyes as Zeus. He tossed me to the bed, and I landed on my back, propping myself on both elbows. Tracing his fingers down my calf, he kept his gaze locked with mine as he removed my heels, tossing them aside.

"Don't want me digging my heels into your ass anymore?" I raised a wicked brow.

He leaned over me, grinning and trailing his touch over my knees, stopping at my thighs. "If you want to show appreciation for what I'm about to do to you, Keira—use your claws."

My throat became sandpaper as I gazed up at him, the sound of my beating heart pounding in my chest rivaling a bass drum.

He clenched his fists, and lightning began to crackle and swirl his arms, curling over his chest, his neck, and sparking in his eyes. "Lie back," he ordered.

I did as commanded, resting my hands on my stomach. He moved near me beside the bed and took hold of my wrists, forcing them at my sides. He hovered his hand over my chest, and the lightning brightened until a small current struck from his palm, settling into my skin. It didn't hurt, didn't shock me—it was a feeling of warmth and shivers and a passing caress. His hand traveled over my ribs, making my back arch from the bed. The sensations continued to entice my body as he moved over my stomach and settled at my pussy, sending tiny warm strikes one after the other, making me convulse.

I pinned my knees together to keep them from shaking. He walked to the foot of the bed, still holding his lightning power on me before he paused long enough to slide his hands to the insides of my thighs and yanked my legs apart. My breaths quickened, diving into a sensual frenzy of panting as he lowered his face to my folds, the glow of his eyes staring back at me. The lightning coursed over his lips as he lapped his tongue over me, sparking against my clit. As he worked his tongue, darting in and out of me, licking, and surging the lightning power through every nerve with expert intricacy, I gripped the sheets.

"Oh my—" I started before crying out in pure fucking ecstasy, my entire body becoming one tense muscle.

He stood, a confident grin playing over his mouth as he dragged a hand across his lips. The lightning didn't fade away as he crawled onto the bed—want playing in his gaze as he neared me—the wolf coming to claim, to possess. I lay with my legs still sprawled, my chest pumping, the swirling euphoria from coming only moments ago still swelling. He curled his hands on my hips and, in one swift motion, flipped me to my stomach and hoisted my ass into the air. I bent forward, pressing my forearms into the bed, waiting, anticipating, craving it.

Kneading my ass with his palms, he plunged into me from behind. I clenched around his cock as he thrusted, making him grunt with every other stroke. He slapped my ass first with one hand then both, leaving behind a pleasuring sting. I rocked my hips back every time he pushed forward, our bodies making the satisfying *clap* every time they met with each hard motion we made together.

He grabbed both of my arms, holding them behind me as he continued to fuck me, harder and harder. I pressed my face into the sheets, panting, screaming in pleasure, letting him use my arms as handles. He let go and switched to grabbing my hair, yanking my head back, my gaze peering up at the eagle looming above us. He slammed into me, digging his fingers into my ass, his lightning now swirling over *my* body. It sizzled and hissed, circling my arms and legs, skirting over my chest. A sort of tingle prickled the back of my neck before whizzing down my spine, and heat flushed in my chest, making me gasp.

Zeus paused behind me, panting. He let go of my hair and pulled me up by the crooks of my elbows, rocking in and out of me, slower this time, deliberate. "Did you feel that?"

"Yes," I whispered, moaning. "What was it?"

He traced a hand over my stomach, trailing down to my clit and circling it with a finger. "The bond." He massaged one breast, pinching my nipple between two fingers. "We're officially connected for as long as we both live, Keira." His hand moved over my collarbone, lightly wrapping around my neck for a moment before cupping my chin, turning my face to look up at him. "Even if you don't choose me, I'll always be a part of you. When you make yourself come at night, it'll be *me* who invades your every thought."

My body ached for him, even with him already inside me. With a whimper, I grabbed the back of his head, pulling his mouth down to mine, kissing him, raking my nails over his skull. With his fingers between my legs and his languid thrusts pulsing in and out of me, I came undone for the third time that night, moaning and groaning into his mouth.

He pulled out of me and guided me to lay on my back, his body crawling over me as soon as my head hit the pillows. Grabbing both of my wrists in one hand, he shoved them above my head, pressing some of his weight to hold them there. The lightning fizzled away, his blue eyes returning as he took all of me in—lingering over my breasts and stomach before returning to my face.

"Fuck. You'd make such a Queen." He kept my gaze as the tip of his cock teased my entrance, rubbing against it.

"Shut up, Zeus," I said, breathy and lustful.

He glared at me, his hand gripping my wrists tighter.

"Tonight, you fuck me. Keep showing me what I'd be missing." I bucked my hips, forcing part of him inside me. "Tomorrow, we can talk."

He grinned, a deep chuckle resonating from his chest before he thrust forward, filling me to the hilt. As he pumped in and out, rolling his hips, the motion turned from feral overtaking to—something else. He let go of my arms, fingers tracing the side of my breast, my ribs, and to my hip. I stared up at him, trailing my hands over his back muscles, before finding my way to the muscular ass I'd been drooling over, digging my nails into it.

His blue eyes became two rushing currents, pulling me through the rapids with nothing to grip. And I welcomed the chaos, opened my heart and soul to it. Another tingle, but more intense than the last, jabbed at the base of my neck, trickling down each vertebra until it reached my tailbone, sizzling. I arched from the bed, burying Zeus's head into my breasts, encouraging him to lick them. His tongue lapped over one nipple and bit it, the cool air in the room making it harden.

Pinching my knees at his sides, I shivered, quaked, and screamed so loud it hurt my ears as the euphoria erupted in my core. He trailed his nose over my chin and to my neck, taking a long-drawn breath, smelling me. His thrusts quickened, pounding into me, pushing my body toward the headboard. With a ferocious snarl, he gave one final thrust and spilled himself inside me, biting the side of my neck but not breaking the skin. He slowly pulled back, staring down at me with a wicked glint in his eye.

"What?" I smiled, my skin flushed and beading with sweat.

"You felt it a second time, didn't you?" Still inside me, his cock pulsed.

I locked my ankles together behind his back, holding him captive. "Maybe."

"You want it, Keira. You want me. You want all of it." He traced his thumb across my bottom lip.

I pressed a finger over his mouth. "I said tomorrow."

He nipped at my finger.

"You called me something earlier. Started with a 'v.'"

He stiffened. "You heard that, huh?"

Using my legs still locked around him, I pulled him closer. "What was it?"

"Vasílissa," he whispered against my cheek, the way the word rolled off his tongue making my stomach clench.

"Is that Greek?"

He nodded as he rubbed his cock between my legs before slowly slipping inside me again. "It means—Queen."

As I took a sharp inhale, I snapped my gaze to his, my grip tightening around his neck.

The faint sound of nails scraping against hardwood sounded from the side of the bed. A pair of big brown eyes peeked around the corner.

"I'm honestly surprised he stayed in his room," Zeus said with a smirk.

I turned my head to look at Levin. "Let him sleep with us."

"I—I mean, shit, what a cockblock you are, Levin."

Playfully swatting him in the shoulder, I trailed my fingers over his chest, and traced each abdominal muscle. "Nothing's stopping us from exploring every other room in this place when we can't sleep in the middle of the night. The kitchen. The floor. The balcony."

"Is that a promise?" His cock twitched.

I gave a soft kiss to his lips. "A promise."

He groaned, kissing me one last time before pulling out of me and slipping us both under the sheets. "Come here, Levin," he grumbled.

The dog came trotting to the bed, his large pink tongue flopped from his mouth as he jumped up. After working a corner of the bed in a circle several times, he curled up, satisfied, and closed his eyes. I nestled my ass against Zeus's hips, moaning as his large arms wrapped around me from behind.

"You're such a tease," he whispered, his breath coating my ear.

"And you love it," I whispered back, feeling his smile against my cheek.

With a fizzle of lightning striking from his palm, the lights went out. We didn't wind up fucking in the middle of the night as I promised because, for the first time since I was a kid, I slept to morning, wrapped in the god-king's embrace.

SEVENTEEN

KEIRA

I'D EXPECTED TO WAKE up to a room filled with darkness, but instead, a faint light peeked through the blinds from the rising sun. The scent of sandalwood surrounded the air around me and a strong tanned arm curled over my body, his hand cupping one breast. His beard tickled the back of my neck as his nose trailed my skin.

"Good morning," he whispered, kissing my ear.

I ran my fingers down the dark hair scattered on his muscular forearm. "Good morning. I can't remember the last time I slept like that. I don't think I woke up once."

He moaned, pulling me against him tighter. "Mm, I don't think I did either." His cock hardened as he rolled his hips against my ass.

I smiled as I bit my knuckle, recalling what happened last night with vivid, visceral detail. Closing my eyes, I lifted my leg, welcoming him. He grinned into my hair, moving one hand to my stomach while the other held up my leg from my inner thigh. The tip of him pushed at my entrance and I moaned.

A whimper sounded from the side of the bed and I flew my eyes open. Levin's head rested on the sheets, his body sitting on the floor.

Zeus sighed behind me, his forehead pressing into the back of my shoulder. "He needs to go out. I'll take him for a quick walk and be *right* back."

Biting back a smile, I scratched Levin's head, feeling the bed dip as Zeus crawled out.

"Who'd have ever thought the King of the Gods would be thwarted by a mortal canine." Zeus shook his head, chuckling as he swirled a hand around himself, appearing in a simple pair of jeans, sweater and boots.

Biting my lip at the sight of him, I curled the sheets to my chin. He was beyond sexy in a suit, fucking sin naked, but in this get up? He looked so normal and so at ease I wanted to eat every inch of him up.

Zane grabbed a leash hanging on a peg by the door and whistled at Levin. "Come on, boy."

Levin ran so excitedly to Zeus he slipped several times on the way over.

"If I come back and you're still here plus all of my valuables, I'll take that as a sign you like me." Zane flashed a charming grin.

I guffawed, grabbed a pillow and hurled it at him, laughing.

Zeus winced and ducked out the door with a chuckle, the pillow colliding into it.

He could've created a companion for himself, I was sure of

it. Some divine animal that would live forever and possibly even fly or something, but he decided to own a mortal pet. One that came with the same responsibilities as any human being—food, water, all the necessities. He *chose* to care for him. He showed me a vulnerable side to him, and I believed there was more buried deep but he feared bringing it to the surface. Yes. Feared. I refused to think even divine entities didn't fear something, didn't have weaknesses. It's what made the world turn. The balance.

I sat up, letting the sheet fall away and hanging my legs off one corner of the bed. His apartment left no clue a Greek god dwelled within. It wasn't simple by any means, but I suppose I shouldn't have thought a King would settle for any less. Every piece of furniture, every fixture, even the selections of alcohol in the bar were all top of the line. Did he fabricate the money himself? Earn it? Make it appear in his pocket whenever he needed it? So many questions and barely enough time to ask them all before the inevitable. Immigration would be knocking on my door soon, throwing my illegal alien status in my face. And the worst part of it? I didn't know when.

The door swung open and I turned my frown into a smile, sitting up straight, and pressing my palms to the bed between my legs. Levin ran past me, heading straight for his room to chew on a toy. Zeus paused at the doorway, his eyes turning carnal once he spotted me naked and waiting.

"This is certainly a sight to come home to." He chewed on his bottom lip, not tearing his gaze away from me as he hung the leash up and locked the door.

My nipples hardened as I watched him cross the room to me,

pushing his sweater sleeves up, and sinking to his knees. He placed his hand on my ankle, delicately dragging his touch up my shin, circling my knee with a single finger, and tantalizing my thigh. I let my head fall back with a moan. He grabbed my left ass cheek before giving it a light slap. Grazing his lips up my ribs, he kissed, nipped, and sucked. His hand cupped one breast, massaging it as he playfully bit my ass with a growl.

As he traced his callused palms over the tops of my thighs, he gave a quick subtle lick to his lips. "Would you believe me if I told you, you are the most gorgeous woman I've ever seen?"

My heart missed a beat as I gazed down at him.

Lust. Admiration. Respect.

"Considering how old you are, I'd say it was hard to believe." But his emotions didn't lie. It had me reeling.

"Believe it." A devious grin tugged at his lips. "You're positively filthy, however. You could use a shower."

Shoving his shoulder, I laughed and pushed to my feet. "Well, I guess I'll head in there alone then if I'm so filthy."

"Oh, no." He stood and snapped his fingers, making his clothes disappear. "Who else is going to show you how to properly scrub behind your ears?"

My eyes unabashedly dropped straight to his already hard as granite cock asking for attention. I trailed my gaze over the body I wanted pressed against me now, tonight, tomorrow, possibly forever. "Lead the way."

He took my hand in his and led us down the hall to a massive marbled bathroom complete with hot tub and a shower wide enough to fit eight people. I dragged my fingers over the smooth countertops—swirls of black, grey, and white. He slid a hand to my lower back, leading me into the shower, his hand waving above us. The squared chrome showerhead sprung to life, sending a high-pressured downpour of simulated rain.

"If I would've stayed in Argentina—" He lightly shoved me against the tiled wall in the same motion as when I'd been sensually pinned to the tree. "—how do you think this moment, *right* here, would've played out?"

The steaming hot water poured over our heads, our hair, making our naked bodies glisten from the one light illuminating above us. I skirted my right leg up his thigh, wrapping it around his waist—the same leg that showed from the slit in my dress.

"I would've let you have me right there against that tree. Fuck everything else." Gazing up at him, I roughly tangled my fingers in his soaked hair.

Groaning, he gripped my chin, tracing his thumb over my bottom lip, catching on it. His hand slipped to my ass and unlike last night where he would've claimed me with one thrust, he pushed himself in inch-by-inch, grinning as he made me whimper. He pressed the other hand on the tiles by my head, starting slow rolls of his hips.

"And it wouldn't have bothered you if someone saw you getting railed in a public park? At a wedding reception no less?" Pumping, rolling, writhing inside me, he brushed his lips over my cheek.

"No. Just because I take what I want, doesn't make me a whore. It makes me empowered." I pressed my head against the wall behind me, groaning as he rubbed that spot inside me so feather-like it caused tremors and tiny quakes within my belly.

His thrusts grew in intensity, urgency at my words, the hand on my ass pulling me onto him further. "I'd never call you a whore. Unless of course, you wanted me to behind closed doors." He smiled against my neck, before licking and kissing it.

Dirty, filthy, talk.

"Use it," I breathed out, digging my nails into his shoulders.

As if being able to read my thoughts or sense my need, the lightning pulsed over his skin, traveling to mine, entwining us in an electric embrace. The water from the shower made it hiss and smoke, filling the shower with an ethereal lit fog. I bit my lip, waiting for the sensations to titillate my skin, my nerves, my insides. It started at my lips as he kissed me, sparking against my skin before traveling over my breasts, through my stomach and finally—a pulsing radiation intensified by his thumb circling my clit, crackling the lightning directly over it.

I cried out and not just a cry—I fucking screamed in pleasure, digging my nails into his back, scratching him. If he'd have been mortal, I would've scarred him. He growled and pumped inside me harder, firmer, sliding my body up the wall, the water splashing around us. The lightning didn't stop, still cracking and surging around us—our union. As he pumped his final thrusts, he settled his hand around my neck. Not gripping it, simply rested it there, taking my gaze with his lightning blazed one as he came undone inside me.

We spent the next several minutes taking an actual shower, his hands still roaming my body as he sudsed me up, bathing me. When we finished, he made himself instantly dry, but I still stood on the mat, dripping wet.

"Are you not going to dry me off too?" I asked, snickering.

He canted his head to one side, taking me in with those sensual sapphires he called eyes. Producing a fluffy grey towel, he handed it to me with a grin. "I would but you look so fucking sexy right now."

Smiling, I yanked the towel from his grasp. It was perfectly warmed. Hugging it to my chest to relish in the heat wafting from it, I dragged it over my skin, drying myself as he watched me.

He folded his arms and leaned on the doorway, letting out a deep sigh. "Have you made a decision yet, Keira?"

My smiled faded and I crinkled my brow, tying the towel around me, suddenly feeling exposed. "What?"

"You know what I'm talking about. You've heard my offer. I've answered your questions. You've experienced what *else* I can offer, multiple, multiple times—" He cut his gaze to mine. It wasn't ruthless or conniving, but serious. "—it's time to cut a deal…or not."

Fury exploded in my chest and I pushed past him, back to the living room and away from the steam and heat of the bathroom. He followed behind me, directly on my heels.

"I can't believe you. You're making this sound like some sort of business transaction," I snapped, leaning on the bar top with my back to him.

He shoved his hands in his pockets, the skin between his eyes wrinkling with no hint of a smile. "It is."

Impatient. Nervous. Irritated.

Taking a quick inhale, I turned to face him, still leaning on the bar. "How could you possibly say that?"

"It's more than that, yes, but at the end of the day it's an arrangement to help us *both*." He shook his head, holding one hand at his side.

Arrangement.

"I'd eventually be just another Hera, wouldn't I?" A lump as coarse as coal formed in my throat.

He rested his arms at his sides, and grabbed a fistful of his hair, tugging it once as he took a step forward. "No. This is different."

"Is it?" My sinuses stung. "This is arranged. We'd be jumping into it sooner than we'd have ever done in a real situation—so what's to stop this from fizzling out a year from now? Ten? A thousand?"

He furiously rubbed his chin, his eyes dropping to his feet before cutting back to me. "That won't happen. This. Is. Different."

Storming forward, I fumed up at him. "How?"

His mouth opened and closed several times, but nothing came out.

Confusion. Rage. Slightly frantic.

"I—" He paused to loosen his tie, his jaw tightening. "I don't know what you expect from me. This is who I am, Keira. You either take it—" Sucking in a deep breath, he lifted his chin. "—or leave it."

Hurt. Anger. ...sadness.

My eyes blurred with tears as I stumbled backward. "That's it then, huh?"

With a discomfort that flowed from him like a waterfall, he rubbed the back of his neck, dragged a hand down his face and after locking eyes with me, raised his hand, fingers ready to snap.

He was going to port away. "Don't you dare, you son of a bitch." I jolted forward.

He snapped his fingers, drying me off, clothing me, and… disappearing.

Growling, I circled the room as if he were still here. "You fucking coward," I screamed into the void, panting and on the verge of sobbing.

I dropped to the floor in a slump, curling my knees against my chest, letting the tears roll down my cheeks. Levin approached with his ears drooping, tail between his legs.

Coaxing him over, I wrapped my arms around him and stroked his soft white fur. "It's okay, boy. How do you deal with him every day, hm?" I smirked. "That part's obvious I suppose. Non-verbal communication is the key to your relationship with him, huh?"

Whereas with us? Talking was the *only* solution.

And like that, it was crystal clear to me. I couldn't do this. Who in their right mind would agree to this? The possibility of leading a lonely, loveless marriage was too great to risk—right? But he kept repeating it was different for us. All I want him to do is tell me why.

Why?

Having no idea when or if Zeus would come back, I had to head to work, but couldn't in good conscience leave Levin in the apartment without food. After rummaging through the kitchen cabinets and drawers, I couldn't find any dog food nor even any real food in the fridge. What was I expecting? He was

Zeus. He could create anything his heart or canine desired in a blink of an eye.

I ran to the convenience store down the street, bought some kibble, and gave Levin a heaping bowl of it. My hand was on the door knob, ready to leave, when I realized—the door would be unlocked. Anyone could waltz in and rob him blind, or worse yet...steal Levin. Frowning and against every cardinal rule I imposed on myself, I moved into Zane's bedroom to search for a spare key.

Hovering my hand over the first drawer in his armoire, I held my breath. Would it be so much to ask I'd only find socks, boxers, and condoms? Maybe a bottle of lube or two? Hell, I'd even be okay with butt plugs, but what exactly did the King of the Gods store in his drawers?

Biting the bullet, I yanked the drawer open.

Nothing.

Not even a lining of any kind, just bare wood with nothing inside it.

The rest of the drawers were the same. And so was the nightstand.

The entrance to his walk-in closet stared back at me like a luring web of darkness. Gulping, I flipped the light switch, revealing immaculately organized rows of suits, shoes, watches, and cufflinks. I traced my fingers over the suit jackets, sighing at the feel of the fabric against my skin. Designer brands always had the softest materials but I could never afford them, having to settle for the scratchy imitation varieties.

Licking my lips, I reached to the shelf above the clothes, feeling around for a key. My fingers brushed something rounded and rough, and I grabbed it. It was a large black rock with letters carved on the back. The symbols resembled the letters a, p, n, and c. There was only one god whose name started with an A and had four letters I could recall.

"Ares," I whispered, running my finger over the haphazard carving that resembled a child's handiwork.

So much more to Zeus than he let on. If he'd just talk to me, truly talk to me, I wouldn't feel so hesitant about taking the plunge. I wouldn't. Smiling, I put the rock back and continued to feel around until a cool piece of metal brushed my skin. Bingo.

With key in hand, I turned off the light, gave Levin a quick kiss to his head, and whisked out the door to distract myself with piles of paperwork.

I'd been sifting through case files for the Daniels case when a light knock sounded at my office door.

"Come in," I said flatly, squinting at a storage facility invoice.

"Are you still not talking to me? Because I'm not sure how much longer I can take this torture," Olivia said, grinning at me from the crack of the door.

Sighing, I waved her in. "I'm sorry, Ollie."

"Uh-oh. You don't look like a woman who's been sufficiently screwed. What happened?" She shut the door behind her.

Oh, I'd been screwed, in far more ways than one.

"It was Zane. I slept with Zane and I thoroughly regret it."

Her jaw dropped and she sprinted to my desk. "There is no way in hell I believe you regret sleeping with the King of the Gods for one bloody second."

"You—" I narrowed my eyes at her, dropping the papers to

my desk. "You said you didn't believe me."

She snapped her hands to her hips. "I never said that. Can you blame me for needing some time to let it process? To do— research?"

"So, you believe he's Zeus and I'm a demigod?"

She folded her hands in her lap. "Yes. Read me if you must."

I searched her face, her body language, and a small smile managed to work its way over my lips. "No need."

"Now that that's out of the way, what's really going on, Keira?" She nudged my shoulder.

Who else would I talk to about this?

"He offered to marry me to keep me from being deported and damaging the career I've built here in New York." I couldn't look at her when I said it.

"I'm sorry, hold it, hold it, hold it." She moved around the desk and leaned into my face, pressing her hands on the armrests of my chair. "He offered to make you *Queen*?"

"Yes."

She blew out a breath, laughing. "Leave it to you to not only stew this long over an amazing offer but also look depressed about it."

"Ollie, it's not that simple. He's only doing it to save his own ass in the process. Hera left him. Their marriage never ended in love. It ended with them living separate sexual lives while staying married for politics' sake." I couldn't help the worry and fear displaying on my face as my forehead cinched and my throat bobbed.

Pouting, Olivia shook her head. "I see what's going on here. You're scared the same thing will happen to you."

"Yes, but—" I stood and dragged my hands through my hair. "It's not only that. This whole thing started out of a selfish act for him to save his own goddamned ass. A lot of the myths about him may have been warped and fabricated but his arrogance and self-centeredness? That's all there."

"I don't know. He may have spun it as selfish, but if you look at it from a different perspective it's an arrangement that benefits you both. You need a husband to stay here, he needs a Queen to keep his power and title." Olivia shrugged and leaned her hip on the desk. "He could've married anyone, Keir. Hell, he could've asked *me*. But he's asking to marry *you* because I'm going to guess one: he likes you and two…it's more than marriage, it's *helping* you."

Here I was, the powerful prosecutor who could solve some of the craziest cases, and I couldn't even navigate a relationship. But Olivia? She's always been so good at thinking outside the box.

"Wait. How do you know he needs a Queen to keep his power and title? He never even told me that." I stood in front of her, folding my arms.

"I told you. I researched. Gaea made a clause when he became King. There always has to be a Queen. If there's not, he has a certain timeframe to find another. If he doesn't…he loses part of his power *and* his crown." She leaned back on her palms, crossing her legs, and bouncing one foot. "Textbook fantasy irony, really."

My heart raced. How long did he have? The Greek gods without Zeus as their King? It seemed absurd.

"Ollie, what timeframe? How long does he have?" I grabbed

her shoulders.

"It didn't say. I looked. I couldn't find it. Why? Do you think it's soon?"

Numbly, I let my hands fall away, the rawness traveling to my toes. "It has to be. This morning he sounded so—urgent."

"Keira, sweetie." Olivia appeared at my side, grabbing my elbow to turn me toward her. "The fact you're concerned about this, tells you all you need to know. He's not just doing this for himself. Remember that."

And maybe he wasn't. But was it so much to want to hear *him* say that?

EIGHTEEN

ZEUS

SHE HAD ONE THING right. I was a son of a downright bitch. And not my mother—my father. Now there was a *real* dickwad. We gods aren't unlike mortals—spending the better part of our lives finding ourselves. How much of our parents will reflect in us? Can we stop it? Do we want to? About the only thing I ever wanted that Kronos possessed was his sheer fucking determination. Too bad I'd inherited more than that.

Groaning, I beat my head against the stone behind me, swigging down my third bottle of ambrosia wine. Like an absolute pussy, I'd ported away in the middle of Keira's argument. Disappeared to the one place I knew I could go to be alone and—call a meeting of The Brothers. And instead of telling them precisely where I was, I took the opportunity to get piss-assed drunk while waiting for them.

I couldn't remember the last time I'd drunk this much. It dulled your senses—made you make extraordinary decisions or horribly bad ones, hardly ever in between. The job came first. It always had.

"Tartarus. You look like shit," Hades said, appearing in front of me in a swirl of black fog. His glowing white eyes radiated from the darkness, and he wiped a hand through his fiery crown, making it fizzle away.

I sat on the ground, not caring that the moist cold from the cave soaked through the ass of my pants. Holding the bottle up to him, I belched. "And I *feel* like shit. How ironic."

"How many of those have you had, brother?" Hades swiped some of his long white hair over one pointed ear.

Loosening my tie, I shrugged as I eyed the half-empty bottle. "As reigning sovereign, I pull rank *not* to answer that question."

"Of course, you do." Hades all but rolled his eyes and turned his gaze to the hanging sconces harboring blue flames.

"What the shit?" Poseidon's voice boomed as he appeared in a flash of sea spray. "I thought you called us because the Titans escaped or something, but I get here to find you wallowing in a corner?"

Groaning, I pressed my skull to the cave wall again and sipped more wine, not bothering to greet the sea god.

"What's going on, Zeus? We have better things to do than to stand here and watch you look miserable." Hades folded his arms as both of my brothers loomed over me, their expressions unenthused, borderline agitated.

Closing my eyes, I pressed the bottle against my forehead with a deep sigh. In all the years I'd been my brothers' king—it took a half-mortal woman for it to come to this. "I need—"

A razor tore at my throat, and I gripped the bottle tighter. "—your…help."

"What the fuck?" Poseidon blurted.

I flew my eyes open to see them both eyeing each other sidelong with raised brows. "You really don't need to make this into something more than it is."

"Like Tartarus we don't." Poseidon smirked as he leaned against a stone pillar. "Not once have we gotten to be actual big brothers to you since you took the crown. Not that you ever even wanted us to be."

Nausea coiled in my stomach. I wasn't sure what was worse—trying to sort out feelings with Keira or getting these asshats to help me with it.

"And say we find it in our good hearts to help you despite your years of mistreatment. What exactly is the problem?" Hades's brow bobbed, and his black robes shifted as he folded his arms.

"Mistreatment?" I glared at my brother before rising to my feet, the bottle still in hand. "Where do you get off saying I mistreated you? Do you have any idea what I go through on a daily basis? The decisions that fall on my shoulders and mine alone?" Scoffing, I took a sip, standing so close to the Underworld King, our toes touched.

"How could we? All we have to go from are your actions. You never *talk* about anything." Hades's eyes flashed brighter.

My lightning power coursed over my hands as I subdued a snarl, making Hades's gaze pull into a glare. Forcing it back, I pointed at him with the same hand that held the bottle. "I gave you this kingdom knowing out of all three of us, *you* had the strongest mind for it. Did you know that, *bro*?"

Hades stood firm. "How generous of you."

"Yes, you can't leave on a fucking whim, but you take the job to heart. It would've crumbled within days if either of us would've taken the helm." Nudging my head at Poseidon, I swayed on my heel, gulping more wine and enjoying the liberating feeling of not giving a shit.

"Hey, speak for yourself," Poseidon grumbled.

"Oh, can it, Flipper. You know as well as I do. Are you telling me you could imagine yourself away from the seas except for two weeks out of the year?" I stuck my chest out, challenging him.

He slow-blinked. "I hate you."

"There's the family spirit we've been missing." I threw my hands out at my sides, sending lightning crackling. "Your sacrifice never went unnoticed, Hades. I discreetly did all I could to make you happy. You wanted Persephone?" I snapped my fingers. "I made it happen. She left you, and you were prepared to spend eternity alone. But that's not *you*, brother." I poked him in the chest before lightly beating my fist against it. "You asked for opportunities to surface with your new Queen? To take breaks? I gave you that too. Something I don't even take for *myself*."

His eyes panned to my hand before returning to my face, curiosity, and astonishment flooding his expression.

"I didn't force Stephanie into anything. I disguised what I did as meddling but what you both need to realize—" I caught Poseidon's gaze as I held up a single finger and looked between the two of them. "—none of them can see me as soft. Do you understand?"

Hades clenched his jaw. "I—appreciate you saying all of this, brother."

Nodding, I turned my attention to Poseidon. "And you, Fishsticks—" I rubbed my chin, thinking, contemplating. "—nah. You're still a prick."

Poseidon chuckled and punched me in the shoulder. "Love you too, Bolt."

"What? You fight with a giant fork. It's hard to take you seriously at times." I bit back a smile and hid my mouth with the bottle.

"Spar with me some day and I'll show you what that giant fork can do, little bro." Poseidon shook his head with a smirk.

"You're on." Sighing, I let the bottle fall limp in my hand. "Considering word travels so swiftly through Olympus, I'm sure you both know of Hera's departure?" I finished the bottle of wine before chucking it over my shoulder, making it disappear before shattering to the ground.

"Wait. Have you not elected a new Queen yet?" Poseidon's eyes widened as he took a step forward, the three of us now standing in a triangle.

Shock morphed over Hades's features, his lips parting. "Brother, the expiration is—"

"Tomorrow. I know." I held my head low, rubbing furiously at my temples.

Poseidon gripped my shoulder. "You've fallen for someone, haven't you?"

Was that what it was? Had I somehow fallen for a woman I'd only known for a matter of weeks?

"Shit." Poseidon laughed before slapping me on the back. "Another thousand years could've passed, and I still would've never thought I'd see the day."

Exhaustion pulled at my brain like melting caramel. "Not helping."

"Cutting it kind of close, aren't you? Why not select any mortal? Why not—" Hades started, but I cut him off with a flick of my hand, silencing him.

"We're fated." Unable to meet their gazes at first, I kept mine focused on the ground.

"Olympus," Poseidon breathed out.

"It has to be her. And even if I could find some way to coerce her beyond her own thinking, I wouldn't." I lifted my eyes to my brothers. "Because I *want* her to want this. *Want* her to want me. All of it."

Poseidon gripped Hades's shoulders, and they both stared at me as if I were a younger version of myself and just told them I'd lost my virginity. Jostling my shoulders, I waited for one of them to respond. Anything would do. Even laughing in my godsdamned face would've been better than this torturous silence.

"There's something else." I cracked my knuckles. "She's a demigod."

A single brow rose on Poseidon's face.

"Who's the god?" Hades asked.

"The goddess is Oizys." I cut my gaze to the god of the Underworld.

"Oizys? I barely even see her. When would she have had time to—"

I cut him off. "It was before she secluded herself to the Underworld. Is she accessible? I'd imagine Keira might wish to meet her at some point."

Hades rubbed his chin. "I couldn't say. She hardly has connections with people—deity or otherwise—except those souls she tortures in Tartarus."

"What a lovely woman." I quirked a brow.

Hades smirked. "Who are you telling?"

Pinching my lips, I let my gaze drop to my feet with a sigh.

"You wish to know how to win her favor," Hades whispered.

Rubbing the back of my neck, I let out a deep sigh. "I suppose that's what I'm asking, yes."

"And you're willing to potentially lose your crown if she doesn't decide in time?" Hades canted his head to the side while Poseidon shook his shoulders with a wide shit-eating grin.

It didn't register in me until Hades said the words aloud. What had this woman done to me? Was she an enchantress?

"Yes," I pushed out, my voice gravelly.

"This is serious," Hades mumbled before swirling his arm, making us all appear in his fire-lit Gothic-themed living room.

I sat alone in a black lounge chair and instantly slumped in it, resting my head on my hand as my brothers loomed over me like investigators ready to interrogate.

"Why do you like this woman?" Hades asked, clasping his hands behind his back.

I'd never had a mortal headache, but somehow, I felt this conversation was bound to give me one. "What do you mean why? She…intrigues me."

Fucking Tartarus. The same damn answer I'd given her, and

it went *so* well the first time.

Poseidon made an obnoxious buzzer sound. "Wrong. Clearly, she intrigues you if you're into her; you need to answer the true 'why.'"

Sighing, I leaned forward, pressing my steepled fingers to my lips. "I don't know. She—" I gripped my hair, ruffling it before falling against the back of the seat with a snarl. "She's a damn good lawyer. Better than me if you take the fact she's doing it with a half-godly brain. She's stubborn. Quick-witted. Bold. Works herself to the bone." I paused as flashes of her mouth around my cock as she held my hands captive in my own damn tie coursed through my brain. "And fucking hot as Olympus forges."

"Have you told her any of this? Any at all?" Hades raised a brow.

Grumbling, I folded my arms. "Whatever happened to actions speak louder than words?"

"For shit's sake, Z. You think a woman doesn't want to *hear* things every once in a while?" Poseidon interlaced his fingers behind his head, shaking it.

Tension built in my shoulders. "Fine. I'll craft a speech. What else do I need to do?"

"You said she's a lawyer. Are you both working on the same case?" Hades paced in front of me, rubbing his chin.

"Opposing counsel."

Poseidon snatched a silver unlit candlestick holder from the mantle and tossed it in his palms. "Is your client guilty?"

"As sin." I ground my molars, knowing full well exactly where they were going with this.

"You say she's good. I assume she knows who and what you are now. Can't imagine she'd take it too lightly if you still used your powers of persuasion to work the trial in your favor." Hades took the candlestick from Poseidon and placed it back on the mantel.

I gripped the armrests. "Yes, but—"

"She wins the case fair and square, brother," Hades interrupted.

Growling, I replied, "Fine. What else?"

"It's going to take more than a speech. You need what's called a 'grand gesture,'" Poseidon muttered, scratching the full beard on his chin.

I furiously rubbed my face. "And just what the shit would that be?"

"That has to come entirely from you. Sweep her off her feet. And we don't mean into bed. You're a natural seducer—a charmer. Use it for something else besides sex for once. You might surprise yourself." Hades opened his palm toward the fireplace, making the flames roar.

A grand gesture. Her birthday. New York City. Huh.

"You obviously had a blowup to drive you to come down here of all places. To seek our help. What happened, Z?" Poseidon dragged a hand through his long hair, genuine concern for my well-being playing in his gaze.

It made my neck stiffen.

"She thinks she'll be another Hera. That the passion will fizzle, and we'll end up married but not together as she and I had. She also said I was treating the whole arrangement like a business transaction." I beat my knuckles against my knee, recalling the fury coiling from her—but most of all...the hurt.

"And what did you say to that?" Hades winced.

"The truth. It *is* a business transaction. Offers and reasons for both parties to form an alliance. What the fuck else was I supposed to say?" Pushing to my feet, I raked a hand through my hair and moved to the fire.

Poseidon groaned and patted my shoulders from behind before leaning on one, staring at the fire with me. "Not that, bro. Not that."

"I think…" Hades started as he moved beside us, all three of us gazing at the flickering flames like they were the sparks of life itself. "You need to realize what you want before you can recognize what *she* wants. So, Zeus, King of the Gods, our brother, what do *you* want?"

Extending my hand, I struck lightning within the fire, making a mesmerizing fire-lit show within the hearth. "A partner. A friend. Someone who's going to understand the job at times must come first. We'd fuck like damn rabbits, and maybe, just maybe, she'd occasionally let me fall asleep using her tits as a pillow while she scratches my scalp with her nails."

"Perhaps not put quite as elegantly, but something tells me, brother—" Hades squeezed my shoulder. "She seeks the same things."

Poseidon stood on one side of me, Hades on the other, and for the first time since I dragged them out of our father's stomach, I felt truly part of a brotherhood again.

"I know what I need to do," I muttered, closing my hand, dousing the lightning with it.

"I feel like hugging you right now. You know that, right?" Poseidon nudged me.

"Please don't."

"Nope. It's happening, little bro. Hades, you too, come on." Poseidon pulled us both in for a hug.

Stiffly, Hades and I landed reluctant pats on Poseidon's back.

"The first group hug in almost a thousand years. Unreal. I definitely need to meet this chick soon." Poseidon pulled away with a wide grin.

I adjusted my jacket, redoing the buttons, tightening my tie, and fixing my ruffled hair. "With any luck, it'll happen sooner rather than later. But if not—there's someone I need to talk to."

Bowing my head to my king brothers, I took a step back. "Brothers."

"Good luck, shithead," Poseidon scoffed before I disappeared.

My son Ares seemed to spend more time in his gym than anywhere else. Undoubtedly, the sparring which inevitably led to other activities with his warrior goddess played a huge part. I waited in a darkened corner near the lockers, only emerging from the shadows when he neared.

"Ares." I lifted my chin, fully prepared for a verbal slapping.

Ares threw his gloves to the floor, his bare chest heaving as he walked up to me. "What do you want, maláka?"

"Honestly, I thought you'd calmed down since bonding with Harmony. No?"

Harmony approached us with her arms folded, clad in only a sports bra and skin-tight shorts. It took everything in my power not to scan her body. "He has calmed down. Funny how any mention of you or your presence gets him riled up."

Cracking my neck, I shot my gaze to Harmony's. "You're a good woman, Harmony. An amazing war goddess. But I need a moment alone with my son. I can assure you it won't involve punches and clashes of lightning."

Harm stole a glance with her war god, who gave her a curt nod before slicing a glare aimed at me. "It better not."

Such fire that one. Huh.

"What is this all about, old man? You need me to do your bidding? Came to blow smoke up my ass again?" Ares clenched his fists at his sides.

"I always thought kicking you from Olympus was the best thing for you. The best way for you to channel your anger and use it in other ways." I jingled the keys in my pocket, shocked he hadn't interrupted me already or told me to go to Tartarus. "I still believe it to be partially true but I wasn't entirely honest with you about the *largest* reason I did it."

"This ought to be good." Ares crossed his arms after freeing his hair from the rubber band holding it in a bun.

"I'd like to think I inherited nothing from my father, but it simply wouldn't be true. Much like he cowardly tried to destroy his children for fear of them overtaking his throne...I did the same thing." Sneering at the ground, I clenched my jaw.

"What are you trying to say?"

Forcing myself to meet his gaze, I took a quick breath. "I kicked you from Olympus because you had and still have the power to overthrow me. But I realized recently, you would've never done it—out of respect."

Ares's nose twitched, and he scratched it with a thumb. "You're right. I wouldn't have. Not to mention I want nothing to do with fucking Olympus."

"You've become a better god than I could've ever predicted, Ares." I smirked, playing with the hair below my lip. "And Olympus is precisely what I've come to talk to you about."

"You don't sound like yourself. What the hell is going on?"

"This first bit should amuse you. Your mother left me."

Ares half-smiled, snorted and then frowned. "Wait, what? How's that possible?"

"It's not as if I held her captive, Ares. She's always had the choice, and she made it. Which has left Olympus without a Queen and with a clause to be upheld…by tomorrow." I'd never been nervous about one godsdamned thing in my divine existence but this—fuck.

"So you find another Queen. What does this have to do with me?" Ares poked himself in the chest, the armor full sleeve tattoo tightening.

"As we continue to have more things in common than I'm sure you'd like to admit, I also have what you share with Harmony." Scratching the back of my neck, I waited for my words to sink into my son's thick head.

"You—have a fated bond with someone?"

"Her name is Keira. I believe you, of all people, will understand when I say, it can't be anyone but her. If I settled for someone else, it'd be like removing two of my limbs and giving them to Keira to keep for all of eternity." My lightning crackled in my eyes, my palms. The thought alone made me want to destroy mountains.

Ares took a step closer. "I *do* understand."

"I'm going to try everything in my power to win her over, but son, if this goes south—" Taking a deep breath, I closed the distance between us and squeezed his shoulder. "Olympus is yours."

He shook his head and batted my arm away. "No. Why would she refuse you?"

The irony of that statement. Laughing, I tilted my head to the side. "Moments ago, you were ready to tear my head off with your teeth as your only blade. And now you compliment me by saying there's no way she wouldn't want me?"

"Maláka, no. I figured you'd have used your powers or—"

"They don't work on her, son. And even if they did, she's different. Would take all of the fun away." A weak smile pulled at my lips. "I need you to agree to this. I don't trust anyone else with the reins. No one. Else."

Ares growled and turned away, dragging a hand over his beard and shaking his head. Returning to stand in front of me, he held out his hand. "Alright. But you better have a hell of a plan, old man. Because—" He paused, his teeth grinding together. "I can't see anyone else ruling Olympus besides you."

If that were the one good thing my son ever said to me for the rest of eternity, I'd store it in a fucking mason jar with the date labeled on it.

"I'm going to deploy everything in my godly arsenal." We locked forearms, my white lightning sparking against his red sparks, sealing the deal. "I hope we can spend more time together."

Ares sniffed once, nodding as he backpedaled. "Yeah. We'll

uh—we'll see."

Nodding, I stepped away, making myself reappear outside the courthouse, staring up at the office light I knew belonged to Keira.

Time to perform the seduction of a lifetime.

NINETEEN

KEIRA

SO. FUCKING. TIRED. DESPITE several cups of coffee and a Red Bull, sleep still pulled at my brain, and I rested my forehead on my arm in my office. A five-minute power nap wouldn't hurt anyone.

Ice clanking against a glass sounded in my ear.

"Keira," Zeus whispered, resting the glass on my desk near my head.

Groggily, I lifted my head to see the insanely gorgeous King of the Gods looming over me with a tumbler of scotch in hand that matched the one resting next to me.

"A peace offering." He lifted the glass in a cheers gesture and nudged his chin at mine.

Eyeing the alcohol, I shifted my gaze to his face, glaring at him. "I fed and took care of your dog, by the way."

He rubbed the back of his neck as he stared at his shoes. "Yeah. I uh—I appreciate that."

Embarrassed. Regretful.

With a sigh, I lifted the glass, and we clanked them together. I remained sitting, sipping on my scotch and waiting to see what wondrous words he came up with after how swimmingly our last encounter went.

"I'm a dick. I'm an asshole. I'm a bastard. Whatever name you want to call me, I'm all of them." He crouched in front of me, resting one forearm on the top of my thigh, his blue eyes pulling me to him. "I didn't expect any of this to happen. Not Hera leaving. Not running into you. And especially not… having my entire world turned fucking upside down—by you."

Sincerity. Hope. Admiration.

My grip tightened on the glass as I pushed down the burning sensation in my sinuses.

"I've spent my entire life living a certain way, having that life ruled by Olympus, contrary to what most think is the other way around. You catapulting into that life made me realize it's possible to have both Olympus and—" He squeezed my knee. "—more."

"Is this an apology?" I squinted at him, biting back a grin.

He smirked. "Definitely not." A hint of a smile played at the corner of his lips before he patted my leg and stood. "Come with me." He held out his hand, the light from my desk lamp glinting from his silver pinky ring.

"I don't know, Zeus."

His hand lowered. "That was the first time you called me Zeus without us fucking each other or your life being threatened."

Hope. Flutters. *Actual* flutters.

As I stood, my chest tightened. I hadn't even realized I'd

said it. "I—"

Shaking his head, he brushed his thumb over my lips to silence me, his palm pressing against my cheek. "You don't need to rationalize it. Just come with me. A little birdie told me it was your birthday. You shouldn't be spending it in your office."

"I've spent every birthday since living in New York in my office." I shrugged, nuzzling against his hand still stroking my face.

"That doesn't surprise me and all the more reason you should come with me." He stepped back and tugged my hand. "Now."

Smiling, I grabbed my coat. "So bossy."

"You love it." He helped me with my coat, even going so far as to do up the buttons.

I did love it. Damn it all to hell. I loved it all.

Canting my head, I saw a new side to him—as if he'd opened a hidden passage to let me in, one he hadn't even opened to himself in a long time.

He wrapped an arm around my waist and, with the blinds closed in my office, ported us to an alley near Rockefeller Center. We were blocks away from where I knew the gigantic tree and ice-skating rink were, but even from this distance, the emotions pouring from the crowds of tourists punched at my mind.

"Keira? What's wrong?" He cupped my elbows, keeping me upright.

I hadn't even told him yet. Here I was expecting every bit of truth from him, and I'd left out that tiny detail?

"I can't handle the city right now. I just can't." I shoved my face against his shoulder, trying to drown out the overwhelming feelings of joy and whimsy—emotions that individually caused euphoria but combined in droves made for hysteria.

"Keira." He pushed me back, tilting my head up to look at him. "Talk to me."

"I'm—" Squeezing his biceps through his jacket, I gulped. "I'm an empath. I guess I got it from my mother because it's—intense. So intense all the time when I'm around a lot of people. I can sense emotions, fleeting feelings, and can even tell when someone is lying."

What started as a light chuckle transformed into a glorious masculine laugh—deep and throaty.

I wanted to laugh, but tears threatened to push their way through. "Why in the hell are you laughing?"

"It just all makes so much sense now. Who better to be at my side than someone who can always see straight through my bullshit? For fuck's sake—the Fates are such conniving, intuitive pieces of work." He chuckled a little more and pulled me to him, hugging me, his nose grazing my hair.

"And now knowing you're a Greek god, it makes sense why emotions were so intense from you." I pressed my ear to his chest, listening to his divine heartbeat thrumming like a giant's steps.

"Try something with me," he whispered, slipping off his glove and shoving it in his pocket. He lifted one of my hands, and with a seductive curve of his lip, he removed my glove finger-by-finger.

"What are you doing?"

"I have a theory because of our formed bond." He took my

hand, our skin touching.

I closed my eyes, the copious amounts of emotions around me dissipating with each passing second. Joy melted into my joy—his joy. Wonder morphed into my own. Hope settled into Zeus's hope alone.

His lips pressed to my ear, the warmth from his breath making heat pool in my stomach. "Did it work?"

"Yes," I breathed out.

"Good." He tugged my hand, causing my eyes to fly open. "We have ice skating to do."

"Ice skating? Zeus, I've never skated in my life." I laughed, scanning the busy sidewalks filled with people dressed in wintry attire with their arms loaded with shopping bags. Familiar smells of roasted nuts, baked goods, and hot dogs pervaded the air.

"I'll just get to laugh at you falling on your ass every other minute then, huh?" His face beamed at me as he flashed a grin.

I pointed at him. "You will do no such thing."

He pretended to bite my finger. "No promises. Besides, you might drag me down with you considering I can't let go." He lifted our joined hands—the only thing keeping the emotions from hundreds of people infiltrating my brain.

And he wouldn't let go. Not for anything. I knew it with every breath escaping my lungs. It made my heart swell.

Lit angel sculptures bordered the ice rink with dozens of people skating in circles—some hugged the wall, others skated like pros, and some shuffled rather than gliding. But what stood out most of all was the majestic sight of the glittering tree at the heart of Rockefeller Center, piercing the sky like a towering Titan.

My eyes blurred with tears staring up at it, the chill in the air making my cheeks numb, but I only gripped Zeus's hand tighter.

"All the time I've been here, and I've never seen this. I've been so caught up with my life and work I never stop to breathe—to enjoy the little things." I sniffled, fighting back the tears that threatened.

His thumb kneaded between my knuckles. "If anyone can relate to you, it is me on the grandest of scales, Keira."

"My mother. Is she alive?" I continued to stare up at the tree, trying to keep my voice steady when I asked.

He circled my palm with his thumb. "Yes."

"Do you—" I turned my gaze to him, taking a deep inhale before my next question. "Do you know where she is?"

"Yes." His face softened.

"Do you think she'd want to see me?" I tightened my grip on his hand, terrified of the response.

"If you ever want to meet her, all you need to do is speak with Hades."

My shoulders tensed. "She's in the Underworld?"

"Tartarus."

An overwhelming sadness tugged at my brain. "By her choice?"

"I think, my dear, that's something you'd need to ask her." He offered a small smile as he tugged my hand.

Pursing my lips, I turned my attention back to the tree. "Tell me something. If we do this—tell me it'd be different. The job will have to come first at times, but the times that it doesn't—we make it for *us*. About us."

He pulled me tight against him, yanking off his other glove to cup my face in his hands. "Those words are the biggest part of the reason no one else can be at my side. I physically couldn't stand it."

He only had so long to get this done. What the hell was he talking about?

"What?" It came out like a squeak.

"You take as long as you need. Because I'm not asking anyone else." His jaw tightened as he stared down at me, the sparkling lights hanging from street lamps framing him, paling in comparison to his lightning.

Was he willing to let the time lapse? To give up the crown? It was so…selfless.

"And to answer your question, you'd have to be willing to share my time with the universe, but when duty doesn't call—" He dipped his lips to mine, kissing me, his tongue skirting the tip of mine before pulling away. "—I'm all yours."

All *mine*. Heart. Pulverized.

I smiled against his lips, and brushed my nose against his to warm it. "Care to watch me look like a penguin in a pair of ice skates?"

"Nothing would give me greater pleasure." He chuckled, and after donning our skates, we circled the ice over a dozen times, hand in hand.

Despite his jabs, he never let me fall and only laughed when I let out an infectious bout of giggles from slipping. He used every opportunity and excuse to touch my ass and cop a feel at my boobs through my jacket, grinning like a jackal each time. We also stole kisses too many times for me to count—the faint sound of holiday music fluttering in the background from outdoor speakers.

We'd retreated to a corner, and he stood behind me with his arms wrapped around me, our bare hands still touching. His beard tickled my cheek as he kissed it. "Have you ever seen thundersnow?"

"What the hell is that?"

He chuckled. "I'm going to take that as a no. It's a rare occurrence, but the people of New York City should thank you that it's your birthday because today—they're going to witness it."

His grip tightened on my arms, and with a cue only a god could give, snowflakes fell on my lashes. Grey clouds filled the sky as blankets of white fell from above like static, making the view of the New York skyline with the giant tree in the forefront look like something from a Norman Rockwell painting. Static flowed from him behind me, followed by a subtle electric current.

A crisp, clean, and wondrous bolt of lightning flashed across the sky, its radiance bouncing off the white snow, illuminating a several block radius of the city in shimmering vibrance. The crowds around us gasped, yelped, and wooed at the rare show in the sky—cheers roaring once the boom of thunder followed.

"That's remarkable," I whispered, sticking my tongue out to catch flakes on it.

"Hey now, I need that tongue. Don't get it electrocuted." He bumped his hips at my back, and grinned against my ear.

"This is the best birthday I've had in a very, very long time."

He continued the thundersnow show as people whipped out their cell phones to record the strange occurrence, children laughing and weather nerds shouting about how rare it was.

"Good, because you realize how off-theme a Hallmark moment like this is for me, right?"

I nuzzled against him. "Yes. And it delights me to know you're screaming inside but still doing this all for me."

"Mmhm." He nibbled the side of my face.

"Was I destined to lose the Daniels case the moment you signed on?"

He grabbed my shoulders and turned me to face him. "What?"

"You're not human. You can spin a case in your favor, I'd imagine?" I frowned.

His eyes shut, and he shook his head before flashing his gaze at me. "You said you can tell when I'm lying, correct?"

I nodded.

"You are the best damn lawyer I've ever seen, Keira Bazin. Even with only half a godly brain, you surpass any power I'd have in that courtroom." He massaged my shoulders before cupping my chin with a gooey smile.

Sincerity. Admiration. Lust.

I grinned at him and took both his hands in mine. "I asked you this once before, and I'm going to ask you again. But I want a real answer this time. Newsflash: Saying I'm hot is not part of the answer."

He lifted a finger. "Let the record show, however, that you *are*."

"Fine. Thank you." I rolled my eyes with a smile before

meeting his gaze. "Why me, Zeus?"

He licked his lips, the static still sizzling over my skin as he continued to produce lightning in the clouds. "You challenge me. Ground me. Drive me fucking crazy—"

I playfully nudged him in the stomach.

He grunted with a grin. "*And* I love it. But mostly because— you understand me. See me. Really see me. I can be myself around you."

Sincerity. Hope. Pure happiness.

"And that, counselor, was a solid argument." Smiling, I raised as high as I could on skates and slid my arms around his neck. "Let's do this."

He squinted at me, tensing beneath my touch. "To clarify, by 'this,' you do mean getting hitched, right?"

"Yes."

His gaze turned predatory. "Fuck, Keira." He kissed me— deeply, longingly, his arms wrapping around me and lifting me from the ice.

The lightning show intensified in the sky, crackling, hissing, striking, and booming. All surrounding lights went out, coating the entirety of Rockefeller Center in darkness. He pressed his forehead to mine, and I couldn't see my hand in front of my face, it was so dark.

"What the hell are you doing?" I whispered.

His eyes glowed with lightning. "I need to show you something before we do this and it can't be here." He grinned as he ported us away from the middle of downtown.

We reappeared in his penthouse, minus the ice skates, and he snapped his fingers.

"Please tell me that snap was returning those beloved lights to full glory, right?"

He kissed my temple. "Yes, it was."

Pulling away from him, I greeted Levin as he trotted over to me with his tongue out. "So what could you possibly need to show me? I've seen every square inch of you." I smiled mischievously over my shoulder at him as I scratched Levin's head.

"Not quite." He played with his jacket sleeve. "If you were full mortal, I wouldn't be able to show my true form to you. Mortals—well, sort of spontaneously combust if they were to lay eyes on my divine form."

My throat tightened, and I slowly rose. "Spontaneously combust? Like—" I made an explosion gesture with widened eyes.

"Yes." Zeus's cheek twitched.

"And you're positive my demigod self is safe from this? That'd be quite a damper on the entire situation, don't you think?" I let out a high-pitched laugh.

"You'll be fine. Are you ready?"

I chewed on my lip, shook out my hands, and stood upright before vigorously nodding.

A massive bolt of lightning struck over him from an invisible pocket above him, the brightness almost blinding me, making me wince. I held a hand above my eyes like one would do to shield from the sun. When my vision acclimated to the light, my lips parted.

It was still him, the same face, the same eyes, but—older. No, not older. Distinguished. Ancient. His dark hair turned silver and longer, reaching to his collarbone. His beard matched in color and hung to just above his chest. He was bare-chested and positively majestic, his muscles far more significant than in his mortal form and cut so pristinely like they were carved from marble. A gold metal crown circled his head, the middle rising to a sharpened point. Golden shin guards covered his knees and legs, his feet in sandals. On one knee bore an eagle's head, the other a crown. His muscular, tanned thighs were exposed from beneath the blue tunic circling his waist, golden chains and adornments hanging from his hips.

With my hands cupped over my mouth, I moved closer. He stood still and tall, gripping a sunburst shield in one hand, the pulsing thunderbolt spear in the other. Once I stood toe-to-toe with him, I gazed up at the familiar eyes and placed a single finger on his cheek, followed by my whole hand. Golden beads with carved ancient Greek lettering were woven into his beard and parts of his wavy hair.

"Hey," he said with a grin, the lightning flashing in his eyes more vibrant than when he was in his mortal guise.

I let my eyes roam over his face up close, and my hands, of their own volition, dragged over the bulging hard muscles that made up his chest, his arms, abdominal muscles over abdominal muscles I didn't even know existed.

Dipping my fingers into the front part of his tunic, I slid closer. "Damn. I never knew I could be so attracted to a silver fox."

He groaned. "Like my godly form, do you? You can fuck this form whenever you please. Except if we're in mortal public. That could—kill the mood rather quickly."

I sputter-laughed, slapping a hand over my mouth as soon

as it happened. He smiled at me, and I kissed him—hard.

After kissing me back for far less time than I'd have liked, he gently coaxed me back. "As much as I love where your head's at right now. We really do need to get this show on the road." His gaze lifted to the clock hanging on the wall behind me. "I only have a matter of hours, and we still have someone we need to talk to about this."

"Hours?" I swatted him hard in the chest. "You're cutting it *that* close? Why didn't you tell me?"

"I needed to know that you truly wanted this. No outside interference. I'm a master meddler, Keira." He twirled the thunderbolt in his palm. "I figured you'd appreciate knowing it came down to you and *only* you as well."

This was the man I sensed bubbling under the surface from the day I met him but couldn't pinpoint what it was. This. Right. Here.

"Who do we need to talk to? Hera?"

"No. I've already spoken to her. Trust me, she's fine."

I bit the inside of my cheek to keep from smiling. "You checked in on her?"

"Yeah. I had to make sure she wasn't going to try and come back around and bite me in the ass."

There was no stopping the grin now. "Uh-huh. I'm sure that's all it was. You know, King of the Gods, you can be rather sweet when you want to be."

He scratched the back of his neck with a pointed part of his sunburst shield. "In the right company, maybe. But don't tell anyone."

After making the gesture of zipping my mouth shut, I asked,

"Then who do we have to see?"

Zeus sighed, his gaze lifting to the ceiling with a disgruntled groan. "My godsdamned grandmother—Gaea."

TWENTY

ZEUS

AFTER TRANSFORMING MYSELF BACK to my mortal form, because dear old grandma didn't need yet another reason to be a wise-ass commenting on the godly form I hardly donned anymore, I ported Keira and me to the celestial gardens. A cottage surrounded by all forms of plant life, flowers, fountains, and lawn ornaments appeared in the distance—a steady smokestack puffing from the chimney. Keira gasped and walked toward the cozy-looking abode, but I hooked her by the elbow and pointed up.

What started as a cloud began to morph into overlapping green leaves, floating from the sky in sea waves—flowers bloomed, a deer trotted, sunbursts blazed. The earthy craziness spooled in front of us until finally, Gaea appeared in her human form—long white hair down to her ankles with vines and scattered flowers, and a dress made entirely of willow branches, moss, and far too sheer to my liking.

The woman always had to make a damn entrance.

"Hey, Yia-Yia." A wicked grin pulled at my lips, knowing full well she hated being called any form of grandmother.

Smirking, Gaea played with the petunia flower charm of her necklace. "You've changed so much and yet the smart ass remains."

"Not sure even I could make that stop," Keira said, smiling at me. "Or that I want it to."

Gaea propped her hands on her hips. "A fated bond for the ages, I'd say."

"What do you know? A third attempt at dethroning me—" I stepped forward, sinking my face into my dear primordial grandmother's. "—and you failed. Again."

Gaea patted my cheek and, with one finger, pushed me back. "Oh, grandson. Your mind is still so clouded. I accepted a very long time ago that you are the god most suited for this task. And you earned it. The marriage clause was put into place to ground you, to ensure you didn't become a ruler such as those before you. Also—to make you put your ass in gear when this opportunity presented itself to you."

What was this harpy going on about?

Scowling at her, I moved closer to Keira, making our arms brush.

"Judging from that look on your face, you need me to spell it out for you." A coy grin pulled at her lips as she steepled her long pale fingers.

Keira slipped her hand in mine, sending an electric pulse through my arm into my chest that did *not* come from my power.

"It has been far too long since our kind has driven into a new era. The moment has come for a change. As time changes through the ages, so must we. This is the dawning of a *new* age, and it starts with progression." Her hands fanned above her, projecting images of aligning planets floating above us. "I ensured all mortals were born and paths intertwined through this very cycle with their gods."

"There's been more than just us?" Keira's grip tightened on my hand.

"Oh, yes. And far more to come. But this past cycle has been vital." She slapped her hands together, making the images disappear, and cutting her rainbow-colored eyes to me.

I looked from left to right. "Are you waiting for me to ask you why? Get on with it."

Keira elbowed me in the ribs, causing a satisfying smile to appear on Gaea's face.

"You, Zeus, King of Kings, witnessed sons, brothers, a grandson, a wife—all find the happiness they'd long since given up on, and little by little, it chipped at the metal that's been weighing you down for far too long."

The lightning hissed in my palms, flashing in my eyes as I ground my teeth.

"As we must progress in this modern age, so must our king." Gaea leaned forward with a gleam in her eye. "And Keira was the final piece. Do you both know the purpose behind a fated bond?"

Keira vigorously shook her head.

"Oh, I'm sure you're going to tell us." I rolled my eyes and added, "Always one to ramble," in a mumble.

Gaea made a tree branch slap me in the face, enticing a growl from the pit of my stomach. I'd defeated the Giants this woman threw at me, *and* a fire-breathing dragon, but still could never predict her conniving little outbursts.

"A fated bond is meant as comfort in a union—a completion of one half to a whole. With both of you accepting it, I suspect you've already begun to experience its effects. And once you are married—it will be tenfold." She clasped her hands together with a brightened smile.

Keira leaned toward my ear. "What does that mean?"

"Only pay attention to half of what this woman says, trust me," I whispered back.

"When Zeus was a little boy growing up in Crete—"

Stepping forward, I opened my mouth to stop her from talking, and another branch slapped me in the face, sticking to me this time.

"—he used to pretend he was a baby goat. Made the noises, hopped around on all fours with sticks on either side of his head to serve as horns, but the best part? He even suckled from one of the real goat's teats." Gaea cut me a wicked grin.

Keira bit her lip, trying to subdue her smile and no doubt holding back a laugh.

Snarling, I sizzled the tree branch away from my mouth with one flash of lightning. "Uh-huh. We're kind of on a time crunch here, as you fully know, *Granny*. You have an eternity to embarrass me."

"For once, you're right." She snapped her fingers, appearing in front of us, and slipping her hands over our shoulders. "Keira Bazin, do you agree to marry Zeus, King of the Greek gods, and thereby becoming Queen and the goddess of healed emotion?"

Keira paused, a warm subtle smile edging over her lips before her gaze lifted to mine. "I do."

My heart boomed in my chest, the thunderous echo pounding in my ears.

"Do you Zeus, King of the Gods, ruler of the skies and wielder of lightning, accept Keira as your new Queen to rule at your side as an equal?"

Without a breath of hesitation, I answered, "I do."

Gaea's grip tightened on our shoulders, making Keira wince. A bright light burst from Keira's chest, blasting through her mouth and eyes before an explosion of golden shimmers trickled over us, and Keira disappeared.

Fury. Anger. Fear.

Turning circles, I whirled on my heel, pointing a finger in Gaea's face. "What the fuck did you do with her?"

Gaea placed one palm on my chest. "Your mother says hello, by the way."

My foster mother, Amalthea, was long gone, so there was only one other she could've been talking about.

The anger trickled away, and my face fell. "Rhea? But you—"

Unlike my brothers, I couldn't remember my birth Titan mother. She handed me off as soon as she gave birth to me to be raised without her, to save me from the fates of my brothers.

"She still lives but is one with Chaos now where she has a purpose."

A peculiar tightening pulled in my chest at the mention of my mother. The realization settling in that she'd been alive this entire time.

"In Chaos, is she able to see everything?" I cast my gaze downward, clenching my fists at my sides.

"Yes. Despite the little shit you've been, Zeus, she is still proud of you and bore witness to this union."

I lifted my eyes to meet Gaea's, and puffed my chest. "Where's Keira?"

"Where else would Zeus's Queen be for a royal—consummation?" Gaea raised a thin brow, eliciting a sly smile from me.

Gaea had a naughty side. And here I thought I'd always gotten it from dear 'ol dad.

"She waits for you, grandson." Gaea pushed my chest.

Nodding, I backpedaled away. Right before porting, I kicked over one of several garden gnomes bordering the cottage and could hear the faint whisper of the word "brat" as I disappeared.

The perfectly formed white clouds and skies of purple and orange welcomed me as I set foot on Olympus marble for the first time in a decade. It had little purpose now, with most of our duties being upheld elsewhere. Perhaps now with this "new age" Gaea spoke of, Olympus could have its uses again. Pillars lined the path leading to the thrones, spires of white and gold towering from the mountains in the distance.

One singular look at her—my new Queen and I transformed into my godly form. My body would accept no other form for the first time I'd be with her. The first time I'd *fuck* her as a goddess, my wife—my. Queen.

She sat on the throne next to mine with her legs crossed and exposed beneath a long white dress. A golden brooch held the strap of white fabric coiled around her neck right above her left breast, and a matching gold belt cinched at her waist. She brought an apple to her lips, her eyes glowing with an orange hue as she bit into it, watching me walk toward her. Golden armbands hugged each of her biceps, and ornately-designed sandals with crisscrossing leather ties traveled up to her knees. As she shifted her waves of blonde hair over one shoulder, my dick got hard.

"Mighty bold of you making your new Queen wait so long alone on her throne." She tossed the apple in her palm, fingernails tapping the gold armrests.

My greaves clanked as I took step after step, not tearing my eyes away from her for anything. "I couldn't agree more. You should allow me to make it up to you." I plastered a devious smile across my lips.

She grinned back, tossing the apple over her shoulder, making it disappear.

Producing ambrosia in my palm, I stood in front of her, outstretching my hand. "Eat this so we can consummate this marriage properly."

She dragged a finger over her lips, still smiling at me as she slowly opened her mouth.

Leaning over her, I slipped the ambrosia in, her tongue licking the length of my finger. My dick twitched, and I groaned. Once she swallowed it, immortality seeping into her bones from the ambrosia's power, she gasped. Her hands gripped the armrests, legs uncrossing and widening as the light and shimmer swirled around her, delivering my wife goddess in only a matter of seconds.

She'd closed her eyes, and once the transformation settled, they flew open, the glowing radiance intensified in her stare. She pushed from the throne, leaping into my arms, curling her own around my neck, kissing me with such force it made me stagger back. Her fingers tangled in my long hair, tugging it. I cupped her ass with both hands, the wide belt hanging over my hips grinding against her.

She pulled away from the kiss, my hair still wrapped in her grip. "I recall an arrogant god telling me he could at any moment port me to Olympus and fuck me on his throne."

"That guy sounds like an asshole." I licked and kissed her neck, tickling her collarbone with my beard.

"He's no asshole."

I lifted my godly gaze to hers.

"He's a dick." She grinned as she slid down my body. Once her sandaled feet touched the marble floor, her finger dipped into my tunic, making my cock throb for her as she pulled me to the thrones. "I want to hold him to his claim—but fuck him on *my* throne."

This. Godsdamned. Woman.

She pushed me to her throne, forcing me to sit on it, more strength behind her movements than her demigod self. Spreading my legs wide, I shifted the tunic to free my cock, stroking it as I watched her saunter over to me, pulling the dress up to her hips. The sight of her bare pussy had me growling, and I dug my fingers into the armrest as she straddled my lap. As I moved my hands to her ass, guiding her, she slapped them away.

"This is my show, god-king," she whispered, nipping at my ear.

Fuck. Me.

Moving her hands to my shoulders, she slowly began to lower herself. As the tight warmth passed over the tip, it sent a tingle down my shaft, straight to the fucking base of my spine, and I groaned. Once our hips met, she stilled, my cock pulsing inside her. She moaned and began to rock, grinding her clit against my stomach as she damn near milked me.

She was so tight and so fucking wet it had my spine stiffening. With a snarl, I let my head fall back, fighting everything in me not to touch her—to squeeze her tits, her ass. The bond pounded through my chest, settling over my brain like the static aftershock from thrown thunderbolts in a heated battle. Keira gasped and pressed her face against the side of my neck, breathing me in.

"Touch me," she whispered.

Seeing as this woman never had to command me to do *anything* twice, I took her face in one hand, our glowing eyes sparking at each other before I kissed her. My other hand grabbed her ass, pulling and pushing her on and off me, deepening her thrusts. Traveling my touch up her back, I yanked the top of the dress down, exposing one breast, and broke away from the kiss to suck on it, flicking my tongue over the nipple before biting it.

Pressing a hand to the back of my head, she rocked back and forth, whimpering and gasping. White lightning crackled in the sky, brought on by my powers going into overdrive from the bond—the connection—my fucking gorgeous Queen writhing on top of me. Her nails dug into the back of my head, her pussy clenching around me as she cried out, coming on me. A small streak of orange lightning blasted through the sky directly above us—silent with no thunder to accompany it.

That…didn't come from me.

The familiar pressure built at the base of my cock, and I grabbed her hips, taking over the thrusts, bucking against her as it built and built. The glorious torture churned until an uncontrollable roar burst from my lungs, and I came inside her, my hips locking. Waves passed over me until finally, I sunk into the throne, holding my new Queen in my arms and keeping her from falling backward with that glowing satiation in her eyes.

"I felt something I've never felt before." She combed my beard with her fingers.

I traced her exposed breast. "The bond?"

"That was far more intense, yes, but this was as if I had an electric pulse radiating from my chest and not settling *over* it like when you use your lightning on me." She caressed my chest.

"The summer lightning. That was you," I whispered.

I'll be damned. I'd given her some of my power through the bond and didn't even realize it.

She sat up straight, my cock still inside her hardening again as she tightened. "I have lightning powers? How?"

Shifting beneath her, I pulled her closer. "Transference, I'd guess. Suppose we should add Wielder of Silent Lightning to that ever-growing list of titles you have, hm? Though I believe *heat* lightning would be more appropriate considering how it happened." I grinned and traced her jawline with a single finger.

She smiled and kissed my lips, starting to rock on me again. "I never got to thank you for saving my career properly."

Moaning, I massaged the back of her neck. "Nor I, you."

We fucked each other senseless for hours amidst the silent halls of Olympus—the marbled floor, the thrones, the atrium, even on the damn mountain's edge. And when we were finally spent, we slept for even longer. And yes, she *did* let me use her tits as a pillow. With our royal consummation duties solidly upheld, tomorrow would lead to other concerns. Our alter-egos had to get married as well. I've heard the weather in Vegas this time of year is perfect for a quickie wedding.

TWENTY ONE

𖥔𖥔𖥔𖥔𖥔𖥔𖥔𖥔𖥔𖥔𖥔𖥔𖥔𖥔𖥔

KEIRA

THE FIRST MOMENTS TOGETHER with my new god-king husband were what could only be described as legendary. We transgressed from fucking to making love and fucking again in all forms and locations across the wonders of Mount Olympus. At one point, I asked him simply to *sit* there. To sit on his throne as the king, legs spread wide, spear in hand. He did as I asked and stared me down with a feral gaze as I danced in front of him, slowly removing my new Queenly attire with every other sway of my hips. He looked *glorious* on his golden throne. Powerful. Commanding. And he was all *mine*.

Tingles. It was the best way to describe how my skin felt whenever I read emotions with my new powers. Static water beads trickling over my skin. But one single touch from him—my husband, my king—would make the world go silent.

Blissfully quiet. I'd thought my empathic abilities would somehow work differently as a goddess, but instead, they became amplified. And sex with Zeus? The sensations were tenfold and made me ravenous for him at any given moment.

Two Greek gods sitting on a curb in Las Vegas, waiting for our turn to have a man dressed as Elvis Presley marry our mortal guises. Weeks ago, the notion of it would've had me laughing hysterically, and though it still enticed a snicker, I couldn't imagine a better way, nor could I imagine it happening with anyone else.

Zeus sat between my legs with his back to me, his arms wrapped around my thighs.

I trailed my fingers through his hair, pausing here and there to scrape his scalp with my nails. "The media is going to have a field day with this, you know?"

"Fuck the media," he grumbled, kissing my knee.

"How are we going to explain this? The next court date is tomorrow, and we show up inexplicably married?" I tensed, resting my hands on his shoulders, and staring at the slew of hardened gum littering the sidewalk.

"Hey." He tugged my arm, bringing my gaze to his. "Come here."

I lowered my face, and he brushed a kiss over my lips, his hand cupping my cheek.

"Master meddler, remember? I got it covered." He grinned, jiggling my chin between two fingers.

"Vronti and Bazin?" A man from inside the chapel called out.

Zeus stood first, holding his hand out to me, helping me stand. I brushed dirt away from my ass as we made our way inside. It was gaudy and quaint with only several rows of bright white pews, dozens of heart decorations, and a rounded arch with fake flowers where our minister, Elvis, stood waiting.

Elvis walked up to us, clad in a black jumpsuit decorated with ornate patterns and red rhinestones. He adjusted the oversized gold sunglasses on his nose, and as he bobbed his head, the black wig shifted. "Thank you all for choosing our chapel. Thank you very much."

I bit my lip to keep from laughing at his horrible impersonation of Elvis's iconic voice.

Zeus hugged me to his side, curling one hand over my hip. I opted to wear a simple floral dress, and he donned one of his many suits.

"Before we begin, do you both have rings?" Elvis pointed between us with a curl of his lip, his one large golden ring glinting from the overhead fluorescent lights.

Shit.

I slipped my hand behind my back, Zeus mimicking me, and we both used our powers to make rings for the other appear in our closed fists.

"Yes, we do," my husband responded with a charming grin.

Elvis leaned to one side, glancing behind us. "No guests?"

"We're kind of in a hurry," Zeus replied with a wink.

Considering the magical ceremony I'd already had on Olympus, I had no scruples in the slightest with making our mortal ceremony as quick as humanly possible.

"I like your dedication. Let's get on with it then, yeah?" Elvis snapped his fingers and shimmied to his spot under the altar, motioning for us to follow.

I was a living, breathing goddess now, a Queen, married to one of the most powerful men in the known universe, and—I'd *already* married him—but yet my stomach fluttered with anticipation.

"If you two would hold hands and face each other?" Elvis made a circling gesture with his hand.

With a sensuous curl of his lips, making my stomach twist even more, Zeus took my hands, running his thumbs over my knuckles. Elvis sang *Love Me Tender* offkey as the accompanying music played over the speakers.

"You ready to do this, counselor?" Zeus winked at me, dragging his middle finger over my palm with languid strokes.

For the second time, for the hundredth time, I'd say yes to marrying him countless times.

"This is the easy part." I smiled at him, squeezing his hands.

"Groom, if you would put the ring on her left hand, ring finger," Elvis said.

Zeus dug into his back pocket and slid a silver band over my finger. Several shimmering stones shined in a zigzag pattern when the light caught it —like lightning.

Zeus pressed his lips to my ear. "Those aren't diamonds. It's captured lightning." He kissed the corner of my jaw before leaning back.

I wiggled my fingers with a grin, making the lightning dance from the assistance of the fake lighting in the room. "It's beautiful."

"Sir, as you look into your bride's eyes, do you promise to love her, respect her, and honor her for the rest of your life?"

Zeus's grip tightened on my hands.

The rest of our lives…eons—eternity.

"Abso-fucking-lutely," Zeus answered with a warm smile.

"Wow. Great answer. Bride, if you wouldn't mind placing the ring on his finger," Elvis replied before turning to me.

I slipped the ring I'd conjured from lava rocks, its dark grey coloring a stark contrast to my brighter ring, onto his finger.

"Miss, do you promise to love him, respect him, and honor him for the rest of *your* life?"

"For eternity," I whispered, tears starting to cloud my vision.

Zeus stole a tear that'd escaped from my cheek with one quick swipe of his thumb. We'd said our vows to each other, promising to take the other through good times and bad, sickness and health, richer or poorer for as long as we both lived. Despite the ethereal nature of our first ceremony, saying the words I'd said before to my first husband made everything so much more real. As the final step, we lit a unity candle together, using our smaller candles to light the larger one in the center in unison. It'd been my missing link all this time. I'd never felt like someone else's crucial half. With Zeus, we were powerful as individuals, but we could conquer galaxies *together*.

"Congratulations to you both. After hearing the vows spoken by both of you, I can now officially pronounce you husband and wife. Sir, you can kiss your wife now."

Zeus flashed a sultry grin before dipping me and planting his lips to mine. I wrapped my arms around his neck, kissing him back, his lightning power coursing through my veins. Elvis sang *Viva Las Vegas* to us as we walked down the aisle toward the exit hand-in-hand. Zeus had fabricated a wedding certificate for us as further proof to immigration once they'd gotten wind of my illegal residency.

Once we were standing outside of the chapel, he slipped his ring off and squinted at the inside of it. "I think your powers need a little more work, sweetheart. Shouldn't that say 'KZ' not 'KB'?" He pointed at the engraving I'd done on the inside of his band.

Smiling, I shook my head. "Nope. I got it right. Keira's Bitch."

He glared at me with a wicked glint in his eye before he let out a roar of masculine chuckles, and slipped the ring back on. He grabbed me by the waist, tickling me, making me cackle before pulling my back to his chest, hugging me from behind.

"Honestly, don't worry about any of it. The media. The trial. Immigration. Big Daddy Z will handle *all* of it." He kissed my cheek and hugged me tighter.

"Big Daddy Z?" I smiled while biting my lip. "I'm not calling you that."

He shrugged, giving my nape a nibble, smiling against it. "Time will tell."

We shared a cab the next day to the courthouse, our hands intertwined, only parting ways once we walked inside. He was off to prep his client, and I was getting used to my new skin— how different it would feel standing in front of a judge and jury knowing I was now a celestial being amongst unknowing mortals.

"Keira fucking Bazin," Olivia shouted, power-walking through the lobby until she stood in front of me.

"Olivia—" I raised a hand, but she batted it away.

"I came into your office with a cake and a gift ready to celebrate your birthday the usual way you bloody prefer, and do you know what I found?"

I opened my mouth to reply, but Olivia cut me a glare.

"Nothing. That's what. And then I don't hear from you?"

Not bothering to speak anymore, I lifted my left hand and wiggled my fingers.

Her eyes widened before snatching my wrist and bringing my hand so close to her face I could feel her breath on my knuckles. "Did you or Zane or you and—" She rolled her neck, her eyes still wide.

"Both." My stomach clenched as an image of my god-king sitting on my throne in his full Zeus form flashed through my mind.

She tugged me closer. "Wait. So you're—"

Taking a quick scan of the area, I leaned forward, making my eyes spark with orange lightning.

Her grip tightened on my wrist as she stared up at me. "Holy shit, Keira."

"It's all happened so fast it's enough to make my head spin." I waved my fingers, making the lightning in my ring glisten.

"Wait. You all eloped, and I didn't get invited? Where'd you get married?" She threw my hand away as if she were disgusted by it.

"Vegas. We were in a hurry, Ollie. You know I would've asked you to come if it were possible." I rubbed the back of my neck with a frown.

"Vegas?" She slapped her hands on her head, laughing and

twirling circles. "That couldn't be more perfect. Please tell me you at least took pictures?"

My frown deepened. Fuck. I hadn't thought about that. "I guess we forgot."

"Keir, what if immigration showed up *today*? They're going to ask to see photos of you both." Olivia grabbed my shoulders, concern cinching in her brow.

Nervousness. Anxiety. Regret.

"I—" My phone buzzed in my briefcase, and I grabbed it.

Several texts from Zeus. Photos of our Vegas Elvis wedding. Smiling to myself, I scrolled through them. Us holding hands, facing each other, both smiling. Zeus in mid-answer of his vows with me glassy-eyed. Him dipping me as he kissed me.

Zane: I told you. Don't Worry. ;) – BDZ

Laughing, I shoved the phone at Olivia. "Apparently, my darling husband snuck in photos I wasn't aware of."

She snatched it from me, giggling. "Oh my—you did an Elvis one? Keira, this is too rich." Pressing a hand to her chest, she sniffled. "You look so, so happy. Legitimately. Look at the way you are absolutely swooning over him."

She wasn't wrong. From the first day I'd laid eyes on him, even when he was just a crummy defense lawyer with a pretty face—I was smitten. At the time, I couldn't make sense of the emotions, the carnal power radiating from his skin, the spark in his gaze that had nothing to do with his lightning. It'd been a destined meeting preconceived in the universe, and who were we to deny its pull?

"Before the trial starts, here." Olivia shoved a small box wrapped in snowflake paper into my hands. "Happy belated birthday."

My chest tightened. I'd gained a husband, godhood, and immortality for my last birthday as a mortal. The thought brought a warm smile to my lips, and my fingernails dug into the paper surrounding the box.

"What is it?" I flashed her a devious grin, knowing she hated whenever I asked that.

"I'm not sure you'll have much use for it now, but—I mean, the thought was there at the time." Olivia folded her hands in front of her and averted her gaze skyward.

Squinting one eye at her, I tore off the paper and flipped open the brown box hidden within. I pulled out a small white ceramic elephant holding a marker with its trunk and folded cloth with its tail.

Grinning, I held it up. "It's adorable. What's the marker for, though?"

Olivia held her hand out, and I rested it on her palm. She removed the marker and wrote something on the elephant's side before showing me.

"File your damn paperwork," I read aloud, laughing.

"It's a dry erase elephant. I figured it'd look cute on your desk *and* serve a purpose. Multi-functional." She rubbed the words away with the cloth and handed it back to me.

"It's perfect, Ollie. And I'll still use it, but maybe more for naughty encrypted messages or something." I winked at her, slipping the elephant into my case.

"I like where your head's at. Ready for what I hope to be

one of the final days of this damn trial?" She curled her arm with mine.

After taking a deep breath, knowing Zeus and I's marriage changed the dynamic, I let my godly intuition calm me as I breezed into the courtroom. Zeus already sat at the table with his client, immediately moving his gaze over his shoulder to grin at me.

What were you up to?

Giving a subtle smile back, I took my seat at the table only to rise seconds later as the judge entered the courtroom.

"You may be seated," she announced, adjusting her glasses and shuffling papers.

Zeus cleared his throat, remaining standing. My heart boomed in my chest. What was he doing?

"Mr. Vronti, is there something you need to address before we proceed?" The judge eyed him over the rim of her glasses.

Zeus adjusted his tie. "I'm sorry, your honor, but I've briefed my client, and with her consent, another partner will be taking over this case as—" His eyes cut to me, fully smiling before turning back to the judge. "—I'm now married to opposing counsel."

My cheeks flushed and I sunk into my chair. I'd wanted to make an announcement, knew we had to tell them, but did *not* plan to make it a spectacle. Considering I knew who I married, it shouldn't have surprised me.

Melissa Daniels' face scrunched, and she shook her head. "We never—"

Zeus waved his fingers behind his back at Melissa, making her face neutral, followed by a firm nod.

"Well, in the thirty years I've been doing this, I can honestly say this has never happened before. Thank you for bringing this to our attention. In light of the change in defense, we'll adjourn the proceedings until tomorrow." She slammed her gavel.

Olivia smacked me in the shoulder with a grin. "He's *so* good."

Oh. I know—the charming, gorgeous asshole.

Zeus approached me as I stood, his hands jiggling the keys in his pants pocket. "I know that's probably not how you wanted to announce this, but I wanted them to know I'm stepping down." He leaned in, unabashedly sliding an arm around my waist now that everyone knew. "Win the case, my Queen."

A sensual shiver shot up my spine, fluttering over my skin.

"And now, to handle the slew of media I know lurks behind that door." Zeus smirked before holding his hand out for me to take.

"Olivia—" I started, flicking my gaze over my shoulder to her.

She held up a hand as she gathered papers into her briefcase. "I'll catch up with you. Trust me. I'm elated your first instinct isn't to go straight to the office to over-prepare." She tugged one of my jacket lapels as she passed and grinned up at Zeus before pointing a finger in his face. "I don't care who you are. If you hurt my best friend, I'll do bad things to you."

"Careful, Ollie. Don't threaten my husband with a good time, or I may get jealous." I smiled at her, offering a tiny wink.

Zeus squeezed my hand.

After Olivia guffawed, she slapped my shoulder. "Yup. I like this version of you. Call me later."

I elbowed Zeus. "Quick work with those photos."

"Mmhmm." He bumped his knuckle under my chin. "What did I say?"

"That you had everything under control." I bit back a smile.

He held up a single finger. "That *who* had everything under control?"

Glaring at him but still smiling, I said, "Big Daddy Z."

"That's right." He kissed my brow.

No sooner did we step outside of the courtroom cameras and reporters swarmed us.

"Miss Bazin, did you ever imagine yourself with a defense lawyer?"

"Mr. Vronti, what does this mean for your career?"

I stepped closer to Zeus, squinting from the flashes going off in waves.

"I'm sure you all have a lot of questions, and we'll answer all of them in due time. Considering this is so new, however, you'll respect us if we wish to enjoy this momentous occasion— alone." Zeus's voice commanded attention, everyone falling silent as soon as he opened his mouth and nodding in agreement without asking anything else.

"Miss Bazin, we *will* expect you to answer a few questions, however," a man's voice said from nearby.

When I turned to face him, he flipped his wallet open, revealing a USCIS badge, making my throat tighten.

It was only a matter of time.

"Miss Bazin, is Mrs. Bazin-Vronti now. She's legally in the country with her marriage-based green card." Zeus said, holding up our joined left hands.

"Be that as it may. We'll need to take you both in for questioning due to the urgency and convenience of your marriage to ensure its legitimacy." The man stepped aside and held out his hand. "If you'd both follow us to the immigration office."

Zeus dropped his lips to my ear. "You're a Queen goddess now. Use that charm for questions we'll undoubtedly be unable to answer. Unless the person interviewing us is a man, then maybe tone it back a tad." He grinned against my cheek.

Let the interrogation commence…

The officers led us to the same room with a single desk, overhead light, and three chairs. I cleared my throat as I adjusted in my seat, purposely playing with the new band on my finger to show my immediate familiarity with it. Zeus sat next to me, but they'd made us far enough apart we couldn't hint answers to the other.

"It may have taken us longer to catch wind of you were it not for going through customs after your quick trip to Argentina," Officer Miles said as he twirled a pen on the desk.

I folded my hands and calmly placed them in front of me. "I wasn't worried about it because I knew I was already marrying Zane."

Zeus grinned and bobbed his brows at the officer.

"You seemed to have a short engagement. Care to explain?" Miles cut his gaze to Zeus.

Zeus casually leaned back in his chair and bent forward, resting his forearms on the table. "Do you believe in love at first sight, Officer Miles?"

"No."

"Well, then how could you possibly understand why we were ravenous to make it official?" Zeus spied me out of the corner of his eye, smiling at me.

Ravenous.

I bit my lip and crossed my legs with a flick of my hair.

"How does he take his coffee?" Miles narrowed his eyes at me, tracing his gaze over every expression and gesture I made.

"Black. No lid," I answered quickly.

Seemingly satisfied, Miles nodded and turned his attention on Zeus. "And hers?"

"Black, but I've also seen her sneaking a packet of sugar in now and again. When she wants to be hyper-focused."

He noticed that?

I didn't want the officer to catch the surprised expression on my face, so I hid it behind a smile.

"What side of the bed does she sleep on?"

"That all depends on which position we finished in." A glint flashed in Zeus's eyes.

My stomach flipped several times.

"Any children from past marriages?"

Zeus stared at the officer before squinting. "Can you repeat the question?"

I slid a hand over my mouth, grinning behind the guise of my palm.

"How long has he been in his current state of employment?" Miles tapped the pen against the table as he shifted his gaze between us.

I shrugged. "Years, but honestly, sometimes it feels like—forever."

"And the wedding, where did it take place?"

Zeus slid his phone from his back pocket, pulling up the gallery of photos he'd fabricated from his memories. "A chapel in Vegas." He pointed at his phone. "They streamed it on Facebook, too, if you need further proof."

"Have you planned the honeymoon?"

I frowned and traced my thumb over my lightning ring. "We haven't talked about it." Stealing a glance at my new husband, I caught his gaze, and he too frowned.

"Have you met each other's parents?"

We both turned our attention back to the officer and responded in unison, "They're dead."

The officer clucked his tongue against his teeth and tapped the pen faster. "What about your spouse's best friend's name?"

Frustration. Annoyance.

Zeus shifted forward. "Olivia."

"Levin," I said, grinning at the god-king when he raised a brow at me over his shoulder.

"Do you live together or plan to live together?"

Live in my tiny apartment with painful memories of my divorce? Fuck that. Besides, I still had half my shit packed anyway. "I'm moving into his penthouse."

Zeus nodded. "Mostly because it's soundproofed."

I choked on my spit, holding back a laugh, and coughed into my fist.

The interrogation continued for another fifteen minutes, and we newlyweds answered each question with ease and precision. The officers informed me I could maintain my green card, which would expire ten years from the current date. We strolled out of the USCIS office holding hands.

"So, you're moving into the penthouse with me, huh?" Zeus tugged my arm.

"Damn right I am. Hope you're prepared for that—hubs." I kissed his cheek.

"So bossy." Zeus flashed me a grin as he slid his sunglasses on.

"You love it."

"Speaking of bosses, we need to introduce you as everyone's new 'co-boss' formally." He brought my hand to his lips, giving a quick peck to my palm.

"How do you propose getting everyone in one place?"

"It's been a very long time since I called everyone home—to Olympus."

TWENTY TWO

ZEUS

I SAT ON MY golden throne comprised of two eagles, their wings making up its back. My gorgeous Queen sat next to me, casually crossing her legs, wrists dangling off the edge of her armrests. The jewels hanging from her hair shimmered and jangled when she turned to look at me, smiling that she caught me staring at her.

"What is it?" Her glowing orange eyes pulsed.

I leaned toward her, resting the thunderbolt I had clutched in my hand on the ground, perching it against my throne. "It's only been a matter of days, and already this role suits you."

"My foster mother always used to say, 'It might take a day. It might take a year, but what's meant to be will always find its way.'" She smiled at me, fucking radiant and ethereal.

"Sounds like a well-spoken woman."

Foster mothers. Workaholics. Passionate. A fated bond made more and more sense with each passing day.

"She was." Keira kept smiling as she turned her head to the other gods as they began to appear in the great hall.

I knew not all of them would or could come, but even a handful of gods to bear witness to me placing the new crown on the new Queen would suffice. It almost seemed bizarre having an official ritualistic ceremony after so long. Gaea said the changes were far from over—that our fated union would pave the way for progression. Whatever the fuck that meant. I think my grandmother delighted in knowing more than any other deity. It continuously gave her leverage over every one of us.

After a dozen arrived, including Apollo, Artemis, Athena, Demeter, Poseidon, Hermes, my enforcers, and even Ares—I couldn't wait any longer.

Standing, I picked up the thunderbolt and waited for the murmurs of conversation to die down. "Those of you who heeded my call know it's appreciated. We could have upheld this tradition with only the Queen and I and my brothers as witnesses, but I propose we make use of Olympus more often again." Displaying my arms wide, I swiveled. "For how could we continue to call it a Great Hall when it remains silent?"

More murmurs and nods floated amongst the gods.

"As you all know, Hera has stepped down as Queen, which led me in the search for another." I paused to look at Keira, who lifted her chin, grinning. "Little did I know when I set my eyes on her, she would not only be my future Queen but that I had found my fated bond. A bond I never knew existed."

Several of the gods gasped, but I kept my gaze on my

goddess.

"She has accepted the role of Queen, goddess of healed emotion, and agreed to be my wife, but she has yet to be properly crowned." Resting the bolt and shield on the seat of my throne, I produced the baroque crown I'd created for her in my palms. Golden metal curved into ornate patterns from Hephaistos' forge, blackened gems and lava stones matching the wedding ring she'd given me.

Keira pressed a hand to her chest, a small whimper fluttering from her throat. She hadn't expected this, and her sincere reaction had my heart singing. Moving behind her, I held the crown above her head and looked to the other gods, most of them my family, now *her* family as well.

"Bear witness to your new Queen, gods of the Greek pantheon. May you respect her, honor her, and obey her not only as Queen but as my equal and my wife." I sparked lightning in my eyes as proof I'd smite any of them for any misdeeds toward her.

They all raised their fists to their chests, pounding in unison. With a slight nod, I lowered the crown to Keira's head, sending a shimmer of gold dust and coils of lightning encircling us both, white and orange hissing vibrant and strong. Keira took a deep breath, her chest rising, before settling into her throne once more.

"May I speak, Zeus?" Keira's thin brows raised.

I cupped her chin with a warm smile. "You never need permission for that." Holding my hand out, I urged her to address the other gods.

Rising, the thin fabric of her white dress curling around

her like floating silk, she stepped to the front of the raised platform holding our thrones. "Gods. Family. I know I must seem like a stranger—a stranger taking over the second most powerful standing amongst the Greek gods, but I can assure you it doesn't come without rhyme or reason." She glanced at Apollo and Ares, knowing full well they'd brought other mortal women into our world.

She held her arms out. "Gaea told us that this is to be a time of progression, and I plan to be the stepping stone for that new age. I come from the modern world while having a piece of this world unknowingly inside me, and I believe with every fiber of my being—" She turned to look at me, crossing the way to take my hand. "—combined with Zeus's immense power, the dawning of this day…is today."

Fucking Tartarus. I thought the way she carried herself in a courtroom was a sight to behold but her as a Queen? Nothing compared.

"Now that we're done being all formal—" She waved her hand, making a table littered with food and ambrosia wine appear near the other gods. "—what's a celebration without food and drink?"

Once the other gods began to attack the table, I pulled her against me, kissing her, trailing my hands up her back and into her hair.

She pulled away, curling her fingers through my long silver hair. "Did I do alright?"

"Alright? You fucking showed *me* up." I chuckled and kissed her.

A chill settled in the air, followed by trickling embers and ash in the center of the atrium. Eris. Godsdammit.

"You have one thing right. You *are* a stranger on the throne," Eris spat as she glared at Keira.

My shoulders tensed from her bone-chilling voice. Growling, I turned on my heel, coaxing Keira behind me on basic instinct alone. "What the Tartarus are you doing here, Eris? I made it explicitly clear you're not welcome in these halls."

She flicked her long black hair, the red streaks in it igniting a newfound fury in my gut like a bull readying to charge. "I'm offended I wasn't invited to this little soiree. The invitation must've gotten lost in the mail." With a crooked grin, she narrowed her eyes at Hermes and waved.

Hermes cut his gaze to me, eyebrows raised, and cheeks full of food.

"Leave. Now," I made my voice boom, echoing off the stone pillars surrounding us.

As she stepped from behind me, Keira's fingers grazed my elbow and she stood at my side with her chin held high.

Eris appeared in front of me in a flash of embers, hissing and pointing a black claw in my face. "All of these new goddesses and none of us had a say in any of them. Particularly—" She cut her gaze to Keira. "—the Queens."

You ever regretted something so profusely it makes your balls ache, knowing it's where it came from? I care for all my children. But Eris? She's always been a fucking *challenge*.

"You don't need a say." I dipped my face into hers. "I'm your King. And if you think I'm incapable of putting someone worthy on the throne to rule beside me, I dare you to say it." Lightning flashed in my gaze.

She sneered at me, making her lip curl. "It was bad enough when a previous mortal joined the ranks of war gods, but to make *this* harpy, Queen? You've grown *soft*, old man."

Ares stepped forward with clenched fists, baring his teeth like a snarling grizzly.

I held my palm up to him, keeping my focus on Eris. "I got this handled, son."

After several nostril flares, Ares gave a curt nod and stalked away.

Fury shot down my spine, and I lashed lightning around Eris, pinning her arms at her sides. "Talk about my wife like that again, and I'll banish you to the furthest nebula to be forgotten. Do you understand me? She is your Queen. Get the fuck over it or get out."

"Banish me?" She cackled and stared at me with those lifeless midnight eyes. "Do it."

Keira's hand slid over my forearm—her calming touch soothing me. She gave one light bob of her thin brows, and I released Eris from my electric grip. After nodding to Keira, I stepped aside.

My Queen took charge as she stood tall in front of Eris with her head cocked to one side. "When Zeus mentioned you before, I hoped we'd meet Eris."

"Why?" Eris scoffed.

Keira stepped closer to her. "So I can help you."

"Help me?" Eris snickered and flicked her hair. "I don't *need* helping."

"Pain. Resentment. You're imbalanced, Eris." Keira's gaze roamed Eris's face.

"How did you—" Backing away, Eris shielded her cheek with a hand as if one of us were going to slap her.

Keira followed her. "Chaos, too, needs balance. And it's up to you to do it—to find it."

"Oh? And how do you propose I do that, my *liege*?" The words dripped from her tongue like snake venom.

My nostril bounced, and I coursed lightning down my arms as I glared at Eris and her wise-ass little mouth.

"The same way as Ares and Zeus. They opened their hearts to two mortal women and in turn balanced themselves the same way they balanced us." Smiling, Keira glanced at me over her shoulder.

Still letting the lighting coil around me, I grinned back.

"You've got to be kidding me. You're telling me to go find 'love.'" Eris rolled her eyes after making air quotes.

Keira stuck out her chest. "I'm not telling you. I'm ordering you. It may not even be love for another person but yourself. That's for you to figure out. Uphold your duties, Eris. Zeus doesn't make empty threats, and neither do I."

Damn. That's my wife, folks. *Mine.*

The surrounding gods widened their eyes as whispers and light chatter amongst them followed. Eris narrowed her eyes at my Queen before scanning the other gods around her. She dragged a hand down the front of her leather corset before lifting her chin. "Consider it done—" Eris took a deep breath before ever so slightly bowing her head. "—my Queen."

Before we could reply, Eris disappeared with a grimace, leaving floating bits of embers and ash spiraling in the air.

Keira let out a breath, and I stepped behind her, pressing my bulge against her ass, and grabbing her hip. "If we were alone right now—" I growled against her neck.

"I wasn't too harsh on her?" Keira snaked her hand behind my head.

"I think you're incapable of being too harsh." I drummed my fingers on her waist. "Except with me. Something tells me you'd hand me my own balls if I did something to incur your wrath."

She pulled my lips to hers. "And don't you forget it."

Ares cleared his throat as he approached us. He bowed his head and pressed a fist to his chest. "I wanted to welcome you personally to the family, my Queen."

"Ares, I know it's been a long time since you've been back here. I appreciate you making an appearance. It means the world to me." Keira bent forward and pressed a kiss to my son's forehead.

"To us," I corrected, holding out my hand for Ares to shake. "Thank you, son."

Ares glared at my hand at first, clenching his jaw before slapping his hand against my forearm, shaking it. "Don't expect me to call her stepmom or anything." He pointed at each of us with a hint of a smile.

"Noted." I chuckled but let it fall away, only to be replaced by a stoic expression. "But you *will* call her that if she one day wishes it."

Keira squeezed my arm and laughed. "Ares, I wouldn't expect that. I'm not taking over anything of your mother's. I think of it more as picking up where she left off in a new era."

"Much like me with my goddess, I can see the bond at

work." Ares looked between us before bowing his head. "And speaking of which, I should get back to her."

Keira leaned against me, running her fingers along my bared skin. "You two are so much alike it's almost uncanny."

Grumbling, I responded, "I know. I think it's why we've butted heads for eons."

The day went by with each of the gods introducing themselves to Keira, Apollo playing music on his lyre—an actual lyre—versus his modern-day guitar. As they disappeared one-by-one, Poseidon finally approached us with a wide grin.

"Well, well, hello, *sis*." He stood with his hands folded behind his back and winked at me. "You did good, little bro."

Keira smiled and extended her hand. "Poseidon. I assume you're one of two reasons for Zeus's grand gesture?"

Poseidon chuckled, covering his mouth with a hand as his green eyes brightened.

"Hey. I was more than capable of thinking of that on my own." Feeling my nose twitch, I cut Poseidon a glare.

Keira curled her arm with mine. "Maybe now you are, but at that precise moment? You needed the push, hun." She rose on the balls of her feet to kiss my cheek.

"I'm going to push something alright," I mumbled, narrowing my eyes at Poseidon over Keira's head and out of view.

"Can you two come to the Underworld? Hades and I wish to speak with you." Looking between the two of us, Poseidon cracked his knuckles.

Nodding, I slipped a hand to Keira's lower back and ported us to Hades's throne room. He sat on his throne, talking with his own Queen, Stephanie, seated upon her throne. Stephanie smiled and trotted across the black sand to greet us, taking Keira's hands into hers.

"It is an absolute pleasure to meet you, Keira." Stephanie bowed her head and did a small curtsy. "My Queen."

Squeezing her hands, Keira replied, "I appreciate you saying it out of respect, but please call me Keira."

Beaming, Stephanie stood tall and stepped to Hades as he approached us.

"Keira has a similar power as you, darling." Hades squeezed Stephanie's shoulders.

Stephanie gasped. "You see auras too?"

"I guess emotions can also be associated with auras, but no, I'm an empath. I can sense emotions from anyone mortal and immortal alike. And since becoming a goddess, I can project any emotion I wish on mortals." Keira ran the skirt of her dress through her fingers.

"She's selling herself short. She was a powerful empath before becoming Queen and now, well—" I paused, at a loss for words. No form of verbal description could possibly do this woman justice.

"Little bro, we were thinking." Stepping beside me, Poseidon wrapped a hand over my shoulder.

"Here we go." I pinched the bridge of my nose.

"You raised a valid point when you said you granted me the means to take breaks but not yourself." Hades lifted his chin.

The idea of leaving Olympus in anyone else's hands made my neck tense.

"It's because I can't afford to take breaks. Those moments are for you and your Queen to make you happy, Hades. It doesn't have to be fair on all fronts."

"Bullshit, Z," Poseidon barked.

I tossed him a glare over my shoulder, the lightning swirling in my eyes.

"Do you not think you're deserving of happiness, brother?" Hades rose a single brow, and Stephanie rested her head on his shoulder.

Keira's hand slipped over my arm. She was beautiful, there wasn't a doubt in my mind about it, but the tiredness I could feel floating from her was too distinct to ignore. Combined with my own exhaustion—it was enough to make me audibly sigh.

"What are you proposing?" I lifted my gaze to Hades.

"Take a week. Go on a honeymoon. Go wherever you wish, but leave knowing Olympus is taken care of and in good hands. Relax. Rejuvenate." Hades stepped forward, curling his hand over my shoulder. "Between the three of us, Olympus will be *fine*."

"I don't know. It's not only Olympus. It's all of the gods, the universe, mortals. How will you handle any of that from down here, Hades? Hm?" I held my arms out, swiveling my hips as I referenced the Underworld.

"You'd be surprised at all of what I can do from here. We have it handled."

Licking my lips, I scratched my chin. "What about Levin?"

"Cordelia is already at your apartment taking care of him as we speak. You know how my wife is with animals. He's in good hands." Poseidon crossed his arms and leaned into my face. "Stop making excuses and go."

My gaze shifted to Keira's eyes—the hope swirling in them.

If I felt any ounce of being undeserving of happiness with all I've done in my past, she *did* deserve to be happy.

Holding my hand out to her, I smiled. "Bali?"

Stephanie clapped her hands and hugged Hades to her side.

"Anywhere, Zeus. Anywhere." Keira interlaced her fingers and beamed up at me.

"If Olympus is in ruins when I return, I'm making you live in a desert for a week." I pointed at Poseidon, followed by Hades. "And you'll be forced to smile for twenty-four hours."

"Oops," Hades said right before waving his hand at us and making us disappear.

No sooner had we landed in the lobby, it took Keira an entire five minutes before finding an unhappy couple arguing at the front desk. She'd tried to be discreet, casually waltzing past them, but she forgot who she married. And judging by their sudden change in demeanor, going from fighting to googly eyes the moment my wife passed them, it was fairly obvious.

"By Olympus, you're worse than me." I pulled her to me, wrapping my arms around her. "We're supposed to be *relaxing*, love. Not working."

"I know. I promise that was it. Besides, I couldn't let them feel like that in paradise. It didn't seem right." She poked me in the ribs. "And you think I couldn't sense you checking on your brothers moments after arriving?"

Busted.

"They're asshats. One last little check calmed my growing

anxiety." I shrugged.

"First time your children are being babysat jitters, huh?" She grinned up at me as she elbowed my side.

I kissed the top of her head. "Something like that."

When we appeared in our room in Bali, it was in such seclusion Keira could scream her lungs out, and only the birds would hear it. I planned to make the most of it during our stay here—the most of the unburdening of our work, the most of the open floor plan, and definitely the most out of the tub I'd coaxed her into within minutes of our arrival.

"I've seen Olympus itself, and yet this place still looks like a thing from fairytales to me," she whispered as she twirled her finger in the steaming water filled with rose petals, her blonde hair pulled in a bunch on top of her head.

The tub was situated underneath a gazebo on the deck outside of our room, giving us full view of the valley of palm trees and fog collecting in the air. Two lounge chairs and a private pool also faced the trees. A king-sized canopy bed rested in the bedroom behind us inside, the pale purple comforter littered with the same rose petals in our tub water.

I curled an arm around her from behind, pressing beneath her breasts and pulling her back tighter to my chest. "Never lose that sense of wonder, Vasílissa."

Queen.

Smiling, she reached for her flute of champagne resting on the nearby table. "Were you close to your foster mom?"

"Very." I grabbed a bottle of oil, pooling some in my palm before massaging her shoulders, her neck. "It angered me to no end when she died."

She closed her eyes and let out a contented sigh from my touch. "Do you think that's why you were so ruthless in your youth? Lashing out?"

"Possibly." I kneaded a tight spot in her neck—the same place I always seemed to form a knot. "But I wouldn't want to blame my choices on someone else. At the end of the day, *we* make the choices. No one else."

"And that is why I wish you'd somehow make the world know about the true Zeus." She rubbed my calf beneath the water.

"It's not my place, sweetheart." I kissed her cheek and brushed my nose over her jawline. "Mortals have been the ones to depict us. If someone wants to envision me differently someday, I'd be fucking ecstatic, I truly would, but I've accepted it." Pinching one nipple, I kissed her neck, lightly biting it. "You know me. That's all I need."

"I haven't been able to make lightning since the day on Olympus. How do you conjure it? Especially with such precision?"

Grinning against her cheek, I trailed my fingers down her stomach until I reached her clit. "You mean when I do this?" Calling to my power, I flickered it over her, making her cry out.

She laughed. "Yes. Exactly."

"The precision has taken hundreds of years of practicing, but this—" The lightning swirled over my arms before crackling across the grey sky above us. "—is easy to master."

"Show me," she whispered, rubbing her cheek against a knee I'd poked from the water.

"Everything starts here." I traced my finger between her breasts. "You can feel it building up, sizzling, waiting for you to release it and direct it where to go."

She closed her eyes, and I could hear the hissing emanating from her chest.

"I can feel it."

"Good. Now pull it out of you, guide it, using this." I dragged my fingertips over her forehead. "It'll start at your arms, but if you want it in the sky, *tell* it to go there. Command it."

Her forehead wrinkled as she concentrated, her nails digging into my leg as she fought to control the bit of lightning I'd passed onto her. Slowly, the orange electricity pulsed over her shoulders and after several moments of grunting and further nail digging into my flesh, a silent flash of heat lightning overtook the clouds.

"I love the way that feels," she murmured, her eyelids heavy.

"Oh, yeah?" My white lightning bubbled in my palms, fanning over her skin in short languid bursts of electricity. Goosebumps covered her arms, and she bit her lip, her eyes closing, back arching. Chuckling, I doused the power and kissed the corner of her brow.

She moaned and sunk further into the water. "Tell me to sit on your face."

My cock twitched against her ass, and I couldn't help but chuckle. "I'm sorry?"

"Just say it. Please."

Pressing my lips to her ear, moistening it, I whispered, "Sit on my face, Keira."

Her hand found my cock under the water, idly stroking it as she kept her eyes closed. "Now repeat it, but command it."

This. Godsdamned. *Woman.*

"Sit. On. My. Face," I growled against her neck.

"Mm, that's so much sexier than my dream."

Chuckling again, I groaned at the feel of her hand still stroking me. "You dreamed about me? When?"

"On my way to Argentina. And don't sound so surprised. You probably commanded Morpheus to do it."

I nipped at her ear lobe. "As much as I would love to take the credit for that little gem, I really would. That was all you, sweetheart."

She turned in the water, pressing her tits to my chest with a brightened smile. "I guess I couldn't help myself."

"You know what would be far sexier than me saying it, Keira?" I scooted down in the water, encouraging her to stand over me.

We continued to act out her salacious dream in vivid detail, taking it a step further by fucking both on the pool deck and in it. We spent the week showing our appreciation for the other in every held conversation, every position imaginable, and slept more than either of us had in several lifetimes. I'd have to thank my brothers for this, which annoyed the shit out of me, but these days...I had *a lot* to be grateful for.

ЄPILOGUЄ

ᕭᕭᕭᕭᕭᕭᕭᕭᕭᕭᕭᕭᕭᕭ

THREE MONTHS LATER...

KEIRA

IT TOOK ME MONTHS to work up the courage to ask my brother-in-law to escort me to Tartarus. The looming question of whether my mother would even want to speak with me hung over me like a raincloud—not to mention the emotion in this place.

Agony. Pain. Suffering. Remorse. Regret.

Gripping my head, I paused, causing Hades to turn and squeeze my shoulder. "Keira?"

"It's too much. Can you drown them out somehow?"

I could've asked Zeus to come with me, and none of this would've bothered me, but this was something I needed to do by myself. *For* myself.

"For a time, but you won't have long. These souls are too

strong for me to dampen it permanently." Hades waved his hand.

Like the deafening aftermath of a nearby explosion, the emotions overwhelming me fizzled away.

Sighing, I stood straight. "Thank you."

"If she wishes to see you, she'll be through this door." Hades displayed a doorway leading into nothing but darkness.

Nodding, I stepped through, never being one that feared the dark or the creatures that lurked within it. Flames flickered around me, creating enough illumination in bursts to see shadows of people. As I ignored the wails and cries from the tortured souls, a woman with long blonde hair the same color as mine emerged from the blanket of darkness. A breath caught in my throat.

"Why are you here, Keira?" Her long flowing black dress made her float above the ground. Two black orbs served as eyes, and her teeth were jagged and deadly.

"You really have to ask me that?"

No regret. No remorse. Only sadness.

A tiny smile pulled at her lips. "You inherited the gift of emotion reading."

"You didn't know?" I wanted to be mad at her for abandoning me, but how could you resent someone you never knew?

"I suspected it. But I imagine there are two questions you seek answers for. Why I didn't raise you and who your father is." She cocked her head to the side, floating in front of me, and raising one pale hand to my face.

I recoiled at her touch, stepping back. "Yes."

"I wasn't supposed to be able to have children, but the Fates had other plans. A destiny that I could've only given with the gifts I possess. I was in no place to raise you and wished only to protect you from the meddling of Olympus. The mortal couple I left you with, they treated you well, yes?" She folded her hands in front of her.

"Yes. They did." Tears stung my eyes.

Did Gaea plan for my birth from the very beginning?

"Your father. You have his eyes, his nose—" She traced her fingers over her face with a small smile. "I loved him. He never knew you existed as he died before you were born. Cancer." Her glistening black gaze fell to her feet. "It was another reason that drove me here. The pain of loss."

"Did you know I had a fated bond to Zeus?" I clenched my fists at my sides.

At first, she didn't speak, and her inward gaze lifted to mine. "Yes."

"Yes?" I yelled. "You knew and you kept him from me? With the spell you put on me to keep my lineage a secret, what if— what if we had never found each other?"

"In one way or another, no matter what—you would've found each other, Keira. Fate always figures out a way. Always." She floated closer. "You must understand I did that to protect you as a child. You were able to grow up as a mortal and have a carefree childhood."

"Carefree? You think it was carefree? I didn't have anyone around to explain to me the tidal wave of emotions I felt whenever I was in public. No one to explain a way to control it. I had to figure it all out on my own." I pointed to the ground, my tone turning more infuriated with each passing word.

"And for that, I can only offer you an apology, but it shaped you into the woman you are today. A goddess. My Queen." She bowed her head.

Shaking my head, I stepped away, the agonizing emotions from the surrounding souls starting to seep their way back into my bones. "And you wish to stay here, Oizys? As an enforcer to Hades?"

"Yes, my Queen. My powers are most suited here." She bowed her head further. "One last thing before you leave. You may find yourself connected to the moon and darkness given your family ties. It may even increase your power versus the daylight."

Being the ultimate night owl made a lot more sense.

"Then so be it. If you ever wish to see me again, to get to know anything about me besides what you knew to be prophesied, inform Hades, and I'll come."

She didn't answer me one way or the other, lifted her head, and stared at me with those lifeless eyes.

Frowning, I called to Hades with my mind and instantly appeared on the banks of the river Styx.

"I'm gathering the visit didn't go as well as you hoped?" Hades squeezed my arm.

"I'm not sure how I expected it to go, honestly. I'm just thankful for some answers."

He nodded, and I glanced at my wristwatch. "Shit. The mortal job calls."

"Say something derogatory to my brother for me, would you?" A hint of smile pulled at Hades's lips before fading away.

Grinning, I made myself appear in my office at the courthouse. Already feeling his presence behind me, I pushed my fingertips against my desk, the office door creaking shut. Zeus stood behind it, casually leaning against the wall with his feet crossed at the ankles.

"Why, your honor, have I misbehaved again?" Raising a brow, I turned to face him, sitting on the edge of the desk.

When Zeus had stepped away from the Daniels case, it wasn't too difficult for the prosecution to establish a win. The evidence had only continued to pile up against Melissa, including a testimony I managed to get from her accomplice, Jimmy, under the agreement his own sentencing would be less severe than hers. That combined with computer evidence showing her searches for "acid to digest animal tissue" when her shop only worked on soil-based items. The proof of her ordering over a year's supply of sulfuric *and* hydrochloric acid, and proof of purchase of the blue chemical barrel right before the incident—it was a shoo-in. She received life without any hope of parole, and I kept my winning streak.

Not soon after the trial ended, Zeus announced that Zane Vronti would no longer serve as a defense lawyer. He ran for a judgeship and won by a landslide. Zeus, King of the Gods, and god of justice seemed so much more fitting as a judge at any rate. Not to mention it allowed us to work in the same building and have lots and lots of scandalous office sex.

"Very. I may have to resort to drastic measures this time around." He peeled back his jacket, tapping the metal clasp on his belt.

Biting my lip and smiling, I outstretched my arms for him to hug me. Obliging, he wrapped his burly arms around me, his beard tickling my cheek as he nuzzled it.

"How'd it go, sweetheart?" He asked, his nose brushing my ear.

"I could've misinterpreted it, but it almost sounded as if Gaea made sure Oizys would get pregnant with me. She wasn't supposed to be able to have kids," I mumbled against his chest.

He pushed back, holding onto my shoulders with a scrunched nose. "You don't have a father?"

"She didn't pluck me from her head or anything, Zeus." Poking him in the chest, I gave a tiny smile. "I did have a father. He died before I was born."

He rubbed my arms. "I'm sorry. I know you hoped to meet him."

"Shit happens. I've got enough family to last me an eternity now, I suppose." Smiling, I dipped my fingers into his belt, pulling him between my legs. "Now about that punishment."

He lowered his lips to mine as he grabbed my ass, pulling me forward. I dipped my hands into his shirt, making the top two buttons pluck away as I greedily groped his chest.

"Sorry for interrupting, Keir. Sorry," Olivia said, ducking her head through the cracked door, her hand firmly over her eyes but peeking through her fingers.

Zeus held his head low with a gruff sigh. A warranted reaction considering this was the fourth time this week we'd been "disturbed." After patting his chest, I stood and adjusted my skirt.

"Why do you have your hand on your face, Ollie?"

"Not taking any chances anymore, Keir. Not doing it. You walk in on your best friend making out with her husband one time, and that's quite bloody enough." She waved a folder of papers at me. "Just take it, and I'll be on my merry way."

Grinning, I snatched the folder, and she slipped away, shutting the door behind her. I threw the folder to my desk, knowing there were other matters to attend to before my mortal job duties.

"My turn to make the rounds, right?" I slid between Zeus's legs who'd changed positions with me. He was sitting on the desk now.

"If you're up for it. I can always do it again." He kneaded my hips with his strong fingers.

"We talked about this. Shared responsibility so neither of us burn out. Remember?" I bopped him on the nose.

He chuckled and drummed his fingers on my ass. "Then off you go."

Leaning forward, I placed my lips to his, kissing him tenderly. "Promise we'll pick up where we left off at our place later tonight?"

Our place. The penthouse I'd sneered at for months and now considered my sanctuary from the world.

"You know I'm always good for anything you ask. Especially if it involves fucking you." He slapped my ass. "Now go so you can get back."

Stepping away and blowing him a kiss that he caught and placed on his dick, I ported away laughing.

I enjoyed making rounds the most of all as part of my Queenly duties. Not only checking on all the other gods to ensure they were doing their jobs but also tuning into their well-being. Tap into their true emotions and aid if necessary. Everyone needed to be their best selves if what Gaea said was true—that the paving of progression started with Zeus. We'd all need to be ready for our world to go *beyond* anything we knew.

THE END

Well, not exactly
Us Greek gods do love the attention.
Especially Me.

Sincerely Big Daddy Z.

Characters from
the Contemporary Mythos series
WILL return.

STAY TUNED!
WWW.CARLYSPADE.COM

Catch the first book in the Contemporary Mythos series:

HADES

The King of the Underworld may have found a woman
truly capable of melting his cold, dark heart.

HADES (Contemporary Mythos, #1)
BUY IT ON AMAZON

ALSO BY
CARLY SPADE

Be sure to check out Carly's Celtic urban fantasy romance with Celtic mythical heroes, creatures, and a run-in with The Dullahan, a headless death god.

POWER OF ETERNITY
(DRUID DUO, #1)

Available on Amazon

ACKNOWLEDGEMENTS

FIRSTLY, TO MY HUSBAND, who leant so much to this story I could never thank you enough for making it the best it could be. The King of the Gods himself owes your input to shedding him in such good light.

To someone who shall remain unnamed but they know who they are, I sincerely thank you for giving the inside scoop on The Acid Lady case as it made incorporating it into this story so much easier, and gave it a sense of authenticity.

Jeanette, I'm unsure if I'd have been bold enough to publish a lawyer romance without your expertise as a criminal prosecutor yourself reading this over! Sincerely, thank you from the bottom of my heart for correcting my assumptions and helping make Zeus sound like the badass lawyer he is.

To my handful of alpha readers, there was no surprise that my nerves were on high when I started the concept for this book two years ago. It took TWO YEARS to figure out what angle to play with Zeus and how to turn him into a romance hero. The underlying fear of, also, is this too much spice? He's Zeus. There should be. It's warranted. But still. So, thank you for helping me dissolve my anxiety and being my cheerleaders!

To my beta readers who've been in my corner since the release of Hades. You've read six of my books, given countless amounts of feedback, and improved each and every one of these stories with it. Zeus was no exception and made for extra content I was glad to write because I didn't want to say goodbye to these characters.

To my dedicated readers of the Contemporary Mythos series, whether you've been here since the release of Hades, are starting with this book, or you recently binged to get here… from the absolute bottom of my heart, THANK YOU! Greek mythology has been a passion of mine since I was a kid and I never imagined reimagining them this way. To think this all started with my love of contemporary romance but feeling constricted in not being able to incorporate fantasy or magic. It's sad to call Zeus as "The End," but I promise you—it's a short-lived melancholy because I have zero plans of saying goodbye this cast. But the plans I *do* have…go beyond the contemporary world.

ABOUT THE AUTHOR

CARLY SPADE is an adult romance writer who has been writing since she could pick up a pencil. After the insanity of obtaining a bachelor's and master's degree in cybersecurity, creating worlds to escape to still ate at her very soul. She started writing FanFiction (which can still be found if you scour the internet), and soon felt the need to get her original ideas on paper. And so the adventure began.

She lives in Colorado with her husband and two fur babies, and revels in an enemies to lovers trope with a slow burn.

Find her online:

WWW.CARLYSPADE.COM

Printed in Great Britain
by Amazon

38700513R00182